HOPE
Knocking

Nova Mann

Jan-Carol Publishing, Inc
"every story needs a book"

Hope Knocking
Nova Mann
Published May 2022
Little Creek Books
Imprint of Jan-Carol Publishing, Inc.
All rights reserved
Copyright © 2022 Nova Mann

This is a fictional narrative based on actual events, and the views and opinions expressed herein by the author are the sole responsibility of the author and this material does not represent the views of the publishing company.

This book may not be reproduced in whole or part, in any manner whatsoever without written permission, with the exception of brief quotations within book reviews or articles.

ISBN: 978-1-954978-43-0
Library of Congress Control Number: 2022938728

Jan-Carol Publishing, Inc.
PO Box 701
Johnson City, TN 37605
publisher@jancarolpublishing.com
www.jancarolpublishing.com

*Dedicated to people around the world
who lost their lives during the Covid-19 pandemic.
Please continue to love thy neighbor.*

Preface

Dear Reader,

I am convinced that practically every human on planet Earth struggled through 2020, including myself. I felt compelled to begin a journal during my two-week quarantine after returning from a trip in the spring of 2020. What started as a way for me to document my thoughts and observations about the global crisis soon morphed into my first book, *Hope Knocking*, which took nearly a year for me to complete. I began to examine buried feelings and question core beliefs in an effort to improve myself. I turned to writing to help ease my overwhelming anxiety as I dealt with issue after issue not only in my own life but also in the United States and world. Those issues include loss of friendship, loneliness, aging, racism, sexism, mental well-being, poverty, and religion.

Hope Knocking also explores the tumultuous American political environment during the Covid-19 pandemic. Seeing my fellow Americans turn on one another has troubled me greatly, and it is my intention to offer hope, not further division, with this book. If we are going to thrive and survive as a nation, we must once again be the *United* States of America. I believe my book will help others, just as it helped me to honestly confront my past, America's past, and the pain and suffering that so many are experiencing right now. As a nation, we are still having growing pains. Will we continue to blindly pursue power over the well-being of people and the planet, or will we finally attempt to be that beacon of light held up high by Lady Liberty?

I realize that some people may disagree with my political stance, which is their right, but I have to speak my own personal truth. It is my hope that we are still able to do this in the "land of the free" without fear of persecution. I hope this memoir will spark healthy conversation and get people to think about and question their embedded belief systems, which is something I am also trying to do.

The global environmental crisis also keeps me up at night. Raging fires, droughts, historic flooding, and monster hurricanes are now an everyday occurrence. As humanity's population continues to explode and people migrate to escape the consequences of runaway climate change, what will become of Earth's other residents? Are they not also entitled to the pursuit of happiness and life? Why do we think this planet is ours alone to save or destroy? How will we save them and ourselves? Will we finally become good stewards of our beautiful blue planet, or will we take these other species down with us?

I live surrounded by nature in the mountains of East Tennessee, where the river sets the pace of my days and the wind racing through the hemlocks is my nightly lullaby. Being connected to the natural world is essential to my well-being. I attempted to express that joy with the written word, while hopefully showing that humankind has a responsibility to the rest of planet Earth. *We are all connected to Earth; we are one.*

In summary, the primary drive of the book is relationships with other human beings. How do we treat each other? What does that say about how we view ourselves? Where does humankind go from here? We can't hit "replay," and we can't seem to agree on what needs to be replayed anyway, so are we doomed to go the way of the dinosaurs? Would that be best for other species?

Hope Knocking explores the relationships that exist in an Appalachian family: Amantha, her elderly mother, Nancy Mae, and Matthew,

Amantha's husband. To give the memoir different perspectives, I included all of their points of view. Nancy Mae and Matthew were both brought up in Appalachia, and therefore season the narrative with many interesting cultural tidbits. Amantha struggles at times to understand their mountain ways, and it is this struggle that plays out within herself, causing her to question her own place among the kinfolk she finds difficult to understand. Will she and Matthew stay put and allow roots to deeply penetrate the rocky ground, or will other circumstances uproot them and scatter them to the westward wind?

I hope you are inspired and energized by my book.

Remember

Remember the sky that you were born under, know each of the star's stories.

Remember the moon, know who she is.

Remember the sun's birth at dawn, that is the strongest point of time.

Remember sundown and the giving away to night.

Remember your birth, how your mother struggled to give you form and breath. You are evidence of her life, and her mother's, and hers.

Remember your father. He is your life, also.

Remember the earth whose skin you are: red earth, black earth, yellow earth, white earth, brown earth, we are earth.

Remember the plants, trees, animal life who all
have their tribes, their families, their histories, too.
Talk to them, listen to them. They are alive poems.

Remember the wind. Remember her voice.
She knows the origin of this universe.

Remember you are all people, and all people are you.

Remember you are this universe and this universe
is you.

Remember all is in motion, is growing, is you.

Remember language comes from this.

Remember the dance language is, that life is.

Remember.

—Joy Harjo

Part One:
Springing into the Abyss

Amantha

Week One of Quarantine

As I trudge up the hill leading to The Nowhere on a warm day in late March, I spot something hiding in the brown leaves on the bank: bloodroot! Its pearly white petals are bathed in the soft mountain sunlight, and it looks like a miracle. Though I always search for this native wildflower, its beauty never fails to surprise and delight me to the core every spring. This year, 2020, in the midst of so much darkness and despair, its innocence makes me want to cry.

I turn right on Mava Road and continue my climb up the empty stretch of road winding beside rocky cliffs, steep banks, and mountainous views that the locals have always called The Nowhere.

I notice our neighbor Frank washing his car, and I try to wave and get his attention so I can inquire about his family. Either he doesn't see me or he's pretending not to, so I turn my back and walk on. Ever since Matthew, Mom, and I moved down to the bottom—over fifteen years ago—the neighbors and I have barely spoken. I couldn't say who's more to blame, but the good Lord knows I have tried...most of the time. I immediately berate myself: *You know, he could be shy, Amantha. Don't be so quick to judge.*

I consider myself to be half hillbilly and half flatlander because Momma grew up here, and Dad's family is from the Deep South. I grew up in the foothills of Appalachia, in north Georgia, but I found my true home when I started my teaching career in the late eighties and moved up to the ancient mountains on the Tennessee-North Carolina border. Even though a few years later I got wanderlust and moved to the Rockies and then South America, Appalachia called me home in 2003, and I found true love with Matthew, who gazed at me with the bluest mountain eyes I'd ever seen. My song "Mountain Heart" explains our meeting:

Many years she had wandered
This world all alone
From Georgia to Spain,
Looked for love in vain

Caroline to Colorado,
A trail of tears
Chile coasts she roamed
Till she drifted back home

<u>CHORUS</u>
In the hills of Tennessee,
My true love waits for me
With blue eyes so clear,
He draws me near
To a mountain heart so dear

Salida, Virginia
In the Appalachian hills
He had never left home,
But he felt lonely still

Hope Knocking

One Saturday night
At a dance in Tennessee,
Two hearts came together
For eternity

Momma—Nancy Mae—came back here too, after retiring from her teaching job in Georgia. She bought a place on the Diamond River, right in the beloved community of her childhood, Mavie. Matthew and I got married on the banks of the river fifteen years ago and now live next door to my mother.

I admit that I don't quite understand my mountain half. At times, I feel like the people withhold so much of themselves from outsiders that the outsiders start to wonder if it's personal or just another queer mountain trait. I guess I'll always be an outsider with connections, like it or not.

Another neighbor's little dog is yapping incessantly, and now I see why: a red fox—a big one, too. The graceful creature darts out onto the road, sees me, and then disappears into the woods on the other side of the road. The den must be in the other direction, or maybe she just wants a better look at me because Ms. Fox quickly crosses the road again, this time scampering up the bank and disappearing.

Since my quarantine began last Monday, I've seen a different animal every day. First, there was the slinky, graceful mink across the river from the tiny house, my quarantine home for two weeks. Matthew built it for momma to use as a guesthouse, since neither one of our homes can accommodate many people. The mink seemed to tell me to tread carefully and quietly through the waters of life. Next, two deer grazing in the new grass on the Diamond's banks warned me to blend in and not make waves. Now this fox. I wonder what lesson she is trying to impart.

Someone has left a box of packaged foods on the side of the road, probably picked up from the food pantry down at Little Mann School. I move it closer to the road, hoping that someone who needs it—and I'm *sure* that someone now needs it—will pick it up before the animals scatter the trash everywhere.

As I continue up The Nowhere, I feel a heaviness envelop me in spite of the pretty day. I feel a need to *do* something, *help* someone, *connect*, or try to *ease* the trouble that the Coronavirus has brought to the world.

There's trash on both sides of the road, and I berate myself for forgetting to bring a trash bag again. I cross the road at the curve, trying to avoid the cars that usually come flying down the road. Today, though, there are no cars in sight. I spy an empty mulch sack that's big enough to do the job, and by the time I get to the old dump site, it's halfway full already. I peer over the steep sides of the former dump and see that people are continuing to dump trash here despite the rocky barrier that was recently erected. They just stop a few feet away from the barrier and unload their trash. Just three months ago, the newly formed "Keep Elk County Beautiful" group came out one Saturday and worked all day, hauling out cars, refrigerators, stoves, car batteries, tires, and mounds of Styrofoam, plastic, and paper. You name it, they found it.

I try to understand the mentality of people who mindlessly toss their trash out their car window, but I struggle to. I suppose poverty has forced them to view their surroundings in terms of survival, not beauty. What can they extract from the land in order to make some money so that they can eat and pay bills? They only think of how the environment can best serve them, not how they might help the environment. Maybe they cannot appreciate the beauty that has surrounded them their entire lives. Generations have dealt with trash this way—bury it, burn it, or toss it over a cliff. Why pay a dollar a bag to drop it off at the dump?

It all seems so hopeless to me today, but I cross the road and continue to fill the sack as I retrace my steps home. I hear a car approaching behind me, so I step into the ditch, nearly hugging the steep rock face of the cliff.

My third cousin Trula, who is in her bright yellow Jeep, slows down to a crawl and says, "Are you out yet, Amantha? I heard you were in quarantine for a couple of weeks."

I notice she's wearing a mask—the first one outside our home that I've seen in Mavie—and blue plastic gloves.

"No, I've still got one week left. I'm getting my walk in and trying to do something useful," I say, glancing at my bulging sack. "Are you heading to Billy Joe's?"

Trula was the home health worker assigned to old man Bill, who lived down the river from us, before Hospice was called in. He was the first to succumb to the virus in Mavie.

"Yeah. The family wants me to clean up the place so they can sell it, I guess. Tell your momma I said hi, and I hope you'uns will all be okay."

"You, too, Trula. Love you!" I yell as she drives away.

My bag is now filled to the brim, mostly with Dr. Enuf, Mountain Dew, beer bottles, Styrofoam take-out containers, and lots of straws. I barely manage to drag it down the hill to the garden shed, where I leave it until it can either be burned or hauled off. I need to drink something and check on Mom. From a safe distance, of course. I make my way past the garden, walking alongside the Diamond River, and I see her sitting under the shed. I pull a chair out into the sun and sit six feet away.

"I'm glad you're back. I always worry about you when you walk up there," she said.

I give her my standard response: "It's still too early for the drunks and druggies to be up and about. I did see Trula, though, and she said hi."

She tells me that North Carolina has closed all its borders and that five people have now died from Covid-19 at the Med Center.

"I feel so depressed," I tell her. "This all feels so surreal."

Momma smiles reassuringly at me, and her big blue eyes light up. I can tell she has something important to say. She looks out at the tumbling river as she turns her thoughts back in time.

"This virus brings to mind the TB epidemic. We lived right across the road from Aunt Oda and Uncle Oliver and played with our cousins every day. Sometimes we even spent the night there. They had eight children. Four of them got sick, and so did Uncle Oliver. Three of our dear cousins died of that terrible disease, while our family didn't lose one soul. I'll never understand that, but I remember how scared I was that my sister Maddie—just a baby then—would get it and die. She would crawl on the floor right where they were spitting their bakker juice into coffee cans. I'd carry her into the bedroom away from the filth, but she'd start a wailing and momma would fuss at me to bring her back."

Momma stops talking and the only sound is the Diamond River making its way downstream. I think she's done and I start to get up, but her intense blue eyes look up at me then, and she says, "We survived those hard times and we'll get through these, too."

I smile gratefully at her and we enjoy the sunshine and each other's company without conversation for a while, and then she tells me it's time for one of her judge shows and she leaves. As I watch her slowly ascend the bank up to her house, I think about the new Coronavirus as I take in the sunshine and the gurgling river.

Personally, I think this is nature's way of getting things back in balance. There are too many humans on the Earth, and we greedily use up all the resources while ruining the planet with our pollution, causing mass animal and plant extinctions and runaway climate change. Now, during this Covid-19 outbreak, which started in China in 2019, people are buying up everything for themselves. I couldn't believe the empty shelves I saw when I returned to the mainland. They were bare of bread, rice, meat, bleach, sanitizer wipes and gel, beans, and the most hoarded item—toilet paper. I figure we can use the newspapers we've been saving for the garden if it comes down to that…if there's no Charmin to be found.

I walk back to the garden shed to get the strawberry plants I bought from Cerro City the other day, and notice the bee balm coming up. I like to harvest the fragrant leaves and flowers to make a wonderful herbal tea that's good for inflammation. I mix it with lemon balm, which I have growing in a tub up at the Treehouse, my name for our house that sits at the top of the property and looks out over a canopy of hemlocks, white oaks, sassafras and dogwoods.

Matthew and I hadn't planned on doing a garden this year at all, but this crisis changed our minds. I bought enough seed, along with a few plants, in Cerro City to cover the recently plowed soil and hoped the seedlings we normally bought—tomatoes, peppers, eggplant, and basil—would later be available. I was glad I found red potato seed, as all potato seed has been hard to find. Matthew was told by two different places in Betsyville that the government was buying up all the seed, which was why they didn't have it. Who knows if there's any truth to this or not? There are *so* many rumors these days.

While I was in town, nobody but me was wearing a mask. I thought one man was going to confront me about scaring his young son, but he kept his mouth shut. No one was abiding by the six-foot rule, either, but I suppose that very few of them had just flown in a plane or been in a crowded airport like Dallas Fort Worth. I had, which is why I'm doing a two-week quarantine away from everyone in the tiny house, that I've named Bear Necessities, because of all its black bear décor. I do not want to infect my eighty-six-year-old mother or sixty-year-old husband, so quarantine I must.

I plant four rows of strawberries next to the perennial patch of asparagus and rhubarb. Yesterday evening, Matthew and I planted cabbage, onions, and peas. Peas are one of my favorite vegetables from the garden, although we've never had any luck with them. I keep trying each year. Maybe the good Lord will provide us with tasty peas to go with the new potatoes this year. Maybe He'll take pity on us considering the *mess* we're in. Maybe not, though.

God may have decided to teach all of us a lesson about being good stewards of the Earth. He wants us to stop being selfish and greedy and to learn to be thankful. I've been pondering the purpose of the pandemic. I believe everything has a purpose. We just need to slow down enough to learn the lessons that are available to us every day. He did say, "No more water, but fire next time." Did He mean the fire of fever? As the song says, "Oh, Mary, don't you weep no more."

*　*　*

Two Canada geese awaken me the next morning with their trumpet sound. Little Bit, my sixteen-year-old cat who has involuntarily become my quarantine companion, is scratching himself on the bed, wanting to be fed. I must get him to Dr. Baker, if he's open, for another flea allergy shot. I feed the orange tabby a few spoonfuls of his diminishing supply of wet Friskies and make my coffee. The comforting routine of making and drinking coffee takes me back to Hawaii.

In Maui, my routine was to let the birds awaken me. First came the soft crowing of the wild roosters, which were *everywhere* on the island. Then came the loud, vibrant chorus of what sounded to me like doves... on steroids. They were so alive, and I loved the sound of them every morning! I'd make my coffee, laced with Aloha honey, and take it back to bed and watch the day begin.

I miss the taste of that honey! Maybe I'll try to get some on Amazon if it's available and not too expensive. In the mountains of East Tennessee, I use mountain honey, which is good, but nothing compares to Aloha.

The geese are grazing on the new grass and are trying to tell me something. "Listen, Amantha. Slow down. Smell the coffee, the roses, the *stink* of Little Bit's box!" *SHEW-WEE!* It's no use. The spell has been broken for now. I hope the geese are patient teachers and will return with their important assignment when I am ready to receive it. Off the geese go, perhaps in search of more receptive students.

The birds remind me of the Nene, the geese found on the slopes of the Haleakalā volcano in Hawaii. They are actually related, but the Nene have developed webbed feet to help them adapt to the rough volcanic rocks.

I feel like crying right now but do not face these feelings, instead creating some tasks to do. The sadness doesn't go away, though, so I give in. I think, *Who are you, sadness, and what do you have to tell me? Remember the geese and how they calmly went about their day, grazing, enjoying the sunshine, joyfully surviving.* The simple beauty brings on the tears, and I let them flow like a river.

God will always bring a rainbow. Meanwhile, take it one day at a time. Help each other. We are not alone, nor are we meant to be. Graze together. Bask in God's beauty. Weep if you must, but then rejoice.

Amantha

Week Two of Quarantine

Matthew's now working second shift, so until I return to our Treehouse on April 6th, I'll hardly get to see him. I call up there to see if he wants breakfast, but he just wants me to fix him a dinner to take to ClothTreat, a factory that treats fabric for various companies. We are fortunate to get N-95 masks and gloves from the company to wear during this viral outbreak. They are impossible to find, even for the stressed-out healthcare workers who depend on them to save their patients' lives and their own lives.

As far as we know, Covid-19 started back in the fall of 2019 at a live animal market in China, transmitted from animal to human. It became a global pandemic in early spring of 2020, and its first victims in the US were residents in a nursing home in the state of Washington. Now, it has supposedly peaked in China and is wreaking havoc in the rest of the world.

I meet my husband at Mother's house, all of us masked and at a safe distance from each other.

"Can you believe ClothTreat is now forbidding the line workers to enter the main office?" Matthew rants. "The workers are also starting to complain about having to work when everyone else around here is laid off with pay. The supervisors are threatening to fire people who don't show up. They're all scared. *Anyone* would be. At least I don't have to work Saturdays anymore."

Matthew is considered an "essential worker," one of the many new terms that has come out of Covid-19. The cloth his company treats is now going to the healthcare industry to be made into HAZMAT suits.

The essential healthcare workers have it so bad right now. There is a shortage of PPE (personal protection equipment), such as masks, face shields, gloves, ventilators, and even test kits. States are being forced to compete with each other for these resources because we have a president who says there's no problem, no shortage. POTUS says he doesn't even plan to wear a mask, that it's optional. He has said that Covid-19 is no worse than the flu and has accused Democrats of creating this "fake news" to keep him from being re-elected.

Getting re-elected seems to be all the president cares about right now. His daily CV briefings have the flavor of slick campaign ads, with him stating how wonderfully his administration is handling it all. He says that everything will be back to normal by Easter. Somehow, his approval rating has risen slightly lately. I suppose he *could* get re-elected in November. Anything is possible. He did win the presidency in 2016, though he did not win the popular vote—something that seems to really bother him. He seems to have an unhealthy longing for approval, much to the detriment of the people now dying from the Coronavirus.

Matthew and I do our long-distance smooch routine, and he's out the door. I'm so scared for him, but I try not to let him hear the panic in my voice as I follow him out to his truck and say, "You hang in there, sweetie pie. And wear your mask, even if those bozos don't. I love you, honey. Be careful."

He reassures me that he'll wear his mask, gets in Big Red, his fire-engine red pickup truck, and leaves.

* * *

Mom and I do a writing exercise together. She has written six books during her retirement, but now, at eighty-six, she says she's done. I sometimes try to stimulate her brain, get her away from the TV and its increasingly morbid news.

"Remember how depressed we both felt on Sunday? Just like Kris Kristofferson's song about how Sunday makes a person feel alone. Let's use our senses to write about how we felt, okay?"

She reluctantly agrees but seems to thoroughly enjoy the activity once we get into it.

Sight

Mom: New life continuing non-stop. Joy and hope carried by the river.

Me: Bloodroot highlighted by rays of sun, swaying gently in the breeze.

Sound

Mom: Animals making joyful noises—birds singing, dog sighing. The wind rustling the trees.

Me: Beaver felling a tree that crashes into the river, awakening me, reminding me that life ebbs and flows whether we are there to witness it or not.

Touch

Mom: Caution! Limits on touching other humans, but you can pet cats, dogs, and smooth river rocks.

Me: River soil between my fingers as I cradle new cabbage plants and feathery-soft sage roots, which offer their protection against diseases that threaten life.

Smell

Mom: Soft breeze brings damp, warm smell of river, animals, plants, and new life.

Me: Sanitizer gel burns my skin and nostrils, drying me up like an apple core left unattended in the sun.

Coronavirus

Mom: Anxiety, hope, and remembrance of desperate times in the past. Faith in nature, people, animals, and plants. Recovery, renewal, and healing.

Me: Nightmare that refuses to release me, bringing fear, death, and isolation. Yet it frees up my days, a release from so-called important appointments. Inspires me to consider others and what they must be feeling. Such sadness.

* * *

I return to Bear Necessities, where Little Bit is waiting to be let out again even though it's a cold, wet, drizzling day. He wants back in immediately. He seems more and more unhappy every day, not seeming to understand what we're doing down here. I try talking to him, explaining everything, and I tell him we'll all be back together again soon. Things will get back to normal. I think I'm trying to convince myself of this, though. In reality, I know it's going to take more than a two-week quarantine for life to stabilize. I'm sure it'll be comparable to 9/11; we'll discuss life *before* Covid-19 and life *after*. Hopefully, so long as they keep making Little Friskies canned food, he gets to go back home with Mommy *and* Daddy, *and* we take those "things" off our faces, my cat will be okay.

After our little chat, I listen to about an hour of *NPR* on my alarm clock radio, and Little Bit curls up on the bed. The radio is my only connection to the world other than the house phone. Mom and I share the phone. We've worked out a system where she picks up right away at her house, and if it's for me, she has them call back and lets it ring. Mom forgot our system after a few days, though, and I can tell the whole thing is irritating her.

According to *NPR*, New York is in terrible shape. They're now using refrigerated trucks as morgues, confiscating them from poor truckers who are trying to make a living delivering food. Funerals have become a thing of the past, as social distancing must be maintained. Graveside services are limited to only ten immediate family members...for now.

Every day, something changes. At first, people were encouraged to get outdoors and exercise, but now popular trails and parks are closed. People just won't stay six feet apart. Just three weeks ago, high school and college students were still going on spring break. It was as if they hadn't heard of the Coronavirus, or they just didn't care, figuring that only the elderly and sickly could get it. Those students brought home more than a tan, forcing colleges and high schools to close their doors.

My sister, Eileen, an adjunct professor at the University of Washington, is now teaching her computer classes online from home, joining other higher education institutions around the world. I suspect this may become a permanent solution for many schools, even after this has ended.

NPR interviews a scientist who believes that Covid-19 will probably disappear from the US in the summer but return next winter. Hopefully, there will be a vaccine by then.

I really wonder if I had Covid-19 this past winter. I was the sickest I'd ever been. It had started after my hiking trip to Utah. First was a terrible hacking cough, which is a telltale sign of Covid-19, and then I got a viral infection. They told me I had bronchitis, but were they sure? If there was more testing available, I could find out if I'd developed antibodies, and if I had, that would probably mean Mother and Matthew had them as well. So we'd all be immune, right? There's so much they *don't* know about this virus.

I can't take the gloom and doom any longer, so I turn off the radio. I'm hungry and decide to make a healthy soup with celery, carrots, chicken, onion, brown rice, pepper flakes, cilantro, and lemon. I eat a big, steaming bowlful and give Little Bit his Friskies fix. After I eat, I take a large helping to Mother.

Mother tells me that my cousin Bart, who lives alone in public housing, thinks he has the virus. She gave him the 1-800 hotline to call if you're showing symptoms, but he's completely illiterate and couldn't write down the number. I tell her I'll call him tonight to determine if he has the fever and tight chest, symptoms that accompany the cough.

We are both in bad moods, so I don't stay long. Upon returning to the tiny house, I notice ants in Little Bit's water bowl. I kill them immediately. Then I wonder why I did that. I speculate about how it would feel to have some giant reach down and squash the life out of me. I do regret murdering the ants, but if any stink bugs make an appearance, there will be no mercy.

Before bedtime, I look out at the river and see what first appears to be a bear cub. However, it is actually a very fat beaver. I watch him swim. He propels himself from one submerged rock to another, then dives underwater. I don't think beavers do that, which makes me think it's actually a muskrat. But they don't have flat tails. I wonder if it was a beaver with an identity crisis. I try to figure out what message he's trying to send me, but I just do not know.

I call my cousin Bart, and he really sounds freaked out. He tells me that he doesn't have any tightness in his chest, nor does he think he's running a fever. I do my best to convince him that he has a cold, and I tell him to ask his son, Brad, to buy him some cough medicine.

The next morning, I see the same animal with a rhododendron branch in his mouth, so now I know my second hunch was right. It's a beaver. I think his message is that things really are what they seem to be, at least most of the time. I do wonder about my perception of reality at times, though, because sometimes I get it all wrong. Yeah, like in Hawaii.

Staring into my coffee cup, I think of Mahena, the Maui cat who would visit me most mornings in Hawaii. Solid black and as old as Little Bit, she took to sleeping on the outdoor couch outside my bedroom window, but when she heard me making my morning brew, she wanted in. Of course, I let her comfort me with her purring. There's something about a cat's purring that is so grounding, calming, and nurturing.

Little Bit jumps up on the bed, curls up right beside me and is purring now. His amber eyes meet mine and seem to tell me he's now available for counseling. Tell him all about my awkward vacation blunder.

I stayed with my friend Sarah when I was in Hawaii. Her birthday is March 20th, and mine is the 21st, so she invited me to come celebrate island-style. It was my first time there, and we did some amazing things. We sailed out in the lavender waters of the Pacific to watch the humpback whales, and they put on quite a show! Her friend James joined us the next day for a hike into the crater of Haleakalā. The mist-shrouded volcano is my favorite memory from my ten-day stay on Maui.

Thinking back now, though, I can't help but feel like I'm grieving a lost friendship. From the time she picked me up in Kahului, Sarah seemed withdrawn and a little irritated. I mistakenly interpreted that to mean that she really didn't want me there. She gave up her bedroom for me—I strongly protested, to no avail—and constantly fussed at me when I did things differently from her. I cooked dinner for her and James, and she complained about my method. I cleaned her bathroom and kitchen, and she complained that I used the wrong sponge. I felt there was something going on, but she wouldn't talk to me and seemed sad.

At the time, I figured that, with the virus and all, I'd come at a bad time and should probably make plans to leave a few days early. On my eighth day there, in my typical blunt way, I just blurted out, "Sarah, do you want me to go home?"

My question seemed to anger and hurt her, and I immediately regretted it. She had, after all, been a wonderful hostess. She had arranged for us to play music, hike, kayak, and even go sailing. Plus, she had sacrificed her bedroom, though I *did* protest. Sarah admitted that she was worried about her mother, who lives in the Smokies, *and* me during the pandemic. She had been trying to make sure I stayed healthy during my stay. I tried to express my sincere gratitude to her, but I also communicated that, due to her silence, I was unaware of her worries. I said that maybe my leaving early would alleviate some of her stress. She then completely shut down, and I felt like a complete jerk. I apologized over and over again, telling her I'd apparently misjudged the entire situation, but she became unavailable.

After that, I left her staring out into the garden, clearly upset. I walked into the quaint cowboy town called Makawao, which was practically deserted. I saw only one other person on my walk, a little boy who passed me on his skateboard. I stopped at the park, which was closed, and sat on the steps to make my call to American Airlines. After more than an hour-long wait, I talked to a sympathetic agent who arranged for me to return home three days early—on my birthday, in fact. It began to rain, so I pulled on my rain jacket and continued into town, no agenda at all.

Just walk, Amantha, I told myself.

I'd done it again—alienated myself from another friend because of my false assumptions. I'd reacted instead of considering that my thinking might be flawed. When would I learn to keep my mouth shut? Now I'd hurt a lovely friend who had so graciously opened her home to me. This lesson kept reappearing in my life, I guess because I hadn't learned it yet.

The summer before Hawaii, during Bible School, I had lashed out at Melinda, the woman in charge, because I felt like she was trying to control everything, including the music, which was supposed to be my baby. I thought I had learned then that it just wasn't worth speaking up when it ended up hurting someone.

I realized then, as I realize now, that speaking up had become important to me as an adult because I hadn't felt heard as a child. I get that. I really do. But somehow, I need to learn how to comfort that unheard inner child without striking out at another being whom I believe is trying to hurt me. If only I had taken the time to talk with God and spend some time with my feelings before reacting...

During my walk through Makawao, I realized the Kamoda Bakery was open. I entered and ordered several island delicacies, including guava-filled pastries and, of course, coconut donuts. Since I'd arrived in Hawaii on March 11th, I'd craved coconut and really hadn't indulged *too* much...if I didn't count the coconut candy I bought after the volcano hike or the ice cream I'd scarfed down in Paia. But who was counting? Besides, I'd been bad and needed to beat myself up a little. (Such is my relationship with food—I sometimes use it to reward or punish myself rather than simply using it to nourish my body. But, hey, at least I'm aware that I do this.)

I stuffed pastry after pastry down as I walked past the art market, which was closed, and continued past town, intent on finding the elusive Sacred Garden. The elderly Japanese proprietor of the bakery had said it was "just down the road." That sounded like someone back home saying, "It's not fer. Just over the next holler." Well, it *was* "fer," and after walking for nearly an hour on the side of a highway that had no sidewalks, I turned back.

When I got back to Sarah's, she was more receptive to talking, and she seemed to let it go. We decided to pack up the ukuleles and head to the beach. She taught me a few chords, and I was good to go. (Ukuleles are similar to the guitar, which I know how to play.) We sang and watched the most spectacular sunset.

I thought I'd repaired our friendship, but now, back in Tennessee, I'm unable to reach her. I've called, emailed, and messaged her on Facebook, but she does not respond. It hurts, but I've done everything I know to do, so I leave the ball in her court.

I thank Little Bit for his services, get on my knees in front of the full-sized bed that's just right for one person, and I pray: "Dear Lord, thank you for another day, for the rest, and for the coffee. Thank you for the outlet of writing during this—I won't call it a nightmare because I know now that I'm wide awake—this ordeal. Writing helps to ease my pain, Lord. I pray, too, Lord, that Sarah will forgive me, because I need *all* my friends right now. I pray that you both forgive me for my shortcomings. Help me to do thy will. Amen."

I get dressed and go check on Mother. It's Saturday, and Matthew's still sleeping, I'm sure. I invite her to breakfast, which consists of scrambled eggs, grits, and sweet potatoes with butter and cinnamon. After eating, we look through *Voices of the Diamond*, her book of poetry—her last book, she swears—and find the poem she wants me to read at her funeral.

She was reminded of it earlier, when I met her and Pedro—her aged, faithful black lab, whom she insists is on his way out—and we walked by the river. She was wrapped up in a cape and shawl, looking like quite a character, which she is. I have a treasured photograph of her looking exactly like this present moment: a tall, bent-over woman with silver hair and startlingly big blue eyes peeking out beneath a hooded cape. She was wearing numerous layers of mismatched clothing, which include pajamas and big garden gloves. She was clutching a ski pole that serves as her cane.

I greeted her, saying, "This is how I'll remember you, you know, walking by the Diamond with Pedro."

"I'm going to haint you, I'm sure," she replied, smiling like a sprite.

"Then I'll just leave," I said.

She reassured me that she'd be a friendly "haint," and we left it at that.

Nova Mann

Now she wants to read "Lingering Love" to me.

Walk by the river at the first light of dawn.
Feel my presence. Know I'm changed in form, not gone.
Here by the river when it's neither night nor day,
Memories move along with the low drifting fog.
Past and present merge, and time fades away.
A damp river breeze just caressed your face.
A little burst of wind lifted your hair.
Or was it a touch and a kiss gently placed?
Linger by the river at the first light of day.
Let the past and present merge.
Feel the essence of those who passed this way.
Was that river mist swirling through the air,
Damp fog that licked your face,
Or was it dogs running as a pair?
What was that streak of white that floated by?
Was it the memory of a little dog that played in the sand?
Or was it just clouds drifting down from the sky?
Silent as the grave, fog makes no sound,
Just moves with the flow of the river,
Forming patterns on the ground.
Is that fast-moving mass just fog and clouds?
Or is it a band of Indian warriors marching strong and proud?
Is that Uncle Carter Harmon and his faithful hound dog
Taking their morning stroll by the river he loved?
Or is it just the shadow of that big pine log?
Is that my face smiling down at you?
Does the breeze lift your hair like the touch of a hand?
Can you feel the warmth from tracks in the sand?
If the trees sway and dance as you pass by,
I will be there in the stillness of winter

Hope Knocking

As snowflakes drift to Earth from the sky.
Spring will return and warm the Earth.
When nature wakes from her long winter nap,
Flowers come forth and grace the rebirth.
I greet you in flower planted by my hand.
I am not gone, just changed in form.
My love is everlasting, as is the land.
Love never dies.
You can feel it in the land,
In the waters and the sky.

I can imagine her reading stories to her fourth grade class, her tall frame filling up the room and them attentively listening to her sweet, clear mountain voice. I'm sure they adored her. Everyone does.

I'm also sure that I don't want to talk about her dying anymore. (This has been one of her favorite topics of conversation for the last five years or more.) Therefore, I bid her farewell, pack a few of my belongings in my sky-blue Subaru, which I lovingly call Cielito Lindo, and take everything back up to the Treehouse, anticipating my release from my self-imposed "prison."

Matthew is awake now, eating breakfast on the couch while watching the governor of New York speak about the dire situation there. He says that his state will likely peak next week. The death toll in the US is now over eight thousand. Worldwide, there are more than sixty thousand deaths. The governor is frantically begging other states to send ventilators, as they're now having to hook at least two patients up to one machine.

Matthew and I do our distant smooching routine, and as I go into the kitchen to fill up more jugs of water and wash his dishes, I sneak a longing look back at him. I see stubble on his chin and I long to curl up with him on the couch and rub my cheek against his so I can feel that roughness. There's something so compelling about Matthew. He's a gentle soul, really, but also very masculine—a man's man, as the saying goes. He adores football, auctions, chainsaws, and hunting dogs, but he also likes to sing, dance, study the Bible, and garden. He is also very observant. He noticed I'd circled an article about raised beds in *Mother Earth* magazine, and went out and bought the materials, and made them during my quarantine. What a great birthday surprise!

After it warms up outside, we decide to fill the new beds with garden soil so I can plant the lettuce seed I got from Cerro City. He goes to start the tractor and attach the scoop.

While I'm waiting, I decide to check my voicemail. Before I press "play," I clean my hands with our diminishing supply of Germ-X and disinfect the phone, too. It's funny (but not really) how everything that we touch can become contaminated. I wonder how long we'll have to continue this cleaning routine throughout 2020.

Our preacher called to say he's putting his message on Facebook this Sunday, and he wants me to send him a song that would comfort people right now. I know the perfect song: "Stand by Me." I first heard Doc Watson sing this old hymn at a music festival in North Carolina, and since then it's become one of my favorite songs to sing. I return my preacher's call to tell him that I'll do my best to get the video to him tonight or, at the latest, tomorrow morning.

The second message makes me smile instantly. It's from Becky, my best friend since the beginning of time. I haven't talked with her since my birthday, when she called me to wish me well. I need at least an hour on the phone with her just to clear my head and heart. We somehow always seem to know when the other needs a shoulder to cry on. We have always been able to tell each other everything, and we know we can trust each other completely. I guess this call will have to wait until I get back home since I can't tie up Mom's phone for that long.

I hear the tractor coming up the drive with the first load of dirt. Our project takes five trips back and forth to the garden, shoveling the dirt into the dilapidated wheelbarrow, and then pushing it around the house to the courtyard, where we then shovel the soil into the large raised beds. This is exhausting work, and I know I earned my nickname today.

"You sure look good in those jeans, Manthie Mule", Matthew tells me as I roll the wheelbarrow back for the last time. I hope he calls me that because of my strong work ethic—not my stubbornness.

"It's a good thing I'm still quarantined, sweetie pie, because I'm dog-tired *and* hungry. But I thank you for the compliment. Come on down for supper in an hour or two. I'm going to whip up some meatloaf, boiled cabbage, and mashed taters."

"Mmm, my favorite. I'll be down later on. First, I'm going to smooth out the garden."

After supper, which we all three eat out on the porch at Bear Necessities, I make a final trip back up to the Treehouse to record the song. As I rehearse, I realize that I haven't picked guitar since Maui. There, Sarah, James, a sweet old man named Breeze, a fiddler named Heather, and I would play for hours practically every night. We played gospel, old-time, bluegrass, Hawaiian, alternative...whatever struck our fancy. I would play one of James's guitars or Sarah's ukulele, and James would play the Kora, a stringed African instrument made from a large gourd. Sarah and Breeze were on drums, and Heather danced and played fiddle. None of us really thought much about the virus while playing, and we usually forgot *not* to hug at the end of our sessions. I even wrote Sarah her own birthday song, which she loved:

Here's to our friend Sarah on her birthday this year
May it be filled with joy and presents so dear

CHORUS 1
Presents like love, music, and light
Dancing and singing into the night
Oh, Blessed Redeemer, show us the way

May we learn to be present every day
The present of friendship is a gift from above
When we stumble and fall, a true friend gives love

CHORUS 2
Love lifts us up to the glorious light
Like a lighthouse, it beckons when we're lost in the night
The Master of the sea sent Noah His love
May we learn to embrace that beautiful dove

"Happy Birthday, dear Sarah!" we all sing to you
With the whales in the deep blue sea, we pray peace to you, too

CHORUS 3
Peace like a river flowing with ease
Peace like the sun in your face, your hair in the breeze
May peace caress you like a mother's embrace,
Bring joy to your heart and a smile to your face

Finally, I get back to Bear Necessities. I realize that I'm utterly exhausted, dirty, and cold. I run a hot bath—it can't be too hot for me—add some lavender and frankincense oils, and scrub myself from head to toe. After that, I soak for a very long time before getting out.

Little Bit begs for more wet food, but I only give him dry Friskies. He's too tired to aggravate me much and is on the bed asleep by the time I finally lie down. I figured I'd be too tired to write, but here I am writing again. Maybe it will become a completed book, or maybe it's just good therapy for me right now and will become food for the woodstove next winter.

Oh, dear God. Next winter…Will life be back to normal by then? I wonder.

Hope Knocking

During my tiny house quarantine, I come to realize that the river speaks and is truly alive. I've been awakened every night by a noise that I now know is the river itself. At first, its popping noises reminded me of distant gunshots, and since turkey season opened last week, I just assumed I'd been hearing the shots from way up on Hickory Nut Mountain across the river. This theory was given more credence when, yesterday, while Matthew and I were shoveling dirt, two hunters quietly trespassed across our property, coming from the direction of the Cherokee National Forest, which connects to our land. Matthew thought one of them was Eddie, our next-door neighbor and Cousin Jewell's son, but I wasn't so sure. Eddie's really lean, but this guy was bulked up.

It made me a little uneasy and angry that they hadn't bothered to ask permission to be on our land. We value our privacy so much, as I'm sure everyone does. When we first moved here, it was quite difficult to convince the locals to access the public lands by using the road above instead of walking through our front yard. They had been coming this way their entire lives, and I'm sure they resented us. But nevertheless, the peace, quiet, and beauty are what lured us and keep us on The Nowhere so far.

This morning, it dawned on me that those noises I'd been hearing came from the Diamond, *not* hunters and *not* animals crossing and dislodging rocks while looking for food. It's the sound of the water rolling down its ancient course, moving the rocks along with it. This knowledge has made me appreciate rivers even more than before.

The river has its own language! There's the non-stop light babbling of the water rushing over the rapids. Then there's the menacing roar after days of hard rain. There's also the painful groans it makes when it becomes jammed with ice after days of hard freeze. And now this new sound. Well, I suppose it's only new to me. The river's been popping forever, and perhaps it's only modern-day humans who've failed to pay attention. I'm sure all the animals that the river supports—the trout, wood ducks, muskrats, otter, eagles, and countless others—hear, speak, and understand this language. I'll bet the Cherokee also knew this ancient tongue. I frequently find fragments of their tools in the garden, and their presence is still felt here.

Our presence is felt here, too, and has soured the landscape. It saddens me to think of all the trash that's probably buried at the bottom of the river—tires, cars, glass, plastic, fishing line, and lures. Mom tells me that the old hospital in Banter, NC, used to dispose of its hazardous waste in the Diamond. The hospital's been closed for over forty years now, but I still won't eat any fish that come from the river's seemingly pristine waters.

I am rambling this morning, but you don't care, because you may never read my great American novel. I never really had any intention of writing one, but about five days into my quarantine, I found myself trying to suppress an overwhelming desire to write. Finally, that desire won out, and here we are. There's a great freedom in following your desire, even if it may be a temporary one.

I've never considered myself to be anything but a writer of songs. I've written many, and I even have a light-hearted one about the virus. It's called "Coronavirus Blues."

Can't find a mask or sanitizer gel
This could be bad, folks; this could be hell
They've closed down schools; they're cancelling flights
I'm getting real worried; I can't sleep at night
Toilet paper is impossible to find
A bar of soap might go for $9.99
Don't shake my hand or give me a hug
'Cause I don't want that Coronavirus bug

<u>CHORUS</u>

Hope Knocking

I got the Coronavirus blues
Oh, what should I do if I have to sneeze?
Should I say it's just allergies or just watch them flee?
Either way, I'm not sorry 'cause I'm going to Maui
I'm sailing along with my face to the sun,
Munching on mango and pork on a bun
I've landed in paradise; it's so much fun
If I'm quarantined in Maui, what can be done?

CHORUS 2

I got the Coronavirus blues
Oh, what should I do if I get all flushed?
Should I blame those hula-hula boys for making me blush?
Either way, I'm not sorry that I'm in Maui
They know I'm a tourist 'cause I'm burned to a crisp
I try to speak Hawaiian with a Castilian lisp
I've worn out my welcome, and it's time to fly
You know Aloha also means goodbye

CHORUS 3

I got the Coronavirus blues
Oh, what should I do if I cough on the plane?
Should I hold up my biscotti cookie,
Give it all the blame?
Anyway, I'm not sorry that I'm going home to Mavie
Yeah, I'm really happy that I'm going to Mavie
Because my baby lives in Mavie
And we can do the Hokey-Pokey if we stay six feet apart

Okay, now that I've flexed my creative muscle, I've got to get on with my day, though my calendar remains empty. I do need to start the transition back to the Treehouse. Yes, I name everything around here. It's just something I do. On the way up there, I'll point out the Bottle Room, the Zebra and the Pet Cemetery, which is not hard to figure out.

I'm really starting to get into writing my first book. I think, *What does it want? What is the plot? Is this book for me? Am I to wrestle with my demons, and will I win? Is this book for others? Is it simply a day-by-day account of living during the Coronavirus?* I don't think it's ready to tell me yet, so I just let it be...for now.

Today is Sunday, and lately there's something about Sundays that's been hard to take. Sunday *does* make you feel alone. I know Kris Kristofferson could relate. I feel so tired, too. Why do I feel like I have to take care of everyone? It wears me out, and it's my own fault. I suppose I do it to feel needed.

When I go back home, I make sure Matthew has what he needs for another work week, and I try to spend time with him. We watch Charles Goodman. He really is a good preacher. I don't normally like TV evangelists at all. Even though Matthew and I are together, it feels awkward, and I still feel alone. Maybe we're getting used to being apart now. It seems like we hardly speak at all anymore.

I go down to Mother's to get her *huge* shopping list, because tomorrow I'm going to town to do all of our shopping. I dread it because I know it's going to take most of the day. Aunt Macie calls while I'm there, so Mom and I don't really get the chance to talk, which is okay because I don't feel much like talking right now.

I head back to Bear Necessities to pack up Little Bit and his belongings, as he has visitation privileges with his daddy and is spending the night with him. Then I return to the tiny house to write some more. It seems to be the only balm for my unease right now.

I think part of the problem with Sundays right now is the departure from our routine of attending church. Matthew and I regularly attend Gentry Gap Baptist Church, and now nobody's having church, except virtually. It's pretty amazing how quickly churches are adapting to our new reality. So many preachers have online services now that, unless you have really good internet service, the connection is sketchy. Our connection is bad here in Mavie. My song never uploaded, and the preacher's message didn't, either. They are both floating around in the twilight zone of virtual space somewhere, I guess.

I read online that the CDC now advises everyone to wear masks and that the US is number one in the world for Coronavirus infections. *God, please help us.*

"Stand by Me" finally uploads at four in the afternoon, and I share it with our church members, friends, and family, hoping it will comfort them all.

Matthew and I sit on the porch and do our Bible lesson for today, and we pray. He reveals his anxiety and depression in his prayer to God.

"I've gotta get away from work," he tells me when we're done. "I'm gonna put in for a week off—the week of my birthday. If I don't, I'm probably going to punch somebody in the nose."

I raise my eyebrows and squeeze his hand, which is trembling slightly, and say, "I think that's what you need to do, sweetie."

Perhaps the rumors of imminent martial law will prove to be true, and then everything will close down. Then my husband will have more vacation time than he's bargaining for. I hope it doesn't happen tomorrow, though, because I'm going on a big grocery run. Plus, I'm taking a mask to my friend and former student, Jared, who depends on his job at the dollar store but doesn't want to die for it. If I leave by seven in the morning, I hope to be back by three in the afternoon, if all goes as planned. We live an hour from Junction City, so it's bound to be a long day.

The geese have come to tell me goodbye, and the Diamond just spoke his clunking message, telling me to roll with the current, like water off a goose's back.

Nancy Mae

I carefully place my feet on the cold wooden floor, make my way to the coffee maker, and turn it on. I hear Pedro's nails softly clicking as he approaches to bid me good morning and demand my time and attention. While my brew is percolating and reaching its noisy climax, I let him out into the fresh, cool mountain air.

"Go on now. Go pee-pee," I coax as he finally exits.

I take my coffee black, and I take it in bed. This is my favorite time of day, when I can listen and watch as the new day begins. Another day above ground. By the time I finish my first cup, Pedro—named by Matthew—is ready to come back in and begin demanding food.

My daughter Amantha calls Pedro "Beautiful Brown Eyes," and she even sings her own version of that old song to him. I think it goes something like this:

> *Pedro Garcia's a good dog, he's black as the darkest night sky*
> *He eats and eats just like a hog and has the biggest brown eyes*
> *Beautiful, beautiful brown eyes; beautiful, beautiful brown eyes*
> *Beautiful, beautiful brown eyes, I'll never love blue eyes again*
> *He likes to wade in the river as we walk on its bank every day*
> *His big brown eyes make my heart quiver, and that's why I'm singing today*

I give him some Beneful, fill up my cup, and head back to bed, telling him, "Now, you be a good boy and leave me alone, so I can have my coffee in peace."

He seems to understand and comes to lie down by my bed—after he's eaten, of course.

I can't bring myself to turn on the TV yet. It's nothing but news now anyway—news about this new Coronavirus spreading across the globe. Yesterday, the outbreak even affected my judge show, as the president came on and interrupted it. I don't have any idea what he said, because I could not stand to hear it anymore, so I turned off the TV. He better not try that today.

I get up and fix myself a piece of whole wheat toast, smeared with apple butter that we made last October. That seems like so long ago, and it was so much work, but it was nice to have people over. I wonder when we'll be able to do that again. I start to worry that our big family reunion scheduled for August will be cancelled because of this blamed virus.

Pedro wants my toast, so I give him a little canned chicken and more dry food to see if that'll make him leave me alone.

I get dressed, simply adding more layers over my nightgown, in preparation for our morning stroll by the river. I don't go very far these days—I'm pushing ninety, you know, and I'm getting a little more stooped. I'm really careful. If it weren't for Pedro, I don't know if I'd bother. Amantha says he's the reason I'm in such good shape, but when he goes—and he's on his way out—I'll *never* get another one.

I put on my boots and retrieve my walking stick by the side porch, and we make our way down the driveway. I admire the blooming money plant and tulips by Mary's garden. Mary was my friend and a former Doe High School teacher; she died about six years ago. She gave me a statue, which I think looks like her, and some plants to surround it.

I must remember to tell Amantha who the other statues are of. This one is Amy Rae, another dear friend who died the year before Mary died. This one is my cousin Berthie, and this one...*Oh, dear. Who is this one?* I think. He went to school with me and Amy Rae. I can't remember names anymore.

I slowly make my way up the driveway of my niece Jewell's house. I admire the pink and purple flowers blooming on the bank, but I no longer remember their names, either. Pedro is already eating the food she has thrown out. I've asked her a million times not to do that. One of these days, he's going to choke on a chicken bone, and that'll be the end of him.

I push on and head over the slight rise, making my way down the rocky drive. Ducks, or geese, are in the fields honking at Pedro, but he's such a good boy. He just ignores them as we round the corner near the huge gardens. Later on in the summer, the gardens will be filled with corn, green beans, tomatoes, cabbage, and, of course, potatoes. All of the staples of a mountain diet (because you can't grow Mountain Dew, Dr. Enuf, bologna sandwiches on white bread, and meth).

I make my way back to the Tiny House, but I don't see any lights on yet, so I don't bother my youngest daughter or her mean cat, Little Bit, who terrifies my dog. I'm so glad Amantha's back home from "Hiwahyah"—this is how I like to pronounce it, much to her amusement. It's a bad time to travel right now, and I was so worried she'd be stranded there.

Amantha comes out on the front porch now. "Come on up, Momma, and have some breakfast with me."

By the time I make it up the steps, she has two cups of coffee poured. We try to sit on the porch, but it's way too windy this March morning, so we head indoors. I sit on the couch, right by her suitcase, and she's on the bed across the room.

"It feels good in here. Are you staying warm enough?" I ask.

She nods, and I look around the room, which is decorated in a rose theme. My mother, Pennie, always grew the prettiest flowers around, especially roses. They have always reminded me of her, and there's something about Amantha, who just turned fifty-eight last weekend, that reminds me of her, too. I can't quite put my finger on it, though. It's not so much her physique—she got her father's stout body, not

Pennie's lean, delicate features. It's something in the face, when she's pondering something. I just can't put my finger on it....but I know what it's *not*. It's *not* the rabbit look.

Thank goodness she didn't seem to inherit Mom's nervous spells. My sisters and I called them the rabbit look because when something bad happened—or when she *thought* something bad was going to happen, a look of pure terror would come over mom's face and she would hide in her house like a rabbit in its burrow, refusing to leave for days. Nobody back in those days knew about anxiety attacks, but I'm sure now that's what they were. Poor momma....she suffered so.

Amantha's voice brings me back to the here and now. "I made some hot cereal that's really good, I think. It reminds me of Cream of Wheat, which you used to fix us when we were kids. I always liked that."

She places a steaming bowl in front of me on a tiny round table. We eat at a safe distance apart and talk about how lucky we are to live at No Place on The Nowhere. She says that her two-week quarantine is like having an extended vacation.

I finish my breakfast and get up to leave. "Well, I better go let Pedro in. He's too afraid of this mean ole cat to come up here." Little Bit wraps his tail around my leg, claiming me as another of his humans.

As I make my way home, I realize that today is Tuesday. I wish I could go to the center. You never realize how much something, or someone, means to you until they become absent in your life. They've closed down Birch Mountain Community Center, along with everything else now, because of the virus. It wasn't much. Around a dozen women would gather there every Tuesday to work on a quilt or a hooked rug, or they'd go to listen to Amantha's old-time jam group. Then everyone would gather in the cafeteria of the old CCC school to eat. (The beautiful stone building had been converted to a community center when low attendance forced the K-8 school to close its doors.) Lunch was potluck, and it was mostly edible. I miss the socializing most of all; it was the only place to go around here to talk, laugh, and gossip with a few of the "girls." It got me out of Mavie, at least.

Hopefully, life will get back to normal soon. I sure hope so, because everyone's acting crazy, including Amantha. She acts like she's got the plague, wearing a mask and gloves and using Germ-X like it's an elixir. She's so bossy, too. I can't stand it. I have done things my way my whole life, and she tries to tell me what to do *constantly* now. I know she's worried, but she needs to calm down.

Pedro wags his tail as he sees me coming up the steps, and we go in. He settles down on the rug, and I get back in bed to watch TV. I *love* my TV. If something happens to it, it may be time for me to exit this ole world. It's time for *Family Feud*, one of my favorites. That Steve whatever-his-name-is is pretty funny, and I like to guess the answers.

The phone rings, and I wait to see whose number pops up. It's Jay-boy! My son lives in New Orleans, where he's a professor at Tulane University. Since the outbreak, he's been working from home, and he calls me practically every day.

I pick up and say, "How's my Jay-boy this morning? Are you getting much work done?" I listen for a long time as he explains his worries about the virus.

"Hi, mom. Oh, my God, I'm getting so much work done! I never really thought I'd be able to focus as much at home, with so many distractions to tempt me, like my tennis racket, bike and kayak—not to mention Belinda—but really, I've been a good boy and have graded a crap load of papers. So many places are closed here, too, like the tennis courts, because there are so many infections since Mardi Gras. The governor of Louisiana didn't cancel the madness last month, and Covid-19 cases have skyrocketed here in the Big Easy—one of the worst death rates in the world. It's really hitting the Black community worse than others; more than 75 percent of all cases are in the Black community. And this trend is holding true for the rest of the country, as well.

I think it's because of the lack of health care available to them, plus the prevalence of many other underlying health problems, such as diabetes. You know, once it starts spreading in Appalachia, the same thing is going to happen. So many people up there have terrible health, too."

I get in a few words before we hang up, "They love their bologna on white bread, all forms of tobacco, and Mountain Dew, that's for sure. Well, you try not to work too hard, Jay, and don't worry about us. You come when you can, you hear?"

He pauses before he says, "You know I want to come see you, mom. I'm just not sure if I should."

I tell him he shouldn't, although I'd love to see him.

We have a special bond, this son and me. I can talk with him easily—long, interesting talks that sometimes last for hours, usually involving a drink or two. I love all my children the same, but he's the one I'm closest to. He'd like for me to come live with him and his wife, Belinda, in the winter. I tell him that when Pedro goes, maybe I will. Until then, I just can't make any plans. I don't know if I'd go even then. I'm sure I'd miss my home.

After Jay and I hang up, it's time for one of my judge shows and then lunch. The phone rings again. This time, it's my sister Macie, who lives up north in Connecticut. She's been a nervous wreck since this pandemic began, so I pick up.

"You making it okay, sister?" I ask.

She tells me that her husband, Geoffrey, thinks he has the virus and wants to get tested, but they don't know if they should leave the house or "shelter in place." (Amantha told me yesterday that this term is used in schools when there is an active shooter nearby.) I convince Macie to call the 1-800 hotline, and we hang up.

Macie, our brother RC, and I are the only siblings left out of seven, but she and I are the closest. We are the only ones who left these mountains in search of a better life. The FBI recruited me right after graduating from high school, and I sent for her as soon as I was able.

We both met our husbands in D.C., but I left that fascinating city, and eventually my husband of twenty years, while she stayed up North with her husband. I came back to Mavie after retiring from my teaching job in Georgia, but she very seldom comes, and she never stays for long. I think it makes her sad to think of our hard upbringing. She did come two or three years ago with all of her children and their children, and we had us a big time. If things get back to normal, they'll all be coming back for the reunion in August.

I hear Amantha letting herself in. She says, "I brought you some spaghetti."

"Lord, girl, you cooking again?" I say happily, as that sounds better than peanut butter and crackers.

We crawl back into my bed. She has her mask in place, and I have the plate of food. It's time for the news.

"You know, it's kind of a relief not having TV in the Tiny House," she says. "This is all so overwhelming. I don't think I can bear much more."

She goes into the living room, and I hear her singing "Beautiful Brown Eyes" to Pedro. After watching the weather, I join her, mask in place, and we make plans to go up to Birch Springs cemetery, where most of our family is buried, tomorrow.

"Let's invite Jewell," I say. "She's about bored out of her mind." My niece lives next door to us and spends most days inside cleaning house while her husband works a job in town.

"Only if she wears a mask while we're in the car," Amantha says. "We have to be careful, momma."

"You know she's not going to wear one. I don't want to wear one either. I hate these things! I can hardly breathe!" I pull mine down below my nose, which sends my daughter over the edge.

"*What are you doing?* Pull your mask back up, momma." She stands up, puts her fists on her hips, and waits for me to comply, but I stubbornly hold my ground. Pedro senses trouble and leaves the room.

"Well, forget it. You two just go on without me. I don't care." She storms out the door, angry as a hornet, leaving me alone and dissatisfied.

I go back to my room and watch TV until Matthew comes to deliver my paper and mail. *The Betsyville Star* is not much. I mainly subscribe to it for the obituaries, so it doesn't take me long to read it. I ask my son-in-law if he will hang up a picture in the basement and fix a water leak down there when he has time. Before he heads downstairs, I holler at him.

"Watch out when you go see Amantha! She's in a bad mood. She's becoming a mask dictator."

He pokes his head inside my bedroom and looks at me a moment before saying, "She's just worried about you, Nancy. You *should* be wearing a mask anytime you're around anyone. Sometimes I feel like not wearing one, either, especially at work. Nobody else wears one. They all think this virus is something made up—not real. Some days it's hard to get out of bed and make myself go, but I do, and I wear a mask there because I don't want you or Mantha getting sick."

Matthew's job is essential, which means he won't be laid off like millions of others around the country.

"You're lucky to have a job at all," I tell him, and he stomps off.

The government is supposed to be sending everyone a relief check sometime next month, and I wonder if I'll be getting one. If I do, I wonder what on Earth I'll do with it. I'm sure the Humane Society could use the money, or maybe I'll give it to my nephew Bart. He most certainly needs the money, and he probably won't be getting a stimulus check since he hasn't worked in years.

Matthew doesn't stay long, and I wonder if he hung the picture at least. I hear him close the basement door, start up his truck, and head down to Bear Necessities to visit his wife.

I fix myself a bowl of ice cream and head to my bed. It's finally time for my favorite judge show of all, *Judge Jillian*. She's so mean, and I just love her! She tells people what she thinks, and they listen. In this episode, there's a woman dressed in a ridiculous outfit—one of those awful shirts with holes in the shoulders—and she's suing her landlord because he's trying to keep her deposit after kicking her out for some reason. The man interrupts Jillian, and she lets him have it. She rules in the poor woman's favor.

The second part is not interesting, and Pedro is looking at me, wagging his tail. I sigh, get up, and feed him for the umpteenth time. I clean my teeth, and we go out for the last time so he can pee. I walk past the shed and strain my old eyes to see Amantha stretched out in her favorite recliner—the one that stretches her back—on the porch, and I know what I must do. I slowly make my way up the stairs and join her since the sun is now hitting the deck. Matthew has left, and it's just us. Neither one of us speaks for a few minutes, hearing just the river and my rocker clicking nervously back and forth. Finally, I turn to her and offer an apology.

"I'm sorry I provoked you. I know how worried you are about everything. I'll tell Jewell to wear a mask, and if she doesn't have one, then she can't go."

Amantha smiles and responds, "I overreacted, as usual. We are so lucky to have each other, and these are hard times. Let's try to make the best of it."

I agree, and we both marvel at the new green growth across the river.

"We'll get through this," I say.

Nancy Mae

One Week Later

I'm getting sick and tired of being cooped up here and want to go with Amantha to town to get groceries, but she won't let me, and she has my other children on her side. I know they're just trying to protect me from this virus, but I've lived a good, long life, and I have to go sometime.

To tell you the truth, I think all of us had the Coronavirus already and are immune. Amantha got so sick this past winter and gave it to Matthew, and I got a mild touch of it, too.

My tough, strong body has served me well all my life. I had all the childhood diseases—measles, chicken pox, and mumps—but as an adult I rarely get sick. I only take one prescription, and that's for my underactive thyroid. I never take the flu or pneumonia shots, no matter how many times my doctor fusses at me. I try to stay as far away from those doctors and "horspitals" (as my dearly departed sister Marvie used to call them) as I can.

Now, I do believe in taking supplements. I take cinnamon to lower my blood sugar even though I'm sure I *don't* have diabetes, no matter what both of those doctors tell me. I take fish oil for my heart, garlic for my high cholesterol, calcium for my osteoporosis, and, my strangest remedy of all, gin-soaked raisons for my arthritis. I also enjoy a glass of sweet wine at night to relax. I'd drink more if I could develop a liking for alcohol.

I add cinnamon to my growing shopping list, which I'll give to Amantha this morning. She comes up the stairs at seven, probably hoping to get to the stores before the shelves are emptied.

"Do you have coffee ready?" she asks after she lets herself in. She pets Pedro.

"You must be feeling extra brave this morning if you're wanting my fully-leaded." I smile as I hand her a cup.

She looks over my long list and declares, "I believe this is the longest list I've ever seen. That's good."

"I'll go with you if you let me. You're going to need my help," I plead.

She shakes her head, finishes the coffee, takes my list and money, and gives me a hug goodbye. "It's nice to finally be able to give you a hug," she says and heads out the door.

I notice that her pants are no longer clinging to her shrinking body. In fact, they look quite baggy. Since she retired from her teaching job nearly two years ago, Amantha has lost more than forty pounds. She exercises regularly and eats all kinds of healthy foods, which she doles out to me regularly. I eat some of it, Pedro gets his share, and the rest goes to the compost pile.

I don't complain too much about her giving me healthy foods, because I just *hate* to cook anymore. It seems like so much work now. The most cooking I do now is for my dog, the luckiest in the world. He eats better than most humans on planet Earth. I fix him chicken and rice every day, and I'm about out of both, so I'm hoping Amantha can find these two scarce items today.

I see Pedro's big brown eyes begging me for the daily walk, so I pull on the layers, find my boots and stick, and try not to trip over his big black body as we head down the stairs. The last thing I need right now is a trip to the ER.

I keep my eyes peeled for snakes because it's about time for them to come out of hiding now. There's really only one kind of snake we see around here, and that's copperheads. We try to watch where we put our hands and feet, especially Amantha, who's always working in her garden. So far, we've avoided getting bit. I know they're just trying to survive, too, and they try to stay out of our way.

I love *all* living things. I even had a black snake living in my shed once. I fondly called it Snakesha. I always accuse Matthew of killing her during a family gathering we had a few summers back. He swears it was a copperhead, which I reluctantly allow to be killed when they're found trespassing.

As I tread slowly down my driveway, I admire the Rose Room. Amantha recently added three more roses to the collection, and they are the prettiest coral color. I pass the pet cemetery and remind myself that we have to find a place for Pedro, because he's going soon...hopefully before me. Then I arrive at the Bridal Room, which holds plants that were given to Amantha at her bridal shower nearly fifteen years ago. Matthew and Amantha were married here on the river, and this particular garden room always reminds me of that joyous event, especially when a particular bush blooms. It has white blooms and looks like a bridal veil. I think that's what it is called.

I climb the drive and notice that another bush is decorated with Easter eggs. Is it Easter already? It makes me sad to think that children won't be participating in Easter egg hunts this year, except with their own families in their backyards.

I see my niece Jewell peeking out her window, and she comes out to greet me. "I thought I saw Pedro out here. At first, I thought he was a big black bear."

She tells me that her husband, Ernie, is taking her to the doctor this morning because she's out of medicine. I recognize the inherited rabbit look and hope the doctor can prescribe her some relief.

She goes back in the house, and I cut my walk short, retracing my steps back home. I feel so exhausted these days.

I pass by the Bottle Garden and think of all the glass we've collected to add to it. Elk County doesn't recycle glass, so this garden has been our solution to that problem. But we're running out of room now. Some of the wine bottles will go to my cousin Oliver, who'll use them to make his homemade wine and shine.

I admire the money plant blooming profusely beside the stairs leading up to the house, and I wonder why I can remember its name but not the name of the other pink flower here in the courtyard. I do admit that my memory is going. Although I'll never tell her, Amantha is probably right about the memory loss starting right after I fell out of my bed around three years ago. She thinks I had a small stroke, but I think it was the ham I ate for breakfast. Plus, I overdid it while working out in the yard, trying to clean up the laurel branches those darn beavers had cut. I didn't drink enough water, either, so I was probably dehydrated. She found me later on that afternoon, passed out on the floor, unaware of my surroundings. She called the squad and said I threw the biggest hissy fit she'd ever seen. I remember none of that, nor do I remember the long ride into Junction City. Anyway, they did a whole bunch of tests—I couldn't tell you what all they did—and found nothing. So that just proves that I was right the whole time. She should have just left me alone.

Once inside my house, I fix myself another cup of coffee, grab a donut, and head for bed. I *love* my bed. I practically live in it. It's one of those adjustable ones. I paid a pretty price for it, but it's worth it.

I turn on the TV and notice that it's April 6th. *What on Earth happened to March?* I think. The top stories are, of course, about Covid-19; that is pretty much a constant this year. But today, the weather is also making the news. As if the virus isn't enough, Mother Nature has decided to give an Easter surprise to the Southeast—a huge string of tornados heading from Louisiana to Virginia, and we're right in their path. *Oh shit. I hope we don't lose power,* I think as I listen to the gloomy forecast. As the aged tend to do, I drift back in time and recall with great detail a scary experience that happened when I moved into my newly-built cabin.

Was it 2003 or 2004? Hurricane Something plowed through the Diamond River community, causing a hundred-year flood that ran right below my house, right in my front yard. I kept seeing that brown water rise up and over the banks until it ran down the fields, robbing the gardens of its dark, fertile soil. I didn't sleep a wink, thinking that the water could possibly come up and destroy my new home, sweeping me down that dirty river and into the Cove. I've never liked that lake and sure didn't want to end up dying in its stagnant water.

A character in Amantha's song "Old Bent Town" died in that lake. I think I have a copy of the song right next to the bed. She gave me a copy of it the other day, right after I first heard her play it on her new instrument...the one with all the strings. *What is it called?* She says King David in the Bible played it. I simply cannot remember, and I surely wouldn't remember her song, either, but it's right here where I left it.

"Old Bent Town"

Where the Roe Creek met the Cove, up in Jordan County,
Lay the bustling town of Old Bent, sought by Tennessee Valley Authority
Since the flood of 1940, the government devised a plan
To move all the houses and buy up all the land
Harriet met Henry at Cove Academy
They courted, and they fell in love where Honeycutt's cabin used to be
But he left to serve his country, got shot down in Normandy
Harriet had him buried beneath that white oak tree

<u>CHORUS</u>
Old Bent Town got drowned that day in 1949,
When the TVA released the water that made Cove Lake
The first time they came a-calling to offer her a check,

Harriet replied, "No thank you, sir, my Henry's buried out back"
The second time they made her leave, she returned through the gap,
Escaped authority, climbed that old oak tree
Then they covered up our town
Beneath the clear waters, listen closely to hear
The sighs of two lovers who lay buried here still

You see, Cove Lake, along with many other lakes in Appalachia, was created by the TVA to create jobs and electricity for the poor mountain folk. My dad actually got his first steady job helping to construct it. I remember him being so proud the day our house got electric lights! He brought home our first electric lamp, and I loved being able to stay up reading late into the night, not having to worry about using up the kerosene in our old lantern. It was years later, when I sent home money from D.C., that Dad was able to buy Mom her first refrigerator. Until then, we'd had to rely on our springhouse to keep food from spoiling.

Cove Lake was filled in 1949, covering the old town of Bent, a thriving community before the government forced people to sell out and move their homes to its present location. I suppose mountain people learned to distrust the government then, and they are still bitter about the town's sad past. They even had to unearth the dead bodies in the cemeteries and move them, along with the headstones. *I wonder if they got them all,* I think now. Lakes have always seemed like dead bodies to me. They're not alive like rivers, whose waters are always freshly churning, seeming to cleanse themselves, happily chattering each day.

The Diamond didn't sound happy the day the hurricane passed through, though, which is another reason sleep would not come to me that chilly fall night. It *roared*. I kept looking through my bedroom window at its huge waves, which were carrying entire trees and other debris. I tried to distract myself by watching TV. Then nighttime came, and the power went out. The phone died, too, so I couldn't even call anyone. I have lived by myself since Dan and I divorced, over thirty years ago now, and I have never felt alone...until that scary October night. I worried not only about the rising water but also about a tree crashing into the house. I tightly clenched a wad of paper towel into my fist—my security blanket, Amantha claims—and waited for the dawn to come.

The screaming winds finally began to die down as the light poured into my kitchen window. I'd survived the storm, but what had happened during the night? Before I ventured out, I had to have some coffee, and since the power was still out—and would remain out the entire week—I brewed an awful concoction on top of the woodstove downstairs and drank it down...grounds and all. I exited the safety of home and entered what appeared to be hell. The river was just below the upper bank, right below my house, where the blueberry bushes are now. It ran as far as my eye could see, running down the field below Jewell's new house, and was carrying all kinds of stuff—lumber, dead cattle (poor things!), twisted metal, huge trees, road signs, and who knew what else. I hoped to God no human bodies were in that deadly, frothy water!

I didn't dare venture too close, as I've always been afraid of water. I suppose that is because I never learned to swim. No one around here ever learned to swim. Who had the money for that? You learned to stay out of the deep pools of the river or, better yet, stay out of the water altogether.

I walked to Jewell and Ernie's house, to check on them, I told myself, but I knew it was mainly because I could not bear that day alone anymore.

They saw me coming, and Ernie threw open the door. "Here she is, Jewell. Here's ole Nancy."

I could see the inherited rabbit look in my niece's eyes as she ran up the stairs. "Oh, Nancy, we've been worried sick about you. Did you sleep at all?"

I shook my head, and we decided to go carefully survey the damage. They pulled on boots and rain jackets, and we took the path above their house and walked downriver, where the gardens were covered with water. The barn had disappeared entirely, leaving no trace of its existence. We saw our neighbors close to the water's edge, and we hollered at them to be careful. They rarely spoke to us at all, but they made an exception that day, venturing up the bank to inquire about us and to tell us that they'd heard on their weather radio that people were being rescued from the floodwaters in the Diamond, in the Roe in Betsyville, and in the Cove in North Carolina. When all was said and done, the Flood of 2004 had claimed twenty-four lives. That was a sad, horrible time, and here we are again, this time with a virus that has claimed far more lives.

I force myself back to the present and find myself clutching a wad of paper towels so tightly that they've shredded in my trembling hand. I listen to the grim death toll being announced on the news now. Over twenty thousand people have now died in the US, and New York can claim over half of those deaths. They show the Big Apple's empty streets, and I try to imagine those poor families trapped inside tiny apartments, just like rats in a cage, some of them with small, restless children who do not understand why they can't go to the park for the Easter egg hunt. I'm sure they're driving their parents crazy. What will they do with them on Easter? They better hope the stores don't run out of chocolate bunnies and cream-filled eggs.

The news shows some church in Florida where a preacher was arrested for having services in spite of the stay-at-home order. He made bail and is vowing to have Easter sunrise service next Sunday. "Because God will protect His sheep," he screams at the reporter.

I say that God won't protect *stupid*. Even if God *did* protect them, what about the countless others they come in contact with? Do they even care about that? I think some churches just can't stand having their services labeled as "non-essential" gatherings, and that's why they're acting out. Most churches, however, are being reasonable and are doing all services online.

Amantha and Matthew have invited me to their house on Sunday to watch their church's Easter service on her computer. I'll come for dinner, but not church.

As of now, Tennessee only has one hundred deaths, and there are only five cases here in our area. I'm suddenly glad that we live in the sticks.

Before I turn the TV off, I catch the worldwide death toll—nearly one hundred thousand. *One hundred thousand!* That number just cannot compute in my old brain. It doesn't seem real at all. Will these numbers make us grieve for our fellow human beings, or will they make us numb and empty inside, like the meth-heads under the bridge down at the mall?

I reach for the *huge* copy of the *New York Times* that Jay sends me every week. I finally had to tell him that I don't want it anymore and ask for him to cancel the subscription. It seems like such a chore to get it read. There are some interesting articles, though, like this one about China's monopoly on PPEs. Whatever those are.

Why do humans feel the need to abbreviate everything? I used to think it was only educators who had the sadistic urge to demonstrate their pedagogical knowledge by abbreviating everything—PDP, EBD, ESOL, IEP, PE. It goes on and on. I'm so happy that I no longer remember many of them.

I scan the article, and I have to admit that it worries me. There is a very real shortage of masks, face shields, test kits, ventilators, and other safety gear that those poor nurses and doctors need in order to protect themselves, their families, and their patients. How is it possible that the so-called superpower of the world, the USA, is now at the mercy of the Chinese, who started this whole pandemic? The US states are being forced to compete and outbid each other in order to get life-saving equipment, all because the president will not act or allow the federal government to take charge. I guess he wants to blame the Chinese, the states—anyone but himself—for the horrible predicament our country finds itself in right now. Surely, people will now see that he is completely unfit for the job, and they won't re-elect him this coming November, if there is an election.

Another article discusses the primary election in one of those Midwestern states. The election forced people to endanger themselves by getting out to vote, as mail-in voting was not allowed. This appears to have been instigated by the Republicans, who, I suppose, were hoping there would be a low turn-out, which would allow the GOP to keep the seats. The president says voting by mail can't be trusted, and there's even talk of postponing the presidential election in November. I can't recall a time in my life when that has occurred, but these are strange days indeed.

There's another article about the president reopening our country ASAP and getting our economy going again. At first, he vowed to have us up and running by Easter—a sort of Republican Resurrection, I guess—but he soon had to eat those words. I feel sorry for his team of scientific experts, who have constantly had to correct much of what he has said. I know it must be hard to relinquish power, but I think we really need to listen to the scientists right now. Even they are having to revise information daily as new facts about the Coronavirus emerge.

I recently got into it again with my sister Macie, who just adores our president. We agreed for the hundredth time *not* to discuss politics, because we will never agree. I reminded her of what Mom used to tell us: "Never discuss three things: sex, religion, and politics."

I happily put down the bulky paper and reluctantly get out of bed. I fix myself a sloppy joe. I'm mostly a vegetarian, but I need some protein. I also fix one for Pedro, of course. I sit down in the "man-chair" after I eat to wait for Amantha's return.

The "man-chair" belonged to my brother Jake, who died about five or six years ago. I miss him terribly, though he became quite hateful in the end, probably because he felt so bad. He had a lung disease that was caused by years of smoking and working at the mill down in Betsyville. I'm glad he's not around to see the mess we're in now.

I'm glad that some of my other dear friends and cousins who have passed aren't witnessing this mess, either. Mary, Amy Rae, my cousins Beulah and Juanita, and my friends from Georgia, Dottie and Gail. I miss them all so much. It seems like they all died at the same time, leaving me here to ponder the meaning of it all.

When I leave this Earth, I wonder who will be left to remember me. All my friends are dead. They're *dead, not* passed, *not* gone to glory, *not* in heaven, *not any of that*. I'm going to make sure that my whatever-you-call-it in the paper says that I *died*. That's another thing I need to take care of; I need to write down exactly what I want it to say. But not right now. I'm exhausted, and it's time for *Judge Jillian*. Besides, I'm going to make it to ninety. I promised my favorite nephew, Larry, that I would. I'll write it tomorrow, if I feel like it.

Matthew

3:00 AM
The Day After Easter

I am running through a dark, winding hallway that never seems to end, trying to escape a giant beast—some sort of horrific creature that looks like a vampire. I don't waste precious time looking at the thing; I just run. Other beings try to grab my feet as I run past, but I kick at their claws and break loose every time. The hallway ends abruptly at a high brick wall. I try to climb it before the beasts of hell catch up with me, but when I place one foot on the slippery wall, my other foot slides down, and I make little progress. The wall seems to be oiled with something, and the awful thought that it might be blood comes to my mind. This thought fuels my terrible anxiety. I hear something slithering close to me now, and I think I hear its teeth clicking together. The vampire-like-thing reaches out for one foot, and I kick hard while trying to smash its head with one fist, precariously hanging on to the wall with my other hand.

It is in the midst of this struggle that I feel Amantha holding my thrashing arms, trying to wake me up from another nightmare with this beast.

"Matthew! Honey, it's just a dream. Wake up. It's okay. You're okay. Stop kicking!"

She's clinging to me now, stroking my back soothingly while wrapping her leg around my quivering ones. I am thrust into the present violently, breathing hard as I try to surface.

"Shh, just breathe now. You're okay. Was it the vampire again?" she softly whispers as she tries to comfort me.

I let my breathing calm down before I answer. "He came back with a vengeance, but I kicked his ass this time."

I let my wife hold me for a while, and when I feel her start to drift off to sleep again, I gently slide under her arm and get out of the bed. I head to the bathroom to splash cold water on my face, and I stare at my reflection for a moment or two.

Why do I keep having this awful dream? What's wrong with me? I think.

There's no answer waiting for me in the mirror, so I brush my teeth and listen to the wind howling outside. It has not stopped blowing since yesterday evening, and I know I'll have to be on the lookout for fallen trees, and possibly even power lines, on the dark highway this morning on my way into work.

I get dressed, grab my lunch pail, and head out the door. The darkness of the dawn seems as black as my nightmare, and I still feel immersed in it. I never sleep much at all anymore, especially since the virus started. I just catnap a few hours here and there. Amantha tells me I fight the vampire a lot, and I'm grateful that I don't remember him well. I can't always remember her calming me down, either, holding me, telling me it's just a dream.

I know the pandemic has caused lots of anxiety in everyone. There's so much uncertainty now, and *fear*. Fear that I might get the virus, bring it home to Amantha and Nancy Mae. Fear they'll die and leave me all alone.

That's one thing I couldn't bear: being all alone. I grew up in a big family. There were twelve of us total, if you count Momma and Daddy, so I never had any privacy and never really wanted any. If I did want some time to myself, I would get my old bluetick hound, Molly, and my rifle and head out to Click Mountain, sometimes for days, to hunt coons all night. Then I'd sleep all day, living on potted meat and nabs, or I'd eat cathead biscuits and salted ham if Momma had them to put in my pack. Those were the best days of my life, I reckon. Somehow, I never felt alone on the Click. I relished the freedom of roaming up and down rocky cliffs and through rhododendron hells, the moonlight trickling down through the pines as I tried to keep up with Molly while she hunted one coon after another.

I know those days are long gone. I get winded if I go up and down our stairs. I don't have a dog, because Nancy Mae would probably steal it, just like she did with Pedro. And Amantha wouldn't dream of buying potted meat.

As I reminisce about my glory days, I see that I am already nearly past the lake. The pale moonlight is shining on the rough waves, and I wonder, *Even if I could go back in time, would I?* Momma and Dad died many years ago, along with two of my brothers. I rarely see my other siblings, just at Homecoming every August. They never come see us. In fact, the only time they visited was on our wedding day fifteen years ago. The few times I went to see them, I couldn't wait to get back home. I missed Amantha terribly. She *is* home now. I guess I'm just an old fart whose better days have passed me by, and now I'm feeling sorry for myself. It's about time to whoop my demons and count my blessings.

I pull off the highway, and I put Big Red in park. I allow the tears that I've kept inside for so long fall down my face, and I call out to God, "Father, please help me keep my family safe from this virus. Help me to live in the present, in the *now*, and help me to appreciate all the gifts you have given me—Amantha, our beautiful home in Mavie, my job, my very life, Lord. Thank you, Father God, for *today*. Show me your will for me each moment of today. Amen."

Amantha

5:00 AM

"Peace be unto you all—all people, all creatures big and small." This was Preacher Darrell's Easter message yesterday, and it's helping me cope with my depression, which has become all too apparent to me and everyone who knows me. I long to feel peace, not these dark emotions that are clawing their way to the surface, threatening to scratch anything and anyone who happens to be in the way.

Yesterday, I tried to stay busy by cooking what should have been an unusual but tasty Easter dinner, but I overcooked the scallops. I'm not even sure that Pedro would eat them. The only thing that was palatable was the ginger cake with lemon sauce, so that's what I ate. A *big* piece. Mother and Matthew ate the potatoes and salad, along with the cake. I think they could tell I was in a bad mood, because even Mother didn't complain too much. I felt exhausted, withdrawn, and angry, and I just wanted to go back to bed, so that's what I did, leaving the two of them in the kitchen.

Later, I heard Mother leave, and Matthew got into bed with me, wrapping his arms around me. Soon, I heard his soft snoring. Since I can never nap, I got up, went downstairs to put another log in the woodstove, and fired up the computer. I saw that my preacher's sermon had finally uploaded, so I turned the volume down and began watching his message about God's peace. Matthew didn't nap for long, and he soon joined me. We watched until the power went out.

There were severe storms, and even tornados, being forecast for our area and all of the South last night. We don't normally get tornados here in the mountains of East Tennessee, but climate change has altered weather patterns everywhere. Just three years ago, a devastating storm with terrible straight-line winds shredded the huge white oaks lining the river, and a couple of people lost their lives. There was an actual tornado in Douley Valley—just a few miles away—about eight years ago, and seven people perished in that storm. We've since purchased a weather radio and now have an emergency plan in place.

The thought came to me again that nature seemed to be conspiring against humanity, wanting rid of us once and for all. If Covid-19 couldn't do the job, well, perhaps a path of tornados stretching from Texas to North Carolina would help.

Before it got too dark, I called Mother and convinced her to come to the Treehouse with Pedro to spend the night, just in case we needed to take shelter in our basement. She reluctantly agreed. We put Little Bit in our bathroom to keep him from pouncing on the big, wimpy dog, and then Mom and Pedro quickly settled down in the guest bedroom.

The winds began to roar, and the hardest rain I'd ever heard began to beat the tin roof. It didn't ease off the entire night, and neither did my fears and anxiety. I didn't sleep hardly any. Sometime in the dark night, the power miraculously came back on. I turned on the TV and saw that tornados were ravishing my birth state of Mississippi, Alabama, and Georgia, where I'd spent my childhood. I prayed for all of our friends and family who live there and fell back asleep while waiting for the dawn to come.

Now I see light softly spreading like a blanket across the early spring flowers outside our bedroom, and I get up to make coffee. I didn't even hear Matthew get up to go to work. He's back on first shift this week, and I am sure he couldn't have slept much, either. Four o'clock comes too early. The new day brings sad news; nearly forty people in the South died because of the fifty tornadoes that came this Easter Sunday.

I take Mom some coffee, and after hurriedly drinking it, she takes Pedro and walks home. I join them just to see what old man Diamond did during the night. I am so relieved to see that he behaved and has only come up to the Bottle Garden. We are truly so fortunate, and I feel very grateful. But I also feel like there's so much sadness in the world; so many lives were lost not only because of the storms but also because of the devastating viral attack.

A depression bigger than I've felt since 9/11 is descending on me, and I know I need help. Fortunately, I have a session with Josie, an energy healer I know, this afternoon at two via telephone. Until then, I make myself do my strengthening and stretching exercises to help my lower back, and then I take Mom to the Bent Post Office to mail a few letters. When we return, it's time for me to make the call. I recline on the sofa in the living room, where I can see the wind blowing the big hemlock outside. I can see the birds, too.

Nature has always been my go-to healer, and I am grateful for the beauty of the season. It seems like a God-given consolation prize meant to help us get through the "spiky ball" crisis. (My ex-husband, Sergei, describes the virus as a "spiky ball" because it looks like a ball with spikes on it, kind of like a medieval torture tool.) If this pandemic had occurred during the winter, the stay-at-home mandate would have been so much worse, as we wouldn't have been able to get outdoors as much. It is important to be grateful for every gift, and I have so much to be thankful for.

Maybe this is one of the lessons God is sending all of us right now. We Americans have been so blessed with material comforts that perhaps they have become our idols. God is not pleased and demands our attention.

Josie and I discuss what I want to accomplish during our session. I tell her about the overwhelming sadness I'm feeling and about how

I couldn't stop sobbing on the drive home from Food Lion on Good Friday.

My church had collected food for many immigrant families that had been laid off at the Townsend factory, and I delivered it on Good Friday. Since the immigrants are probably illegal, they do not receive any unemployment benefits, nor will they be getting the relief checks our government is sending out soon. Therefore, their need is great, as was their appreciation. I really didn't think there would be enough food for all seven families that showed up, but it was like the fishes and loaves story in the Bible. The food seemed to multiply, and everyone went home with bags of food! I was so overjoyed by God's mercy and grace. Our diverse group—which included my former student Rosa and her mother, other Guatemalan and Mexican families, my friends and fellow musicians Joan and Melvin, and myself—gathered in a circle, all of us six feet apart, in the parking lot, and we all prayed in Spanish and in English, giving thanks. It was very powerful and seemed to give me a sense of purpose in the midst of the pandemic.

After we all said our goodbyes and I began my long drive home (it is a forty-five-minute drive to any town from Mavie), the tears of joy began streaming down my face. We'd had church in that parking lot! Soon after, however, the joy turned to grief as I realized the enormous need many are facing in our country, and in the whole world, right now.

Immigrants who toil in our fields to bring in the harvest don't have the luxury of staying safe at home right now. If they want to eat, then they must work. They receive no government assistance even though most do pay taxes. Furthermore, many live in crowded conditions—ten or more often sharing one small house—so that they can save money to send back home to families who depend on that income. This lack of personal space obviously puts them at greater risk of contracting Covid.

I also speculate that, in the case of Latino immigrants, customary greetings may also be contributing to the spread. For example, it is the norm to greet friends in Chile with one kiss to the cheek, whereas in

Spain, it's two kisses on both cheeks. Mealtimes are spent together at the table, and dinner can last a couple of hours, filled with several courses and lots of conversation. Even though I adore these customs, I wonder if they factor into the rise of Covid cases for Hispanics, especially for those who can't stay home and quarantine.

In all actuality, I think that America could greatly benefit from the familiarity that's so prevalent in Latin culture. Many former students have told me that their own families never eat together except during holidays. They eat in their bedrooms, on the couch, or even in the car—always in a hurry, always on the run. Perhaps now that families are quarantining at home together, the dining room may once again be used. That may prove to be one of the highlights of 2020.

That night, as I drove over the bridge on 5, I couldn't help but think of the homeless who live underneath it. Shelters all over the country have had to shut down for safety reasons, forcing the homeless to completely fend for themselves. Due to their living conditions, they, too, are extremely susceptible to the virus as well as starvation. They go without meals, soap and water, clean clothing, and bedding, so they definitely go without sanitary gel and masks. I know that when I've gone backpacking, my limit is only about five days without a bath. I honestly cannot fathom the lives of the homeless. It's only by the grace of God that I'm not in that situation.

More than anything, it breaks my heart to see homeless children. Many single working mothers are only one paycheck away from homelessness and must work more than one minimum-wage job in order to escape it. Now, with schools closing due to Covid, many women have had to quit their jobs altogether in order to stay home with their children. I wonder how many are forced into homelessness because of the virus. Mothers who haven't lost their jobs and are able to work from home still bear the brunt of childcare, and they have to help their children adjust to online learning so that they can finish the schoolyear. Many children will not finish the schoolyear. So much suffering and need in the land of milk and honey.

What has happened to the American dream? How can these marginalized groups, who lived from paycheck to paycheck *before* the pandemic, possibly survive this? Covid-19 is rapidly exposing the discrepancies that already existed between the "haves" and the "have-nots." Will we as a country finally step up and help *all* people living in the United States, citizens or not, or will rich corporations continue to hoard all the wealth? America, we are at a crossroads. Who do we choose to be? Can we continue pretending that homeless "choose to live this way?" Are we okay with putting up a wall at our border to keep starving, desperate people out? Will we continue to pay women less and expect them to do more?

After sharing my experience on Good Friday with Josie, she tells me that we are all grieving for our country, and that resonates with me. I also think we are grieving for our planet, now regretting all the destruction we have caused this amazing homeplace, its creatures, and each other.

I feel sorrow when I think of losing Mother, too. I see her strength slipping away, and I am powerless to stop it. I worry that something might happen to her while I'm away from home. Of course, she says she doesn't need babysitting and is in great health, but she is eighty-six and anything can happen. I flash back to that cold Sunday afternoon three years ago, when I found her lying unconscious on the floor. I don't think I'll ever be able to erase that awful image of her from my mind. A towering oak tree felled to the ground. She is nearing the end of her life—something I must acknowledge and allow myself to grieve over.

I'm amazed that God seems to be using this virus to show me areas of my life that need to be cleaned up. My hurt is like a vulture pecking my innards, returning again and again in my life's path, circling in my head and heart, demanding to be acknowledged, demanding to clean up the mess. *How can I help you, my rapacious bird? How can you help me? What sustains you??*

Josie suggests that I have a conversation with my feathered friend to try and find out what she needs. She tells me to be gentle with myself. I agree to try this and thank her for the guidance. I give her my credit card information and make another appointment for two weeks from now. That seems so long to wait.

We hang up, and I pray. "Dear God, help us all. Help us all to learn the lessons Covid-19 is teaching us. Help me to be gentle with myself and with others—every living creature, every blade of grass, each flower, each handful of dirt. Thank you for allowing these lessons to come forth, Lord, and help me to receive them. May peace be upon us. Amen."

After my prayer, I write a new song called "Peace Be Unto You."

Oh Lord, I pray for peace today
May your blessed grace shine upon us all
Let us do good to one another
Lift up each sister and brother
No matter where he's from or what color

God sees our hearts, not the color of our skin
If we're filled with hate, there's no room for love within
So I pray, dear Lord, make me an instrument of love,
For you are love shining down from above

CHORUS
Peace be unto you, my friends
Peace be unto you
May peace and love fill up your hearts,
Bring us all together and never depart

Oh, Lord, I pray for healing today
May your blessed touch take away all pain
Let me have faith as a mustard seed,
Be filled with hope for things unseen
Please make me whole, in body and soul

We must have faith in times of tribulation
Pray to the one who was sent to rule all nations
Just reach out, touch the hem of His garment
If we believe, we shall have peace

<u>CHORUS 2</u>
Peace be unto you, my friends
Peace be unto you
May peace, love, and faith come to the human race
Through Jesus, the finisher of our faith

Purify our hearts! Save us from ourselves!
Justified by faith, we shall have peace

* * *

The next day, I drive to Cerro City to join my friends Sally, Joanie, and Kim on a hike beside Wild Honeysuckle Creek. It's chilly, but we all warm up as we climb the old railroad grade that winds beside the swollen creek. We stop to take pictures of foam flower, trillium, gay wing, and a few other wildflowers we cannot identify. We find a fairy house someone has constructed at the base of a white pine, and this discovery thoroughly delights us. We each leave a token of appreciation: shiny penny, pearl button, pinecone, and quartz.

At the end of the hike, we pull out our camp chairs and sit in a circle, space between us. We ponder over the changes Covid-19 has brought and discuss how these changes may affect us after the pandemic is over. I think that masks will be the must-have accessory from now on, and I believe people will have several in their post-Covid wardrobe, even when they become unnecessary...*if* they become unnecessary.

My hiking friends are all members of the Sunbeam Quilting Guild and have been busy sewing masks since the onset of the pandemic. They have already donated over five hundred beautiful masks so far, with most of them going to the local hospitals. Super Sally, as I like to call her, hands me three masks that she has lovingly sewn for Mother, Matthew, and me. Mine has butterflies, Mom's has watermelon slices, and Matthew's has a masculine *Star Wars* theme.

Joanie speculates that handshakes are now a thing of the past. She thinks that people will use foot bumps instead. We all stand up to try out our foot bumping techniques and say our goodbyes.

When I get back home, Mom tells me how depressed she is, and this makes me feel guilty that I got to be with my friends when she can't. This guilt sparks anger, and I say things I immediately regret. I try to make amends, but the damage has been done for today, so I leave. I feel so bad for her and hope her strong constitution can get her through these difficult days. I am trying my best to do whatever she needs without making her feel like she's imposing on my time. I know how fiercely independent she is and intuitively know that pride is helping to keep her alive right now. I somehow have to learn to balance her needs with my own.

Back home in the Treehouse, I sing "Dear Jesus," which I wrote this winter when I was so sick. I recorded it at Melvin and Joan's house over Easter weekend, and it has received more likes on Facebook than I could have ever imagined, which pleases me.

Dear Jesus, I want to thank you for believing in me,
Even when I didn't believe in you
I was so lost in sin and would not let you in

> *When I'd finally had enough,*
> *I fell to my knees, and I looked up*
>
> <u>CHORUS</u>
> *Lifeline! The love of Christ saved me*
> *Lifeline! He made me whole and set me free*
> *Jesus is the Light this troubled world really needs*
> *Dear Jesus, I want to thank you for healing me,*
> *Even when my faith was weak, too I was sick in my bed,*
> *but your Word kept me fed*
> *When I learned to wait on you,*
> *Amazing grace saw me through*
>
> <u>BRIDGE</u>
> *Holy! His name is holy! All the world shall bow at His throne in our heavenly home*
> *Dear Jesus, I want to thank you for answered prayers,*
> *For lost souls that you might spare*
> *It may take several years and many nights of tears,*
> *But when God reveals His plan,*
> *May she be walking hand in hand in the promised land*
> *Walking hand in hand in the promised land*
> *With dear Jesus*

I think back on my illness, which lasted from Thanksgiving well into the New Year, and wonder again if it was the dreaded virus. If so, am I now immune? With the extreme shortage of antibody tests in the US, it seems unlikely that I'll be able to get tested anytime soon.

The death toll in our country is now over thirty thousand, with very little signs of it slowing down. Even with this grim forecast, POTUS announced yesterday that he had "total control" and would reopen the economy when *he* decided, not when the governors decided. He wants to reopen it by May 1st. The whole country wants to get back to work. If we don't, it will be worse than the Great Depression in 1932. However, we are in a global pandemic, and this virus doesn't care that we have bills to pay. It will continue to spread if given the opportunity. Many states are now banding together, strategizing so they can form a reopening plan based on testing…when testing becomes available. They are asking POTUS to help make the tests available so that they can reopen, but he tells them that it is their responsibility. We are at a stalemate.

Matthew gives me a sleeping pill tonight so I can finally get a good night's rest. I cannot remember when I last slept more than five hours. It knocks me out for ten hours, and I wake up Wednesday morning more determined than ever to make it a good day. After coffee in bed and time with Little Bit, I make myself a healthy carrot, ginger, and orange juice, then do my *Dancing with the Stars* workout. Breakfast consists of asparagus from the garden and one fried egg. It's chilly this morning, so I dress warmly and head down to Mother's to take Beautiful Brown Eyes for a walk.

The geese noisily greet us as they head upriver to greener pastures. I admire the full blooms of the pink, red, and purple azaleas, then remind myself to fertilize the hydrangeas and transplant two more blueberries to the new row I've started alongside the river path. Mother started the blueberry hedge several years ago and didn't even water them after she put them in the ground. I remember thinking that they didn't stand a chance, but like her—someone who started from nothing—they thrived. Now we are able to freeze gallon bags of the delicious fruit and enjoy them all year long. I'm sure they will continue to nourish me long after she's gone.

I am again reminded of her mortality. I've always thought that her death would incapacitate and hurt me deeply, but I now realize that Covid-19, with its constant reminder of death, is showing me a way forward through the pain. I've decided to treasure these days and memories. I'm choosing to honor her strength and legacy by standing instead of falling apart. I can truly know that I have spent time with her, getting to know her strengths and weaknesses, helping her at the end of her journey, and coming to love her unconditionally. We're not there yet, but I feel like every day we're gaining ground in our mutual understanding. When the time comes for her to leave, I'll choose to be okay, for her sake and for my sake.

When Matthew comes home, we watch a movie called *The Warrant*. It isn't nearly as good as *Call of the Wild*, which we watched last week, but he doesn't know that because he slept through both of them. He awakens as the credits are rolling, and we move to the bedroom. He holds me in the dark and gives me love, comfort, and strength. It seems like he has become more resilient during this crisis, while I am struggling. That's a good thing, though, because one of us has to be able to hold up the other, and this time it is him. I confess my deepest fears to him, and he listens. We talk into the night and then soundly sleep.

Nancy Mae

Day After Easter

We made it through Easter, and it wasn't much. Amantha didn't even have ham for dinner, which I dearly love even though I'm practically a vegetarian. She served scallops with rice and overcooked them so much that I'm sure even Pedro wouldn't have eaten them. I didn't say anything, though. I could tell she was tired, upset, and just not herself.

I didn't bring Pedro to dinner because of that mean cat, but I did agree to spend the night there later due to the threat of numerous tornadoes and torrential rains. Pedro and I took shelter together in the guest room, and he was a nervous wreck, causing me to have a sleepless night. I never should have put him through that. I live my life for that dog, but when he goes—and his days are numbered—I'll *never* let anyone dump an animal on me again.

Thank goodness we didn't have the awful winds that were predicted. I just can't stand wind anymore. We did get the rain, though, and I can't wait for it to get light enough outside for me to creep back home and see what old man Diamond did to my property. I finally hurry back home around six thirty or so (as much as an eighty-six-year-old can hurry) and, much to my astonishment, see that Mr. Diamond was a gentleman. His swollen waters did wash up close to the tiny house, though, leaving a trail of debris just a couple of feet from the deck post. I think he's just biding his time, waiting for the right time to strike. Like everything else, I'm sure he's tired of humans—tired of them dumping trash in his home, catching all his fish, building homes too close to his shores, and chasing his inhabitants away.

I expect to see those crazy young men come down the river in their little boats (what are they called?) sometime today. They sure don't have much sense if they'd get in that churning, ugly brown water. The fools even go over the Mavie Falls!

Pedro and I let ourselves in at home, and it is so nice to be back in my house. He starts his non-stop demands for my time, but I'm happy to see that he's calmed down now.

My sister calls, and she sounds more unhappy than usual. I let her rant about everything—, this virus, the economy, the weather—but when she starts praising our government for how it's handling the crisis, I tell her I have to let Pedro out. We've lost over thirty thousand people to Covid-19 so far. That's more than any other country in the world. That fact speaks for itself.

The phone rings again, and this time it's my nephew Bart. He asks me if I think he'll get the $1,200 of relief money the government is supposed to start mailing out at the end of April. If anyone needs that money, it's him, as he has no income. Amantha and I tried to help him get disability last year, but he was rejected for the third time. I tell him I'll ask Amantha to try to find out on the computer. He then starts citing his long list of ailments, and I tell him I have to let Pedro out and hang up. I know I'm going to have to come up with a new handy excuse when that dog dies.

I feel a curtain of depression come down over me as I gaze out the window. I ponder over the current situation in our country and in the world. Death seems to be hovering all around, ushered in with this awful wind. Maybe the wind has come for me, too. I just hope Pedro goes first because he wouldn't make it without me.

I see Amantha climbing the stairs to my house, and I let her in. She sits down on Pedro's couch and waits for me to join her.

"Momma, could you help me with something?"

I look at her with interest, and she goes on.

"Do you remember my friend Janet? She and her husband came to our wedding. They live just over the state line in Beulah."

"Well, no, I can't recall them, but go on."

"Well, she asked me to photograph an old grave that dates back to the 1800s for another friend who's doing genealogy research. The Porter Cemetery is just up the road, but I'm not sure exactly where it is. Would you go with me?"

My interest is definitely aroused. I lean forward and excitedly reply, "I know exactly where that is! In fact, we're related to the Porters."

Amantha pulls out a crumpled piece of paper from her jacket and reads it before saying, "It's not a Porter; it's Hattie McDonald."

"Are you sure? There aren't any McDonalds around here that I know of. I believe we are probably related to the woman in the grave, but she can't be a McDonald."

Amantha snaps at me, "Momma, that's the name Janet gave me. Do you want to go or not?"

"We have Clawsons, Guys, Porters, Lamberts, Hensons, Cables, and Manns, but I don't know of any McDonalds around here."

Amantha has now buried her face in her lap, so I quickly respond, "Calm down, Manthie. Of course I want to go. This sounds like the most fun I've had since this pandemic started!"

How queer (pronounced "choir" in these parts) that a plan to take a trip to the cemetery is the highlight of my week so far! It won't be hard to social distance in a graveyard, that's for sure.

We make plans to go this Thursday, and I also call and invite Jewell, just to get her out of the house, too. I remind my niece to bring a mask, so Amantha doesn't have a meltdown.

* * *

The next day, I'm left all alone as my daughter goes to meet her friends for a hike in Cerro City. I'm glad she's getting out, because she's still just not herself. In fact, I've never seen her like this before. She's always known how to handle her life, just like me, and never really gets too worked up over anything. Until now. I hope she'll be in a better mood when she returns.

I settle down with the newspaper in the "man-chair," and it doesn't take long for me to scan the growing list of names in the obituary column. I do notice that one of them is Ada Miller, who lives—lived—at the bottom of Mavie Road. I call Jewell to see if she knows the details of the death. (I'm sure she does. She always seems to know the comings and goings of everyone in our community, including the people in Mavie, Dark Rise, Birch Springs, Diamond Mills, Dry Branch, and Bent.) She tells me something that disturbs me greatly. Adie did die of the virus, and while the family members were at the funeral home planning her graveside service, someone broke into her home and stole everything of value. People are despicable!

Jewell doesn't have any idea who would do such a thing, but we both speculate that it was probably one of the "walking dead" meth-heads who are occasionally seen down at the Diamond Mills Store, otherwise known as "the mall." Many of them are homeless and live under the bridge on Highway 5. They have been known to live in abandoned houses around here, but we've never heard of them actually breaking into homes. I remember a meth-head whom we called Cowboy because of the hat he wore. A few years ago, he squatted in the old Clawson shack and burned it to the ground, probably while trying to stay warm. I wonder what ever happened to him.

I get off the phone, look out the window, and watch the wind blowing dead leaves around in circles. That old curtain of loneliness comes down on me again, and I wonder who I should call now. I realize I don't really feel like talking to anyone else right now, so I move to the bedroom to watch TV and lie down. I search for something that doesn't have to do with the virus, eventually settling on the Game Show Network, which I'm getting free right now. Since the chocolate ice cream is gone, I get up and fix myself a big bowl of vanilla ice cream.

When I get back to my room, Pedro looks at me expectantly, but I tell him firmly, "You can't have ice cream, so be a good boy."

He seems to understand and lies down beside my bed.

Jay calls, and we have the most interesting conversation. After about an hour, I feel a little better about life. We say our goodbyes because I hear a car in my driveway.

I see Amantha climb the stairs slowly. She must be tired after her walk. She's dressed in long winter pants, a purple jacket, and gray hiking boots. Her hair is braided, and I notice how long it's getting. She reminds me of Mom in some way that I just can't define. It's as if the closer I get to death, the closer Mom is getting to me in my daughter's form. Is she beckoning me home? Where exactly is that?

Amantha and I talk for a while. I ask her to check the IRS online to see if Bart will receive a relief check, and she agrees to. I tell her about Jay's call and describe our theory for why this pandemic is happening. She then explodes in anger, claiming that she told me the exact same thing when she returned from Hawaii. I don't understand why on Earth she's so mad. And what difference does it make who said what? I ask her why she's so jealous of her brother. After all, I treat my children the same and love all of them equally.

"What is wrong with you?" I demand, and she storms off, leaving me hurt and confused.

Why can't we get along, this youngest daughter and me? Pedro senses my distress and puts his head in my lap, giving me comfort. *Animals make so much more sense than humans*, I think. I close my eyes, letting the tears fall onto his soft black coat.

Matthew arrives later with my mail, and I tell him I'm worried about Amantha. He doesn't say much and leaves shortly after. I'm sure he's tired from working so much.

I lie down in bed and read the first twenty pages of Amantha's book. As I read, I find that I'm surprised by her insight, especially concerning me. I didn't think she understood me at all, but apparently I have underestimated her. Her portrayal of me and my thinking is spot-on. She apparently pays more attention than I realized.

I must try harder to get along with Amantha and try to understand what she's dealing with. I know she's worried about her husband getting exposed to the virus, getting sick, and possibly exposing us all. I know she feels responsible for keeping me safe, but I wish she'd realize that I've always taken care of myself and always will. I do not require a keeper. I know that my time on Earth is drawing to a close, and I only wish to know that my children will be there for each other when I'm gone.

I medicate myself with a good dose of wine, watch a couple of episodes of that handsome Perry Mason's show, and turn off the light. Tomorrow is another day.

* * *

On Thursday, we go up Mava Road in search of the grave that Amantha wants to photograph .We find the Porter family plot, which should be deserted since Jimmy Porter died a couple of years ago. Amantha blows her horn anyway, just in case anyone decided to take up residence in the dilapidated camper.

I recall the tall stranger we saw walking down The Nowhere the other day. He was dressed in a black trench coat and hat, looking like the Grim Reaper himself.

We wait a couple of minutes and then get out and begin searching for the grave. We find nothing but old automobiles, trailers, and trash. *Lots* of trash. We decide to ask the next-door neighbors, so we pull into their driveway. Amantha beeps her horn, but no one appears.

"We'd better get outta here. I don't feel like getting shot today," she says as she backs down the steep, rocky driveway.

I suggest we ask my cousin Jolene, so we pull into her driveway. We peek into the windows at her house, and after what feels like forever, her husband, Darrell, comes out. We ask him if he knows where the Porter plot is located.

"I know exactly where it is," he says as he points back up the road. He points at the driveway just past the one we've already searched.

We thank him, turn around, and wave at their neighbor, who just stares at us.

Amantha pulls into the driveway Darrell pointed to and taps her horn, just in case this ramshackle shack has any residents. There's no sign of any life, except for the weeds choking the life out of a few tulips. I jump as a gun goes off nearby.

"What on Earth was that? That sounds close!" I look around but don't see anyone other than my daughter, and she doesn't look worried.

"It turkey season, and I'll bet that was on top of Big Rock Mountain. There's an echo here, and it makes it sound closer," she replies reassuringly.

She tries to help me up the steep bank, but I have my walking stick and make it fine. I do have to stop several times to catch my breath, though.

"I found the tombstone!" I hear her say as I crest the hill to join her.

There are actually two graves, both Porters, and neither date back to the 1800s. The oldest one dates back to 1918, still a long time ago. This person died young, only twenty-three years old.

"Do you think this person could have died of the Spanish Flu, Mom?"

I try to catch my breath before speaking, "I guess it's possible. That was way before my time. People around here have always died before their time, though. They worked themselves to death trying to eke out a living."

"Look, this one here died just eight years ago, and he was only thirty." Amantha is standing over a new wooden cross that has already fallen over into the dirt.

"Well, he died before his time, too, but not from a broken back. Meth took his life."

Too many of our young, in these mountains and all over this country, have been seduced by meth and prescription drugs. They give up on life and end up looking like the walking dead. These walking dead reproduce, and the poor children don't stand a chance, at least not until the grandparents step in to raise them. I personally know at least four cousins and friends who are raising their grandchildren—and even great-grandchildren—and I don't know how they do it. I know I sure couldn't raise kids anymore. I raised four, and that was enough.

"I'm going just over the ridge to see if I can find the McDonald woman." Amantha leaves me in the lonely little graveyard so she can explore the woods behind it.

I think of my cremation bench, which is up the road at the well-tended Birch Springs Cemetery, and hope it will be sat on by my family and friends for many years after I've died. There's nowhere to sit in this awful place, that's for sure, and my legs feel weak.

Amantha finds nothing, so we return to her car. She calls her car Pretty Little Sky, but she says it in Spanish. Amantha was a Spanish teacher before she retired nearly two years ago. She even lived in Spain, and somewhere in South America, too.

We head back down Mavie Road and pull into the old homeplace. Before she turns off the engine, Amantha asks me if I want to get out and look around the remnants of my childhood home. I nod my head in agreement, but can't speak for the lump in my throat.

As we get out, I say, "I haven't been here in a long time, and who knows when I'll get to come back? So I'd better do it even though I'm a little tired and my bed is calling me."

I immediately notice the row of walnut trees that my brother RC planted as a child, and I point them out to Amantha, who takes several pictures of me in front of them. I take hers, too, but my hands are shaky, so I'm sure the picture will be blurry.

Hope Knocking

I move toward the sound of gurgling water, and the old spring takes me down memory lane. I recall the time my brother Jake and I were bored and started pretending to be chickens. We crowed and scratched in the dirt by the old woodshed. Our neighbor Henry was taking the nigh-cut (what we called a shortcut) home through our property. When he saw us playing, he laughed so hard I thought he would surely pee his overalls before he made it to the outhouse. My brother and I got really mad, and shortly after Henry left, still laughing like a hyena, we began to plot our revenge. We decided to take some of Mom's ties—she'd gotten them in her last package from Ohio—and make a pied snake.

(Amantha asked me once what "pied" meant, and I told her it was a mottled-looking snake. I suppose this is another example of a hillbilly word used nowhere else in the world.)

We asked Mom to help with our plot, and she enthusiastically sewed us a couple of snakes—one to place on the path that Henry used, another to play with. We waited and waited day after day for his arrival, and finally, one bright sunny day, he came down the path toward our two-room cabin, whistling all the way. We quickly hid in the bushes by the spring, trying not to laugh. We were rewarded with the loudest blood-curdling scream we'd ever heard, and we died laughing at the sight of our neighbor trying to kill the snake with his walking stick. When he realized he'd been had, he shook his fist at us as he made his way home up the nigh cut.

I can still see Momma on the porch, laughing so hard, tears running down her high cheekbones, saying, "That'll teach him. Oh my, that'll teach ole Henry to mess with my young'uns."

I'd give anything to see Momma again, but she and the two-room shack have been gone a long time. There's nothing left here but old memories. I know Amantha believes in heaven, and *if* heaven exists I know my mother is there, because she was the kindest person I've ever known. However, I have never believed in fairy tales. She's gone, and I'll soon be gone, too.

We don't stay long, as there's nothing left to see. We climb back in Pretty Little Sky and cruise back home to No Place. Today was a good day, and I am thankful.

It's Sunday already, and I don't even know what happened to Friday and Saturday. They went by in a blur. I ride with Amantha over to Dry Branch—another opportunity to get out of the house. She has to drop some money off at a friend's house. We pull into their driveway and walk up to the porch.

Cheryl is in the doorway, and I hear Doug exclaim as he raises his arms, "Is this a hold-up?"

I hate wearing these masks, but my daughter insists that I must wear one if I go out anywhere. She thinks they'll soon be fashionable and is sporting a pretty one with butterflies. Mine has watermelon slices and is prettier and more comfortable than the standard white masks, which have rubber bands that break easily. I can't help but think that a world where masks are required is a world that I no longer wish to inhabit.

I notice that Amantha's friends from church are not wearing masks, and this makes me feel self-conscious. We move the rockers on the porch so we can sit apart from each other. We do not hug or shake hands. We socialize for just a short while and then leave.

Amantha wants to show me some land on a back road I've never been on before. It is really beautiful. Rolling green hills are accentuated by bales of hay and rustic gray barns. I see splashes of yellow flowers that I think are mustard flowers. The white-framed houses nearby are old but tidy, with no signs of the trash or the discarded carcasses of cars that are so prevalent in Mavie. I wonder if taxes here in Jordan County cover trash disposal, unlike in Elk County, where we pay $1.00 per bag at the dump. Our taxes are not used to pave the roads, either; they're just patched over again and again. And the snow is never cleared from the roads when it snows—not that is snows much anymore, not like in the old days.

I remember the Great Blizzard of 1960, when it started snowing in mid-February and didn't let up until April. We had to keep clearing the snow away from our front door, or we couldn't open it. The snow measured higher than Dad, who is six-feet tall! I remember the day we first heard the National Guard helicopters coming to drop food, coal, and bales of hay for us mountain folk who'd been stranded for months. It was like Christmas, but that time we actually got more than an orange and a peppermint stick. The boxes were full of cheese, pasta, and sauce. That was the first time I'd eaten spaghetti, and I've been hooked ever since.

Those were hard times, but somehow now feels harder. Maybe it's because I was only in my twenties then, and your body feels invincible at that age. My days of feeling like Superwoman are over. A couple of years ago, I turned my cape over to my daughters, Amantha and Eileen. They have to be the strong ones now.

In reality, nurses and doctors who are trying to save others from this virus, all the while endangering themselves and their families, are the ones wearing the capes of courage, fortitude, compassion, and mercy. They are the true superheroes of 2020.

Amantha slows down to greet someone from her church. I have to admit that although I don't go to church—nor do I plan to—she and Matthew have found real friends there. They are good people. The one Amantha's talking to now lives close to my brother Jake's old homeplace.

The whole family used to gather at Jake's every summer for huge Harmon reunions. Close to a hundred relatives and friends were there, if I'm remembering right. I ask Amantha to pull into his old driveway, and the engine idles as we imagine Jake and Dena waving to us from the porch. Although the brick house was torn down a few years ago, I can picture Dena's smiling face as she hollered, "You'uns come and sit fer a spell, and I'll fix you something to eat."

If there ever was an angel, Dena was one. She took in dogs, cats, hunters, neglected children, relatives needing a helping hand—every stray creature for miles around—and fed them all. I suppose her big old heart got broken too many times, as she died the very year I retired and moved back. This broke my heart. How many nights had I stayed awake thinking of the good times we'd have together once I returned? Life really does disappoint at times.

The pain of yet another empty homeplace keeps us from lingering there, and so do the posted signs. We leave and head home, winding around Cove Lake and going over the one-lane Bent Landing bridge. I wonder if our No Place will one day join the ranks of unwanted, untended homesteads, kudzu covering up the three houses and the many outbuildings like a shroud.

Amantha drops me off at my unadorned home, leaving me alone with my heavy, smothering thoughts. As I carefully and slowly make my way up the stairs, I wonder if the time has come for me to move in with her and Matthew. I'm spending more and more time alone now, and I know that's not good. Loneliness may kill more people during quarantine than anything else. Thank goodness I at least see my daughter and son-in-law every day. I know I'm way luckier than those unfortunate souls stuck in nursing homes, unable to see their loved ones at all now, except through a window. That's not living. If I get in that kind of shape, I plan to make my own exit out of this world. Until then, I'm grateful for another day, my big black dog, my TV, and my bed.

Amantha

May

Today is Sunday, and Matthew and I try to tune into our preacher's message on Facebook, but it keeps stalling, so we give up. Instead, we read *Jesus Calling*, a book that our friend Tabitha gifted us at the end of our counseling sessions. It has really kept us focused on keeping God in our marriage, and it reminds us to be grateful each day for all things, including each other. I really like the reading for today, April 19th:

"Do not be afraid for I am with you. Hear me saying, "Peace, Be Still" to your restless heart. No matter what happens, I will never leave you or forsake you. Let this assurance soak into your mind and heart until you overflow with joy. Though the earth gives way and the mountains fall into the heart of the sea, you need not fear! I hold you by your right hand, and afterward, I will take you into Glory."

I like it so much that I decide to share it on my Facebook page. I try again to listen to the preacher's message, but it's still live, and there are so many other preachers and church members trying to do the same thing that there must be an overload. I check the status of the song Melvin, Joan, and I recorded on Friday and see that "Bridge Over Troubled Water" has been viewed over three hundred times already.

"Church in the Wildwood," the song we recorded for our church, has two hundred views.

I'm happy with all of the positive comments and likes we've received, but nothing compares to performing live, and I wonder when we'll be able to do that again. I wonder how on Earth professional musicians are able to eke out a living now. It was hard enough *before* Covid-19. The only live gigs we have on our empty calendars are a couple of performances at retirement homes in Junction City. We plan to set up outside under a canopy while the residents sit on their balconies.

It's difficult to comprehend how isolated people in retirement homes and nursing homes must be feeling these days, so cut off from their loved ones, special outings, and even each other. I hope our performance brings them some comfort and lets them know that they are not forgotten. Maybe we'll make this our main focus, other than recording, because I feel sure that, even though a few states like Georgia and Florida are opening back up next week, retirement and nursing homes will not be open anytime soon for anyone other than staff and residents.

My back starts to hurt, so I turn off the PC and yell to Matthew that I'm going down to Mom's. I grab the pan-fried catfish I made for lunch, along with beans, carrots, and cornbread, to take to her.

As I head up Mom's driveway, I notice a few shitake mushrooms ready for picking, so I grab a basket and the scissors from the garden shed and cut them off the oak logs. Matthew and I started the logs at least ten years ago and still get a few every season, but many of the logs are now rotting. Now, after all the rain we've received this spring, would be the prime time to go in search of morels. I usually go mushroom hunting in the Cherokee National Forest, next to Uncle Jake's old homeplace—rather, where Jake's old homeplace *used* to be.

Just a couple of years ago, Jewell and I went over there, hoping to find a few of Aunt Dena's prized red canna lilies to dig up and take home. To our horror, the entire property had been bulldozed, and not even a brick remained.

It seems so sad to return now, though that's where I've found most of these prized fungi. I recall the first time Aunt Dena took me into the woods beside her house to look for morels.

"Now, Manthie, pay attention. Young'un, you just passed five of 'em."

I looked down and marveled at them. "How on Earth can you see them? They look like pinecones and blend in so well with the ground."

She claimed she could smell them. I never developed that gift even though I'm known in my family for my superb sniffer.

I'm brought back to the present at the sight of a big black dog at the end of the drive, wagging his tail at me. I know what Pedro wants, and I relent. Even though it's very windy—the wind seems to blow all the time these days—we go for a walk around the garden and down by the fields alongside the river. Cousin Jimmy's apple and pear trees are blooming now. We climb the slight rise that leads to Jewell's house, and I notice that their car is gone. I know they didn't go to church, as all churches are closed. I wonder where they went. These days, our neighbors' comings and goings add a bit of intrigue to our now dull routine.

Pedro is slowing down already. He never wants to go very far anymore. I know he's used to walking with Mother, and she moves slowly, too. We end up right back at the tiny house, and Pedro gets in the water. The river's come down some since the Easter flood, but there's still a trail of debris marking its rise. I pick up a shiny, smooth stone that just begs to be rescued, then notice the wild phlox popping up everywhere, along with the red columbines that appear above them, right on the cliffs above our homes.

Pedro wants to go home, so we walk up Mother's drive and let ourselves in her side door. She's sitting in the "man-chair," going through the box of photographs she's had forever.

"I found a picture of the walnut trees beside the old homeplace. I'm going to give it to RC since he planted them," she says, showing me the faded black-and-white photograph with the curled-up edges.

I give her a hug even though I know she usually doesn't like to be touched, and she returns it this time. The thought occurs to me that perhaps even she is starving for human contact.

I take the picture and see my grandmother Pennie standing in front of a tiny dilapidated shack, hands on her hips, smiling—actually smiling—for the camera. Back then, mountain people *never* smiled in photographs. They wore exhausted, disapproving looks on their faces, as if they thought the photographer might be up to some mischief But not Pennie. She always smiled, sending her love and approval through the lens of time.

Part Two:

Sunshine Did Not Make It Go Away

Amantha

Three Months Later

I hear the birds welcoming the new day outside the bedroom window, but I don't share their joy, and to tell you the truth, they sound sad to me. The heat of July has brought with it a heavy oppression and nothing but bad news. The United States has had more Covid-19 deaths—we're now up to one hundred and forty thousand—than any other country in the world. Initially, it was thought that the heat of summer would kill the virus and make it disappear, but that has not been the case. Perhaps if people had socially distanced and worn masks, we would have had the success that other countries are now having. But many citizens have just ignored the advice of the CDC and the scientific community, so now hospitals are running out of ICU beds and ventilators, and many states are having to close bars and restaurants... again.

Furthermore, many mayors across the country are implementing mask mandates in their counties because governors, especially the Republican ones, are refusing to act. Apparently, the federal government's pass-the-buck strategy is trickling down to the state level, so now it is up to the locally elected officials to save our country. Lord help them to do the right thing. Even corporations are starting to implement mask mandates in their businesses because the government is failing its constituents.

I do not understand why a pandemic has divided us. This is a time when we should be pulling together to try to defeat the real enemy: the Coronavirus. Fellow Americans are not the enemy, yet it seems like people are so entrenched in their red or blue camps that they do not see the "spiky ball" of death, or they choose not to see it. Those wearing the red uniform only see those "bleeding-heart liberals," "elitists," and "socialists," while those dressed in blue see "fascists," "racists," and "right-wing extremists." We will not be able to defeat this virus if we do not unite and take all necessary precautions that the experts advise to take, such as social distancing and mask-wearing.

I hear neighbors spout off about it being their "personal freedom" to go mask-less, but what about the health of the people they are infecting? Doesn't the right to live surpass personal choice? It saddens me so much to see how unwilling some Americans are to do the right thing and help each other get through this crisis. Bumper stickers and t-shirts are starting to pop up nationwide with the idiotic motto "We Will Not Comply," which refers to the growing, and necessary, mask mandates now being passed.

I'm also disappointed in the young people flocking to bars, beaches, and parties. Some even mockingly call these parties "Covid Parties" in an effort to show that the pandemic is all a hoax and that they won't get sick. Of course, they *do* get sick. Then they overcrowd the hospitals, infect healthcare workers and their family members, and the death toll keeps rising. I think back to my own reckless youth and recall feeling like nothing bad could happen to me then; I felt invincible. However, I like to think that if I had been a young person living through a pandemic back then, I still would have tried to protect others by wearing a piece of cloth over my mouth and nose, even if I may not have seen the need for myself.

Others tout the "herd immunity" approach, in which people are encouraged not to socially-distance or wear masks. This helps them to get the virus, therefore gaining immunity. One problem with this approach is that recent scientific findings show that immunity appears to be short-lived. In other words, you can get the Coronavirus again!

Matthew and I drove to Georgia to see Dad for Father's Day last month, and my brother Dan, his daughter, and his family met us at Dad's home for a dinner. At first, Dad wanted us all to go to a local restaurant to eat, but Dan and I convinced him that we needed to pick up the food and eat at home in order to avoid crowds and socially distance. Tiffany and her family, who live across town and believe that God will protect them from the virus, also came to our gathering—unmasked. They were supposed to eat at the dining room table, while the rest of us ate on the large porch, separated by family units. These plans, though, were trashed, and Dad and my stepmother, Louanne, were coerced into joining Tiffany's family at the table. She said, "Everything will be okay. God will protect us." I'm sure my father did not want to offend them, but I felt furious that she put their health in jeopardy. I expected Dan to speak up and insist on our original plan, but I suppose he didn't know what to say.

After dinner, when Covid-19 came up again in conversation, I made the comment that God expects us to use the brains He gave us and to love one other. This now means wearing a mask and keeping a safe distance. I do not feel like this is such an inconvenience. Everyone should be willing to make this small sacrifice for the good of the whole. I will continue to do so until a vaccine is approved...*if* a vaccine is found.

Anyway, these are my frustrations this July morning. I bow my head and say my daily prayer, giving thanks to God for everything. I do realize how fortunate I am to live in such a beautiful place, to be retired, to have all my needs met, and to have my health.

Just before July 4th, I spent my first night ever in a "horspital." I thought I was going to have a heart attack! All the classic symptoms were there—chest pain, shortness of breath, and nausea—so I reluctantly followed the advice of my primary care doctor, Dr. Smith, and went to the ER. A heart monitor was placed on me all night, and a stress test was ordered. Thank God my heart was found to be in great shape! My Covid test was also negative, and a few days after my release, I felt back to normal.

I've concluded that I caught a norovirus at the Appalachian Trail shelter near Cruz Mountain, as a fellow hiker also had the same symptoms. We had lunch at the shelter about a week before we got sick, and though we didn't touch anything, we both felt oddly chilled right after we left.

The day before yesterday, I felt a chill in my heart when I opened the bill from the hospital. It was over $2,000, and I'm sure it will not be the only one. Still, we have insurance. What on Earth do people without health insurance do? I suppose they don't pay or just don't go to the doctor, much less a hospital.

I'm worried about Mother's declining health, too. She looks bad and complains about fatigue and low blood pressure. Yesterday, she was barely able to walk to the shed, where Matthew and I were breaking green beans. She broke a few before just giving out. I was going to take her to the doctor today, but she called about an hour ago and said that she's feeling better and that her blood pressure is back to normal. I let her be for today, but I'll need to keep an eye on her.

I will, however, make an appointment for Matthew. He's had body aches for a long time and says he never feels well anymore. I hope he can get some answers and relief from a new doctor, as we've both decided to ditch Dr. Smith. She actually charged us for an office visit just to renew Matthew's blood pressure meds on the phone! Plus, she hasn't even inquired about me since I was released from the hospital. I realize she's extremely busy and feeling overwhelmed by this virus, but she just doesn't seem to care. It seems to be so hard to find a good doctor who will listen these days.

These negative thoughts seem to follow me today, so instead of trying to stay busy and therefore covering up these uncomfortable feelings, I decide to dig them up, to confront these dragons. All my life, I've been slaying them, but now I choose to listen instead. I need to do this in order to achieve wholeness. I think, *What are the dragons trying to teach me? What is out of balance in my life?*

I call Josie to make an appointment for an energy session, and it appears that God is freeing up our schedules today so I can do this healing work. She had a cancellation and can fit me into her schedule in just another hour, so I agree to call her then, and we hang up.

I decide to do my *Dancing with The Stars* workout now, as I know that exercise always makes me feel better, and doing it early in the day will ensure that it gets done. Plus, it's going to be hot and humid again later today, so that's another good reason to do it now.

When my workout is completed, I recline on the couch in a spot where I can see the big hemlock and the hummingbird feeder. It always helps me connect to my true self by connecting with Earth. Before I call Josie, I hear a knocking sound downstairs. It's that female cardinal again. She's banging herself against the window. She's been doing this for weeks, and I don't know how to help her. Usually, it's the male that repeats this behavior, most likely thinking that his reflection is another male cardinal. This female bird definitely seems to be trying to get my attention.

I make the call. Josie asks me what I need today, and I tell her that I feel like I have to "fix" other people's problems, like Matthew's and Mother's health issues, and this leaves me feeling empty, unsatisfied, and angry. I tell her about my inner angry bird, and she suggests that I simply allow it to voice its frustrations, showing it kindness, not judgment. This is what we all need and want right now: to be heard and to be treated with kindness. We hang up, and I breathe in gently while she does the energy work from her end. As I breathe in and then exhale, the tears come to my eyes.

I hear the cardinal banging insistently, saying, "Listen, Amantha! I've been knocking on your heart for days, trying to tell you something.

Are you ready to listen? Sometimes that's all you need to do. Just listen. You cannot fix other people, and they don't want you to. They just want to be heard. Listening is perhaps the kindest thing each of us can do right now."

I think, *Thank you, thank you, sister cardinal, for your wisdom. I choose to allow Matthew and Mother to speak their truth while allowing myself to listen with love and kindness. I do not have to do anything other than that unless they ask me to, and then I get to decide if, when, and how much I can help.*

This realization is so refreshing and liberating! I can just be their friend and listen. I don't have to *do* anything. I immediately recognize the pressures I've been putting on myself, as a wife and a daughter, to make *them* happy, which in turn has been denying me my own happiness. I know they love me and want me to be happy, and they never expected me to fix anything. In fact, I'm positive they absolutely resent my meddling. So I will aim to be a better listener, as I know listening is perhaps the best gift one person can give to another.

This realization also makes me think of the Black Lives Matter movement that is sweeping through our country, and the world, since the brutal killing of George Floyd by the Minneapolis police. The movement has inspired protesters—black, brown, yellow, red, and white—to hit the streets, insisting on change. They give me hope, these young people, that change will finally come to our country, fulfilling the promise of America. A promise yet to be fulfilled. Am I naive to think that all people truly are created equal? Am I wrong to hope for racial harmony? No, I am not. This is a movement worth fighting for. How do I, an entitled white woman who is living in a white supremacist nation, begin to help?

I must listen first, I think. Listen with compassion. Really hear the experiences of our oppressed Black brothers and sisters. Then listen to their needs. They're going to need our help. We are all in this together. We must come together as one nation, or we will fall, and this beautiful democratic experiment will be over for the oppressed throughout the world.

Hope Knocking

* * *

The rest of the week goes smoothly, and I feel more at ease in my skin and in our new reality. Sally, Joan, and I hike to Fisher Falls in Seventh Heaven, which is in North Carolina, just across the state line. Even though it is just Tuesday, there are more people than we expected, and we keep having to pull our masks up. It seems to be getting more and more difficult to find trails with few people. I know many Floridians and Georgians have come up here to escape the heat (and perhaps the virus), and I can't help feeling a little resentful of their presence. After all, Covid-19 is out of control in both of those states.

On Wednesday, Mother finally relents and lets me take her to a doctor in Betsyville. We first have to drive up so they can take her temperature and ask her a few preliminary questions in order to rule out Covid-19. Then I let her out and I continue to Ingles, where I make a few purchases.

Every time I've gone into a grocery store lately, I've been so impressed with the kindness and politeness of the young people working there. They don't seem to resent working during a pandemic. In fact, they seem to be thriving. These positive folks make me feel hopeful for our future.

I've started to notice something about the pandemic that makes me laugh out loud. Today, it causes one of the produce stockers to give me a funny look. There's a sort of shuffle—let's call it the Covid Shuffle—that people do when another person approaches them. They slide to the side and turn their backs, pulling up their masks (if they're wearing one) as they ease on past. I'm sure it's going to be the next big dance craze. Maybe I can choreograph the dance to my "Coronavirus Blues" song.

When we get home, I call my best friend, Becky. She's been on my mind, so I know something's up. It's always been that way with us, a sort of telepathy. I guess it's because our friendship has lasted so long—

since fifth grade, in fact. During high school, people always referred to both of us in the same breath. We were always a pair, like peanut butter and jelly, Jekyll and Hyde, Laurel and Hardy. *Did you hear what Amantha and Becky did now?* We were always getting in trouble, and honestly I've tried to blank out a lot of things we did. It all seems a little beneath me now, or at least I'd like to think so. The Good Lord must have had plans for us both considering we're still standing.

Becky picks up immediately and confirms my worst suspicions: she's had pneumonia since Sunday, but she has refused to be admitted to the hospital because of the large number of Covid cases there. (Many hospitals in the South are now struggling to find beds for all the sick, including the hospital I was in just last month, when there weren't any cases at all. Willow Shoals now has thirty cases, and that's low compared to the Med Center in Junction City.) Becky tells me the staff thought she had the virus at first, so they promptly gave her the test. All of the staff members had on full protective gear and took every precaution when treating her. She tells me how scared, alone, and humiliated she felt at that time, being isolated from her family and feeling like a bug under the microscope. She expressed her anger toward China, saying they should have to pay for what they've done.

Becky and I don't talk politics much, mostly because we know we are on opposite sides of the political spectrum. Her side believes that China purposely unleashed this virus into the world and that Covid-19 was manufactured in a lab. Scientists have not found any evidence of this so far. They have found evidence linking the virus to animals, which would suggest that it is *not* manmade. I do agree, however, that the Chinese government was guilty of being secretive when the outbreak started in Wuhan, where the virus was first detected at a live animal market. The scientist who first sounded the alarm on social media was silenced, and the post was removed. He later died from the Coronavirus, which I find so very sad. I suppose it was the Asian custom of "saving face" that caused the Chinese leader to hide the threat instead of warning the rest of the world about the calamity that was coming. Unfortunately, this custom cost humanity months during which it could have been preparing for the plague, and I believe many countries would have used this time wisely.

However, even if there was a warning, I do not believe the United States would have used the time wisely. Even when it was impossible to deny that the virus was here and was much worse than the flu, we failed to act. POTUS was quoted many times saying things like, "It's going to disappear like magic. *POOF!* It'll be gone." First, he promised it would be gone by Easter, and then he said by Memorial Day. Perhaps fireworks would scare it off on July 4th. He seems to place high expectations on holidays. So, in my opinion, placing the blame on China is pointless considering the ineffectiveness of our own government.

I am worried about Becky, though. She's been sick for years with an illness called trigeminal neuralgia. It is a condition that causes excruciating pain in the face due to irritation and the misfiring of the three nerves found in the jaw area. She has been taking some serious painkillers for over twenty years, causing damage to her organs and impairing her immunity, thus making her susceptible to Covid. I hope and pray she recovers from the pneumonia quickly at home.

* * *

I have a day at home on Thursday, so after doing my strengthening/stretching routine to Solfeggio frequencies (I learned these exercises at physical therapy over two years ago, when terrible lower back pain sent me to a specialist, and I now do them twice a week), I head outdoors for a stroll through nature. I pass by the rainbow of daylilies that Jewell just adores. She says she tells them every day how lovely they are and how much she'll miss them this winter. I take many photos of them with the intention of making a new set of cards for my cousin. Jewell's Lilies. That way, on a cold, dark winter's day, she can still have the comfort of her flowers.

It's already starting to get muggy as I round the corner of the veggie gardens. I spot our neighbor Nell tending her garden. I greet her, and we talk about how wet it's been all summer and how poorly gardens are doing this year.

"This time last year, I had beets big enough to eat, but not this year. They're not even forming beets yet," I declare, then bid her goodbye and leave her to whack at the never-ending crop of weeds.

I hear an eagle cry above the river and look up to see him perched high on the mountain, his white head shining in the morning sun. *At least birds and other animals seem to be thriving*, I think. I recall the silence of this place fifteen years ago, when we got married here at the river and began building our home. Not a bird, chipmunk, or squirrel was seen or heard. We have all concluded that Eddie must have shot everything in sight. He does love killing creatures. Who knows why?

Why do humans enjoy killing for sport? I don't have anything against hunting. In fact, I realize that since humans have pretty much eradicated many of the deer's natural predators, such as red wolves and mountain lions, hunting is probably necessary in order to ensure the health of the herd. But to enjoy it is cruel. When a sacred life is taken, thanks should be given whether it is for sustenance or in defense. To kill for sport is inhumane, or is it? Perhaps it is altogether way too human.

Did we become the top predator on planet Earth by wiping out all other competitors? Is this cruelty an inherent part of our gene make-up? Can we change ourselves for the overall good? I can only hope so. Every day, I see evidence of people doing good, so I choose to have faith that we humans will decide to choose life, kindness, connectedness, awareness, and clarity. The time has come to move into the light.

The light of a summer's day is shining fully on the narrow river valley as I wind back around to our home. I pause at the newly dug grave, which has a statue of a black lab with birds on his back beside it. Pedro. He was such a good dog, and I miss him terribly. Mother has lost her companion and is heartbroken. The sweet dog finally quit eating and couldn't even walk, so she made the decision to have him put down. Now Mother barely walks herself and seems to be giving up on life. Everyone in the family seems to think she needs another dog, but she adamantly denies this, saying she can barely take care of herself, and I can see that this is true.

I think the time has come for her to move in with us. I mentioned this to Matthew last night. He completely agrees and has also noted Mom's declining health. The doctor thinks her weakened condition is due to an inner ear imbalance and allergies. The doctor prescribed her a medicine to take, but Mom read the possible side effects and refused to take it. I think her problems are more serious than what the doctor said, but I had hoped she would give the medicine, and her new doctor, a try.

Dr. Cooke is Mom's third doctor in three years, and I can tell Mother is not impressed with her. I'm sure all healthcare workers are completely burned out by the pandemic. They are probably doing the best they can, but this isn't helping my mother.

I've considered that Mother may have Covid even though her symptoms are not the typical ones (cough, fever, and shortness of breath). This virus is manifesting itself differently in everyone. Some carriers are even completely asymptomatic and are unknowingly spreading it to others.

There is a false assumption that children are not affected by Covid. But children with Covid are being hospitalized, and they're having different side effects, such as rashes, than the rest of the population. They are not dying like the people over the age of sixty, but they are still spreaders.

I can't help but wonder what on Earth schools are going to do. Jordan County School System, from which I retired two years ago (I still have to pinch myself!), has already announced that students can return in person on the regularly scheduled start date of August 7th, or they can do at-home online learning. Many working parents will have to opt for in-person learning because they cannot afford childcare. Furthermore, even though the schools are giving laptops to needy students, many homes are without internet connection. The burden of driving children to places where they can connect to the internet is placed on tired parents, and they must monitor students' work when they get home from work *and* get dinner on the table. Therefore, most parents will likely choose in-person learning.

Students who do return in person will not be required to wear masks or socially distance. Do they really think *this* is going to work? Have they been living on Mars since March? Ignoring the virus won't make it go away. I give them until October 1st, at the very latest, until they are forced to shut down.

Other districts are being creative with their approaches. Some are using a staggered schedule where students only go to school on certain days to maintain social distancing. The other days are spent online. Some schools are starting completely online. Other schools have yet to announce their plans. I feel so sorry for everyone and cannot imagine the stress they are facing—parents, children, teachers, administrators, bus drivers, nurses, cafeteria workers, custodians, counselors, and coaches. I say a prayer for them and ask God to help schools across the world come to terms with the virus.

I continue my stroll and arrive at our waterlogged vegetable garden. So far, this season we've put up kraut, relish, bread and butter pickles, cilantro and basil pesto, vegetable soup, tomatoes, green beans, blueberries, and peaches. Today, I'm going to do the shelly beans. I'm so grateful for the garden and its bounty, though it has not done very well this year. The cucumbers bloom, but the blooms fall off. The green beans have rust, and the poor beets are hardly growing at all. It has rained excessively this year—we're already fourteen inches in the surplus. Furthermore, I reckon the soil is worn out. Matthew says it, like us, needs to rest, so we will put a cover crop over it next year and put it to bed for a good three-year sleep.

Hope Knocking

Thankfully, problem insects have not made an appearance this year, unlike last year's plague of flea beetles and squash borers. In fact, I have seen many of the beneficial insects, such as praying mantis, wasps, and lady bugs, resting on the numerous flowers I've planted throughout our organic garden to attract them.

I always plant my favorite flowers—zinnias, marigolds, and sunflowers—and I even have a song about them. It's called *"Bury Me in Zinnias."*

> *I'm sure there are flowers in heaven, where the roses never fade*
> *The Lily of the Valley, such wondrous things He's made*
> *But all around our garden, there are three that I adore*
> *So if I leave tomorrow, one thing I ask you for*
>
> *Oh, bury me in zinnias, marigolds, and sunflowers if I die before you*
> *I'll plant them up in heaven, and when your time has come,*
> *You'll know which mansion is my home*
>
> *Zinnias are the colors of the rainbow, surrounding His throne of gold so bright*
> *Sunflowers look up to heaven, seeking the Son's pure light*
> *Marigolds remind me of the gifts that were laid at His feet that starry night*
> *For the baby born of Mary, our Lord, Jesus Christ*

This year, I also saved cosmos seeds, and the naturalizing wildflowers that I planted last year are coming back strong. There are plenty of black-eyed Susans, along with others that I have yet to identify. The pollinators are all over them, and I just love to stand among the blooms, watching the butterflies, bees, and birds. It does something to me—cleanses me, removes stress and anxiety, and fills me with gratitude and peace.

The words gratitude and peace keep popping up in 2020. Perhaps God has sent the Coronavirus to teach humans to be more grateful for each blessing, to remind us not to take anything for granted. Therefore, as I pick each bean, as I string them and break them, as I labor for each mouthful of precious food, I give thanks to Him. This simple, humble act fills me with peace, for it makes me aware that I am not in control. God is. And I gladly relinquish it.

Humans have tried to control nature before, often with disastrous results. We have attempted to produce more food for an ever-increasing population, and our methodology has resulted in an imbalance in nature. To harvest more food from the fields and to save time and money, American farmers plant one crop—be it corn, soybeans, wheat, or potatoes—instead of interplanting various vegetables, flowers, and herbs. Interplanting draws good insects and pollinators, which are plant protection. Monoculture lacks diversity and becomes susceptible to disease and soil deterioration. The bad insects move in, and pesticides such as Round-Up are then utilized to kill them, which leaves poisonous residue on the food that animals and people ultimately eat.

Furthermore, insecticides do not discriminate and are killing our pollinators. The bees that pollinate our food are dying at an alarming rate. And the animals that feed on the pollinators, including birds, are eating the poison, too. Songbirds are disappearing from our backyards and gardens, along with countless other species. We are supposed to be good stewards of the Earth, and we are failing. We must change the way food is grown and begin to see that everything is connected.

I settle into a plastic chair and make my way through the three rows of October beans, piling the pods into a big tub. I see Mom looking over the blueberry bushes at me.

She says, "I'll help you shell those beans at the shed after lunch, okay?"

I gladly accept her offer to help. I eat a meal of sweet corn, Chilean salad (I just love this mix of fresh, homegrown tomatoes, banana peppers, onions, cilantro, olive oil, and fresh lemon juice!), and baked salmon.

The corn was salvaged early because raccoons destroyed nearly half of our crop. The ears aren't completely full, but they are still so tasty.

I don't really blame Rocky the raccoon, but why couldn't he just sit there and eat the whole ear of corn instead of taking random bites out of numerous ones, therefore ruining them all? We always have a radio blaring at night, and it deters the deer from digging up our taters, but apparently the raccoons are not frightened by the noise. Every night, Matthew has tried to lure the critter into a trap that's baited with peanut butter sandwiches, but some wily creature somehow eats them without getting trapped. Last year, it was a beaver that was too big for the trap. It left its trail going to and from the river, dragging entire stalks of corn with it.

It's always something. Birds have discovered the blueberries, too. I have learned to pick them every other day to try to stay ahead of them.

Blueberries are my absolute favorite fruit, and I know they are great for my immune system, as well. I usually freeze gallon bags every year, but this year I'm getting less and am using quart bags instead. Though there aren't as many, I'm still grateful for each and every berry.

The act of stretching my body; reaching for those elusive fruits way up high in the bushes; slipping on the wet, muddy bank; and enduring insect bites, all while trying not to drop any of the precious gems, is good for my soul. The simple act of harvesting is making me aware of each gift this season is offering my family. Before 2020, I think I *expected* the gifts without really appreciating them, but now I see that God is using this pandemic to wake us up, to teach us not to take things for granted, whether it's a garden, family, friendships, or even democracy.

My generation did not live through the horrors of World War II. We did not witness Hitler's authoritarian regime of hate. We did not see what can happen when a madman is given control over a country. We did not see how quickly things can deteriorate. But we are witnessing it now in the United States. Our democracy is being threatened by POTUS and the Republicans who do nothing to stop him. He is now trying to dismantle the United States Post Office and therefore alter the presidential election on November 3rd. His newly appointed postmaster general, a Republican supporter and donor, is removing mail-sorting machines and drop-off mailboxes, and he's laying workers off. This is delaying mail delivery and is a potential threat to absentee ballots being received on time.

POTUS has been saying for a while now that mail-in ballots are fraudulent. He says that if states are allowed to use them, the election will not be credible. On the other hand, he has already filed to use an absentee ballot in his current home state of Florida, which he says does not have a problem with fraud. Because they voted Republican! Only Democratic states that are issuing absentee ballots to its citizens are being threatened with lawsuits by this administration. States are trying to protect their citizens from Covid-19, but POTUS only seems interested in getting himself re-elected by any means necessary.

It seems surreal that this could be happening to our country. We have always assumed our democracy was safe because we've never had a president who craves power like this one. And he is backed by a party that enables him to do as he pleases. I think these Republicans are on the wrong side of history and are going to pay a dear price for this one day. I just hope that POTUS loses *big* to Job Bright, the presumed Democratic nominee. I hope he loses by such a huge margin that he cannot possibly claim fraud, therefore removing him from the White House. However, I have nagging fears that nothing will make him leave, and I worry that he and his followers will try to take over our country by force. These fears, as far-fetched as they sound, keep me up some nights. People *must* vote. Young people of color must vote. Women must vote. We the people must vote as if our democracy depends on it...because it does.

Nancy Mae

September 1st

Fall is coming, but it feels like winter has come early for me. The seasons of my life are drawing to a close, I'm afraid. And I *do* feel a little bit afraid. Suddenly, it seems like my body is failing me, and I just don't understand it. Is it too much magnesium, fish oil, or cinnamon? I wish it were that simple, but I'm beginning to think there's something really wrong with me now. I've been so healthy all my life, and I'm just not used to feeling sick. I'm losing my patience with it all. I've got to bounce back. I've just got to. There are things I still want to do here on this Earth.

I'd really like to go to D.C. again with my nephew Larry. He and I were talking about my time there just last week. He actually found photographs of both the row house and the boarding house where I lived. I can't believe they're still there! Moreover, I can't believe that I remember their addresses. They just popped into my head!

Memory is a queer (choir!) thing. How can I remember these addresses where I only lived four years? Yet I am unable to recall the addresses I lived at in Mississippi and Georgia, where I spent decades. I don't understand it.

I just want to see D.C. again. I loved that city and the time I spent working for the FBI right after high school. I was so lucky to have been recruited back then. It completely altered my life, and I feel like I owe that city a debt of gratitude. So I want to go back one more time to properly offer my thanks.

I still recall leaving home that fall day, ready to head to D.C., my cardboard suitcase proudly clutched in one hand as I hugged Momma and Dad with the other. I was eager to board that train and start my new life. I never thought once about their feelings and how worried they must have been. I was the first child to graduate from high school and the first to leave. I know they never really understood my desire to fly away, but they didn't stand in my way. Well, not at that time.

Dad had tried to stop me from going to high school years before. He even threatened to whip me if I went, and he had *never* lifted a finger to any of us before. My desire for an education apparently overcame my fear of a beating. I snuck out before daybreak every day to do my chores and make my way down The Nowhere to catch the bus for the hour-long ride to school. I guess Dad's Bay Mule wore him down. He eventually accepted my actions, and he even came to my graduation. I can still see my parents sitting in the bleachers, proud smiles on their faces. Momma even sewed a special black dress with lace on the collar for me. I'm sure that lace was expensive, but at the time I didn't give it much thought. I was too excited, I suppose.

I remember feeling so very grown up on my first train ride, on my way to our nation's capital. I was supposed to be in charge of a twelve-year old girl who was on her way back to the city, but as it turned out, she was much more worldly than I was, and she helped me more than I helped her. She knew where to store our belongings on the train, and she knew how and what to order in the dining car. She even pointed out all the sites we passed.

My confidence disappeared, along with her, the moment we arrived. She was safely escorted home by her parents, and I was left standing on the platform, all alone at last. I looked around the busy station and was reminded of ants on a huge anthill. *Where on Earth did all these people come from, and how am I ever going to find my way to the boarding house?* I thought. I felt butterflies in my stomach and thought I was going to throw up or break down right there on that Washington sidewalk.

Somehow, I managed to use a phone for the very first time. I called sweet Mrs. Greene, the owner of the boarding house, and she told me where to go to hail a cab. I didn't even know what that meant, but she was patient with me, and I found a kind, black cab driver who took me to my new home. I didn't have enough money to pay him the whole fare, but he took pity on this backward hillbilly. I do hope that I thanked him for his generosity.

My life has always been that way. People have been good to me my entire life. I still believe that people are mostly good and are doing the best they can at any given moment. My children don't agree with me. I guess they have had different experiences, which makes me sad for them. Has the world really changed that much? Should I be more cautious? Well, at this point in my life, I do not plan to change. I choose to exit this world thinking the best of humans, though they *are* really misbehaving while the world faces this virus.

Do I have Covid-19? Amantha says I don't have the high temperature, congestion, or severe cough that accompany it, but I do have nausea, and that can be a symptom. You would think that they would have tested me yesterday at the doctor's office, but they didn't. I've pretty much lost faith in our healthcare system. My so-called doctor wouldn't even see me, so I agreed to a teleconference instead. When Amantha came down to check on me and saw how much worse I was, she insisted on taking me to see *anyone*.

I also had to pick up a new prescription for an antibiotic to treat my UTI...*if* that's even what I have. I've never had one in my entire life, but both Jewell and Amantha have had many.. They both agree that's probably what's wrong with me. All I know is that I've been taking medicine for one week, and I feel worse, not any better at all.

My low blood pressure is what concerns me the most. It's been eighty over forty! I'm just so dog-tired, too. I don't have the energy to do anything, even let the chickens out. I call my daughter and ask her if she'll let them out, and of course, she says she will.

I discuss my malaise and tell her that I decided not to take one of the prescriptions because it has so many side effects. She fusses and pleads with me to take it, and I tell her I will consider doing so, but I know that I won't. I make up my own mind, and she will have to let me be. She doesn't push the subject, to her credit, and to appease her I agree to return to the doctor if I don't feel better by Friday. That's three days from now. Surely, I will be better by then. She and Matthew are planning a socially distanced BBQ at the shed for Labor Day, which is next Monday, and I don't want them to cancel it on my account. Besides, I haven't had hardly any company since this mess started, and I do enjoy socializing.

The phone rings as soon as Amantha and I hang up, and I know it's going to be Jewell. She calls me practically every morning around this time. We both discuss our ailments, and as we're talking it occurs to me that I've become one of those people I used to condemn. I've become one of those people who only talk about their health woes, over and over again, to anyone who will listen. I used to think that their ailments were only in their heads, fabricated to get attention. How insensitive and callous my thinking was! I guess it takes walking a mile in someone else's shoes to truly empathize. Now that I'm sick, I see how all-consuming it can be, and sharing this suffering with a friend eases the load considerably. I suppose it's never too late to teach an old dog new tricks.

Pedro. How I miss that sweet black lab! The sound of his nails clicking as he came into my bedroom to greet me each day. His wagging tail communicating his desire to go out or eat. Those big, expressive brown eyes. I had no idea I'd miss him so much. It's been two months since Amantha and I had to put him down, but it seems like just last week. He finally quit eating and walking, so we did what we had to do. Amantha made a real pretty place where we could bury him in the pet cemetery. She put a statue that looks just like him at the head, planted roses, and circled it all with rocks that formed a heart. I think it broke her heart, too. After all, she and Matthew rescued Pedro years ago during that Christmas blizzard, and he found a loving home here on the river.

People tell me I should get another one, but I know he was my last dog. I can barely take care of myself anymore, and animals are a lot of work. Still, he was my steadfast, loyal companion, and I now understand what it means to feel alone. Maybe it is time for me to move in with Amantha and Matthew. Or should I go to New Orleans and spend the winter with Jay?

I cannot seem to make any drastic decisions today, but I do decide to drag myself out of bed and go for a walk—just a small one—so I can check on the chickens and visit Pedro's grave. I carefully descend the basement stairs; grab a coat, scarf, and shoes; and let myself out into the beautiful September day. I detect a hint of fall in the air, and I can hear the peculiar sound the insects make this time of year. I can't say it's louder than in the summer, but there's a sweet sadness to it somehow. Maybe they know they're dying, like me, and have to make every day count. What a good lesson for us all to learn!

The chickens seem to be enjoying the day. They eagerly run to me as I toss food scraps over the fence. They are quite endearing to watch as they sort out their pecking order. I notice them eyeballing me as they consume the leftovers that seem to multiply in my refrigerator these days. I wonder what they think of us humans. I'm sure they don't trust us yet, but they're starting to at least associate us with food. One of the red ones even pecks my shoes when I go into their yard, as if she's trying to eat me. They look like tiny dinosaurs, and although it's disturbing to consider, I'm sure they *would* devour my old body if I expired right here in the chicken yard. I sure don't want to go *that* way, so I exit the coop.

I begin to make my way around to the garden so I can see the cheerful flowers among the tomatoes and peppers. I stop at Pedro's grave and smile. I notice that the rosebush in the middle of his grave has bloomed and is starting to drop its fuchsia petals inside the circle of stones.

I say, "Hi, my sweet boy. I miss you, too. I hope that wherever you are, you are at peace and are being taken care of. When I get there, we can take us a nice walk beside that river over yonder. Would you like that? No, I don't think I'll be long, but be a good boy now and don't rush me. I still have some things that need tending to here. My rose has got a little more bloom left in it."

Amantha

September 11th, 2020

I wake up at around 3:00 AM to pee. Little Bit is already scratching himself, wanting to be fed, but I don't give in to him. He's starting to scratch earlier and earlier. I know the poor thing is suffering, so I must free up some time in my schedule so I can take him to the vet for another flea allergy shot. He's going to have to wait a couple of hours, though. I must get back to my dream!

It's so rare that I dream anymore. This one is so vivid. I'm in another country. The people look Asian, but I'm speaking Spanish and they're understanding me, so it must be Latin America or Spain. I think it must be Spain, because I'm looking for my new high school, and I'm scared to death. I get on the crowded bus and take the only available seat—one that's right behind the driver. But somehow, the gearshift is right between my legs, and I can barely squeeze in. There's a cell phone in the seat, and I pick it up and scan the photographs of what looks like a construction site. I ask the teenager sitting beside me if the phone is hers, and she says no. I ask her if this bus stops at the "escuela secundaria," and she says, "Sí." Before she gets off, I manage to find out the address.

Finally, everyone but the driver and me is gone. He expects me to wash and clean the bus, which I do. As I am cleaning it out, I observe the lack of trash in the aisles—another reminder that I am not in the US. Students in the US trash buses, classrooms, and hallways, and they always expect someone else to clean it up.

Finally, the driver disappears, and another benevolent being, who I am now convinced is an angel, delivers me to the school. It's raining, and I am hovering in line under an umbrella that has magically appeared. There are so many people, and I feel so lost and panicked, but another Aussie-type angel points out the entrance to the school, which is where I should go register. I go through the enormous door and am floating at the top of a huge stairway. I arrive at another line, and this one resembles a ski lift. Students are waiting their turn to climb up this obstacle course to the registrar's desk. Finally, it's my turn, and I can hear people cheering me on as I somehow pant and struggle up to the desk, clinging to clouds to help me ascend. *Is this heaven?*

A male angel congratulates me on my climbing skills, but his smiling face is quickly replaced by a petite, Asian angel. I tell her I'm a new exchange student and give her my name. She seems to know who I am and immediately hands me a strange-looking box that apparently contains everything I need to know. *The book of knowledge?* She then whispers conspiratorially that I will be arrested if I wear my glasses. I try to explain to her that they are only reading glasses and that I need them. People behind me are getting impatient—I think I skipped line!—and I float back down to earth.

This is all I remember the next morning when I wake. I'm so glad I remember this dream, as it seems so significant. I have always thought that dreams are great messengers. I used to keep a dream journal by my side and would record dreams immediately after waking. I haven't done that since I was in my twenties, though.

I need to understand this dream. What was the final angel warning me about? What do the glasses represent? Clarity? Do I need to remove blinders from my eyes? What am I not seeing? I have said that Republicans suffer from a lack of clear vision, that something is preventing them from seeing the reality of this presidency that threatens our democracy. Why is my vision potentially harmful? Will my views come to haunt me one day? Will this book, if it's ever published, be justification for my arrest in a future dictatorship?

This seems implausible, completely ridiculous, but so much has happened in 2020 that *anything* now seems possible. George Orwell's *1984* could become reality, with "Big Brother" watching our every move; monitoring what we watch, what we think, and how we vote; feeding us media junk food on social media; and telling us who to hate, what to think, and what to believe.

Just last week, the CDC stated that the Coronavirus is airborne and that people should be wearing masks even while outdoors if there's a crowd. I guess POTUS didn't like that, as this week that statement has been removed from the agency's website. This agency is supposed to be for us, the people of the United States; it's *not* meant to be altered by the White House.

It's less than two months away from the presidential election, and even though we are closing in on two hundred thousand deaths from the virus, POTUS is holding in-person rallies with no masks and little social distancing. DEAD PEOPLE CAN'T VOTE. Doesn't he know that? I suppose he's hoping they'll vote from their hospital beds.

I hear Matthew quietly let himself out. I know that sleep is impossible, so I, too, start my day. After Little Bit is fed and my coffee's in hand, I head back to bed and drink my brew in the dark, waiting for the soft light to filter through the trees in the backyard. Memories begin to filter through my brain as the caffeine does its job.

I was also awakened very early nineteen years ago, but that time it was because of a terrible anxiety attack rather than an inspiring dream. I remember lying in that tiny twin bed, under a mountain of blankets, trying to figure out what was wrong with me. Was I having a heart attack? My heart was racing, and I had the most horrible feeling of impending doom. What was wrong with me?

I was spending the year in southern Chile, teaching English at a public high school in La Unión after being awarded a Fulbright scholarship. I barely knew anyone and was still experiencing culture shock, as I'd only been there a little over a month. But everything was going very well. The students and faculty were very polite and had gone all-out to welcome me, throwing a huge banquet and dance. I had fun and even danced with some of my new male colleagues. But I did not dance la cueca. Apparently, you cannot fake the national dance of Chile. (I later took a dance class so I wouldn't embarrass myself too much at future dances.)

The students were nice. Similar to the students back home, but much more disciplined. How many US students would stand up to show respect to the teacher as she entered the classroom? Zero. That's how many.

That day, I simply could not explain the horrible feeling, but I shook it off and got ready to go to work. Even though it was spring in the southern hemisphere, it was still cold and damp. (It wasn't crisp and sunny in Chile like it was on the east coast of the United States that fateful day.) Since there was no central heat in the school—and I highly doubted that the boys would have a nice, warm fire going in the woodstove—I bundled up in a coat, gloves, a scarf, and a hat, then made my way through the streets of that small city.

I arrived at the huge school, pressed the buzzer, and waited for Elena to open the door for me. I made my way to the faculty lounge to retrieve my materials from the huge locker assigned to me. Teachers, not students, were given lockers because they were the ones changing classes. I greeted the other teachers and headed up the stairs to 3C, my first class of the day. (I still had to look at my schedule every day to make sure I went to the correct class, as it varied daily.)

The students were noisily chattering as I came in, but they immediately stood up to greet me. When I sat down to take attendance, they followed suit, and we then began a review of basic English greetings.

We asked and answered questions about personal likes, passing around a Smurf ball. They responded with great enthusiasm but struggled pronouncing the new English words. They were so shy. I would sometimes have to scoot up close to the students and cup my ear in order to hear the response. They were getting used to me, though, and we would all come to love each other before the year ended.

Before I knew it, it was time for the ten-minute recess, and I headed back down to the faculty lounge for a quick cup of hot tea. I found everyone gathered around the TV that was mounted on the wall. They told me about the first plane, and although it was horrible, we all assumed it was an accident. When I got back to the classroom, the students also had the TV on (very few had cell phones back then, and they wouldn't have dared to have them in class), and they begged me to let them watch for a few minutes more. When the second plane hit, I knew it was no accident, and the tears fell uncontrollably down my face. Those dear students surrounded me with love, putting their arms around me.

They kept saying, "Miss, Miss, you go home now and call your family."

I numbly obeyed them, barely remembering to tell Silvia, la directora, that I had to leave. I made my way through those busy streets and didn't care that the people there were whispering to each other, wondering what was wrong with la gringa. Once home, I turned on the TV, and for the first time since arriving in that country, I wished to hear my native tongue so that I could be sure I understood what was going on. I tried to call home, but of course, the lines were busy. I cannot begin to explain how devastated I felt while witnessing an attack on my home soil from far away, but I've never felt so alone before. So completely alone.

The doorbell rang, and I looked out the window. I couldn't believe what I saw. There was a line of people outside. Some of them were colleagues and students from the school, but most were complete strangers. They came in one by one, bringing me food, flowers, cards, hugs, and kisses on both cheeks. It was a life-altering event, one that I hope I never forget. From that day forward, I accepted every invitation to visit, to travel, to party, to dance, *to live*.

What a teacher the year 2001 was, especially for Americans. We learned what the rest of the world had known for a long time: the world can be a scary place, and no one is immune to its dangers. We do not live in a protected bubble, and you cannot depend on your government to protect you. In fact, your government can be the boogieman at your door. What a wake-up call! I really *had* felt safe in my country up until then, even through the Cold War era while practicing nuclear fallout drills at school. (What ever happened to those underground fallout shelters? Are they still there, buried underground and just waiting to be resurrected?) I was just a child then, and it just seemed like we were play-acting.

Today, it feels *good* to be awake. It feels good to be alive. Every day truly is a gift, and every person God places in my path just may be an angel, waiting to share infinite wisdom and beauty with me...if I'd just slow down and listen. *Be still and pray.* I pray the Lord's Prayer on this 9/11, all the while hearing the purrs of Little Bitty.

I turn on the news. This year's virtual commemoration is quite somber yet beautiful. I love the stories of those fallen heroes. The firefighters who kept climbing those stairs while others were descending down to safety. The passengers who took control of Flight 93 away from the terrorists, then diverted the plane away from the Capitol before crashing in Pennsylvania. The Pentagon policeman carrying one victim after another out of the inferno. *So many* acts of heroism!

We can be proud of how we came together as a country in the aftermath of those towers falling. I wonder why it is different now. People are further apart than ever before and are acting so selfishly, not even willing to wear masks to protect one another, many choosing to just ignore the science. So many have died since the beginning of the pandemic last winter, and I shudder to think about this winter. If we continue to disregard the well-being of our neighbor, we will be in big trouble. These are such scary times, maybe even scarier than 9/11. Time will tell. Sometimes I have to pinch myself to make sure I'm awake. *America, please wake up!* We are about to cross some invisible line—the point of no return, I fear—if we don't come together as one people. Love thy neighbor.

Amantha

Sunday

Fires are raging in the western United States, horrendous flames just consuming forests the size of some of our smaller states, and another hurricane is plowing up the Gulf Coast. I think this one is named Laura. Meteorologists say they're running through all the names in our alphabet and will soon have to switch to the Greek one. And yet there are many politicians, including our president, who still say that climate change is a hoax. The Earth is screaming in pain, trying to get our attention. Countless wildlife and plant species have been eradicated, and superstorms are becoming all too common. The west keeps getting dryer and hotter, while the Atlantic brews up one monster after another. We're in a vicious cycle now, and it all seems so hopeless. I hope it's not all in vain. Can we turn back the clock?

I roll over to look at the clock and see that it's time for Matthew and me to get up. We are having church in the parking lot these days, and it has been wonderful to get together with our church family again. Even though it's different than being in the physical building, it's still way better than virtual services. There's something about being there in person, in the present that resonates with me. Matthew agrees with me, and we are looking forward to seeing everyone.

Hope Knocking

We have breakfast with Mother, and Matthew is happy because she's fixed his favorite: biscuits and gravy, eggs, and bacon. We invite her to accompany us to church, but we know we're just doing lip service, and we don't press the issue too much. We leave at 10:30 AM, and as we drive past Jewell's house, we admire the asters starting to bloom on the bank. Summer's farewell flower, some mountain people call them. We see our neighbor Nell and roll down the car window to inquire about her husband, Frank. They both got Covid from their grandson a couple of weeks ago, and now Frank's in the Med Center on a ventilator.

"Well, he's still right sick," she says, and we can see the worried look on her face for just a moment, but then a more determined expression lights up her pretty face. "He'll be okay, though. He's tough."

We offer our help and prayers. She says she's making it fine but that prayers are welcome. I make a mental note to take her some apple butter later.

I think back to last fall, when we gathered at the shed by the riverside to make apple butter the old-timey way, in a big copper kettle, stirred all morning by friends and neighbors who came to help with our yearly event. I think of my group playing mountain ballads around the fire, and I now recall one song I wrote called "Apple Butter Pickin' Party."

It's apple butter time in the mountains at Diamond River, Tennessee
We'll peel and core about four bushels of apples; Winesap says the recipe
Friends and family will all gather together
At the homeplace of Nancy Mae,
Who promises to supervise the making of apple butter by Manthie

CHORUS
Add more apples...stir, stir!
A little more water...stir, stir!
A copper penny so it doesn't stick

> *Cinnamon, loads of sugar, and red hots*
> *All together in a copper pot*
>
> *Matthew stirs as he dances 'round the fire, in step to an old-time band*
> *There's a chill in the air in late October; we gather closer to warm our hands*
> *When the butter's ready, we all grab a biscuit,*
> *Just to make sure it turned out right*
> *Then it's all canned in mason jars; we hear them popping all night*

My thoughts of delicious apple butter dissolve like butter on a biscuit as we pull into the church parking lot and park six feet away from the Douglases. We roll down our windows and chat while waiting for the preacher to arrive. Another family pulls in close to us on the other side, but we stay put. I see the preacher waving for me to come sing and play a couple of songs on my guitar.

After, the preacher begins his message. Everything seems to be going fine until he starts in on politics...*again*. This time, he discusses fake news about Antifa (antifascist groups) starting the fires in California, Oregon, and Washington. Then Harold, in the car on our right side, shouts out that the West Coast is reaping what they've sown, and the preacher agrees. What about compassion for our fellow Americans who are suffering through these horrific fires, losing property, livestock, and their own lives? I elbow Matthew and whisper that I cannot take much more of this. Then the preacher says that BLM (Black Lives Matter) embraces violence and anti-government views in its doctrine. I sit there fuming in the warm car.

Matthew whispers to me, "Did I tell you that Deacon Jeff is wearing a Confederate flag cap?"

"*What?*" I forget to whisper, and Freida Douglas turns her attention to me, giving me a sympathetic look.

Freida and I are close friends, and she knows how I feel about the preacher using the pulpit to sway the political opinions of his congregation. I just don't think it's right. Back in March, before I flew to Hawaii, I had words with him on the phone and told him exactly what I thought. This was so hard for me to do! I had sat in my pew for years and just took it, but with all the misinformation and hatred now being spread like the deadly virus, I can no longer be silent. Too many Christians turn a blind eye to all the suffering that's occurring right here in the United States, like on our southern border.

God is about love. I cling to this truth. Anyone who thinks it is okay for our government to put a child in a cage, separating him from his immigrant parents so that other illegals will think twice about making the arduous journey from Central America and Mexico, is *not* about love. I believe that most of these immigrants are truly desperate and would never have made the expensive, dangerous trip if they weren't. Human migration will continue no matter what political party holds the highest office in the land. *People will do whatever it takes to survive.* Most Americans cannot imagine seeing their children starve and cannot understand the constant threat of gang violence or political turmoil. We must walk a mile in their shoes. If we were in their situation, wouldn't we do the same for our children? I think Jesus would open His loving arms and welcome them to safety.

Of course, common sense should prevail. I do think that all people entering our country should be vetted, and not everyone should be allowed in. Obviously, anyone who has a criminal record and any association with gangs or terrorist organizations should be denied entry. I know many people say that anyone coming here illegally should automatically be deported, but I disagree. It is nearly impossible for people with no education or money to come here legally. That's why they come here to begin with: to work. Work enables them to escape poverty, starvation, and death. Work is available here in the US. *We need workers!* Let's face reality: Americans no longer do the jobs that immigrants do. If it weren't for them, our crops would rot in the fields, dishes would go unwashed, and children, yards, and houses would go untended.

My song *"Inmigrante"* was written in an effort to show empathy for the immigrants—*all* immigrants—who have come to our land, which has been a land of opportunity. Will it continue to be?

Inmigrante swims across the Río Grande,
Leaves family, his home, and his friends,
For the land of the red, white, and blue
Might make his dreams come true

<u>CHORUS</u>
But there ain't no welcome mat
They say, "Just turn back
We have problems of our own
Just go back home,
Inmigrante"

Just a mother on her own
Crosses the desert, so hot and alone
Coyote takes the money, and he runs
Her faith in freedom vanished like the sun

<u>CHORUS</u>
And there ain't no welcome mat
They say, "Just turn back
We have problems of our own
Just go back home,
Inmigrante"

After World War Two,
Found a place that welcomed you with open arms
He's your neighbor, the one that looks like you
After all, we're all inmigrantes

Hope Knocking

<u>*CHORUS*</u>
We laid out the welcome mat
We said, "Now don't turn back
Your problems are our own
Please don't go back home,
Inmigrante"

What if Jesus were an inmigrante
Would you turn Him away and cast Him out?
Or His Father, would you tell Him to go away?
America, open your heart
And welcome the inmigrantes

I almost hate to say it, and I pray that I'm wrong, but I suspect that many Americans dislike these hard-working folk because of fear—fear of their dark skin, different languages, and different customs. I wonder, if immigrants were pouring in from northern Europe, would this animosity exist? I highly doubt it. I am starting to see just how deeply racism is embedded in our society, and it troubles me deeply. *I will have no more part of it*, I think to myself.

I try to refocus on the preacher's message, but I know it's no use. The Confederate flag hat has really angered me, and I mentally begin to prepare for my own message to the preacher. Back in March, after confronting him the first time, I knew that he would probably not change and that Matthew and I would be the ones who would have to leave, giving up our beloved church. People rarely change. Life has taught me that. Initially, he told me that we had to follow God's will and that he would pray for us. That did not make me feel good at all! I felt like I was being dismissed, like Matthew and I just didn't matter. So, when the preacher called one week later and told us that he would try his best not to talk politics, I was ecstatic! I had hope for the world and for our country. I thought that just maybe people *could* change, *could* come together.

Well, Amantha, you were wrong. People are more divided than ever, and you have to choose sides. I choose to be on the RIGHT SIDE OF HISTORY, so whatever Matthew decides, I know now that I must leave Gentry Gap Baptist Church, at least for the time being. I will not close that door entirely, not just yet. *I must wait on God.*

I tell Matthew about my decision as we drive home, and I can tell that he's as sad as me. But his words reassure me that he also feels anger and resentment over being subjected to politics at church. "Why, if I wanted to hear Fox News Network, I could just stay at home!" he declares heatedly as we drive down the steep path to our home.

I notice Jewell's car in their driveway and say, "What are we going to tell Carrots?"

We jokingly refer to our relationship with our neighbors as "peas and carrots" because we've all been getting along these days. This has not always been the case.

"Just tell them the truth," my husband replies as we pull into the garage.

I fix chicken quesadillas with fresh mustard greens from the garden, but I can barely eat at all. Matthew eats everything but the greens, so I add them to the chickens' scrap bucket. I cover my plate for later.

I head downstairs to the computer. I find at least nine credible news sources that contradict the preacher's Antifa theory. I go to the Black Lives Matter webpage and find absolutely nothing in their mission statement that promotes violence. I then write a personal message to our beloved preacher, fact-checking him about the fires and BLM and asking him about the deacon wearing the Confederate flag cap. I make sure my tone is respectful and loving before sending him the message, because even though I strongly disagree with him, Matthew and I respect and love our preacher and our church. We would not want to hinder either and absolutely do not wish to cause problems. In fact, we both know that the majority of Gentry Gap Baptist Church supports the current administration, as does most of Appalachia. We just want them to know why we have left.

I sigh, send the message, and head back upstairs to snuggle with Matthew in bed. He's already snoozing, which doesn't surprise me, as I know he's exhausted. He's always worn out by Sunday, especially since ClothTreat has him working most Saturdays now. I quietly get into bed and pray for comfort.

"Lord, I turn it over to you because you are the Great Comforter. I pray for guidance, Lord. Show me which path to take. Fill me with your wisdom, lovingkindness, and knowledge so that I can do thy will. Lord, please help us all. Heal those who have this virus, those who've lost loved ones, and those facing the fires out West. Help the wildlife suffering loss of life and habitat. Help our country and this beautiful planet Earth, which you've given to us as a home. Lord, teach us to be better stewards of our home, and teach us to be better to each other and to *all* creatures. This I pray in your holy name. Amen."

Amantha

Two Weeks Later

It's a gorgeous Saturday morning at the farmers market in Cerro City, where Super Sally's husband, Mitch, and I are scheduled to play music. Everyone wears a mask. How refreshing! The vendors display colorful pumpkins, mums, greens, honey, and soap, and their stalls are all socially distanced. It's kind of strange how the new Covid-19 lingo has seeped into our language with little to no resistance, yet actions like mask-wearing, quarantining, and staying away from others have been met with downright rebellion, mostly by Republicans.

Mitch and I play for three hours straight, and I hardly notice the time pass. You know you love doing something when that happens. The customers and vendors alike show their appreciation by singing with us, tapping their feet, and generously filling my guitar case with money. Many of the vendors put their homemade goods in the case, too, and I am happy to score luscious soaps, honey, dishtowels, mums, and blueberry scones. Sally surprises me with three more masks for Matthew, Momma, and me.

Mine has smiling skulls on it, and I thank her, exclaiming, "I'm all set for Día de Los Muertos! You're super, Sally!"

Day of the Dead is my favorite Mexican holiday. It begins on October 31st and ends on November 2nd. It is similar to Halloween but is much more spiritual. I'd just love to visit Mexico during the festivities, especially to see all the cemeteries decked out with marigolds, candles, incense, music, typical Mexican foods, and families ready to welcome the spirits home to a big party. In the homes, altars are decorated with the deceased loved ones' memorabilia—photographs, favorite foods, drinks, colors, hobbies, and anything else that helps the families remember them. Markets sell a delicious special bread called pan de Muertos, bread of the dead, alongside skulls made from just about anything, including radishes, sugar, carrots, gourds, and wood. In the state of Michoacán, the arrival of the monarch butterflies coincides with the holiday, and many people believe that they are the spirits of the dead returning home.

I think the holiday is so beautiful and respectful to the dead! Some Americans may visit their loved ones on Memorial Day or other holidays, but we do nothing as elaborate as Día de Los Muertos. In fact, I feel pretty sure you'd stir up an awful hornets' nest if you tried to have a party in Birch Springs Cemetery, where most of Momma's relatives lie. You'd probably be asked to leave, and you could expect to be added to the prayer list at the Wednesday night meeting. Then you'd start receiving even more religious material in the mail.

The best America has to offer is Decoration Day, which is still observed in Appalachia by the old-timers, but it has faded from many people's thoughts. This is what Memorial Day was first called, and it was a time to decorate the cemetery with flags and fresh flowers. Families would remove weeds and cut the grass. It was an all-day affair, followed by dinner on the grounds, singing, and preaching. It was a way to remember and respect our dead.

It seems to me that nowadays when people die, they are forgotten. Period. How sad! I know in the past I haven't visited my loved ones' graves enough, but this year, strangely enough, it's been a way to get

Momma out of the house. She *likes* to visit cemeteries, especially Birch Springs, where she'll go when she dies. Maybe most Americans don't visit cemeteries because we don't like to think of dying. Mexicans, and Momma, are realists. They accept death as part of the natural cycle of life, so they prepare for it. One day, I will throw Momma a shin-dig of a party, with roses instead of marigolds, doughnuts instead of dead bread, and old-time music instead of mariachi. I welcome the prayers!

Now, at the market, I give Sally and Mitch huge air hugs and load up Cielito Lindo with all my goods from the market, along with my instruments. I start to drive away but notice I have a praying mantis hitching a ride on my windshield. I pull over and gently place her (it's big so that it must be a female) on the grass next to the walking trail.

I've seen more of these beneficial insects this year than ever before. Earlier this week, I saw two in the bottle garden, one brown and one green, which is a little puzzling to me. The week before, there was one in the vegetable garden soaking in the sunlight on top of a sunflower plant, camouflaged by the green leaves. Right after that sighting, I found one while hiking up on Grandfather Mountain. It was right on the trail, so I moved it out of the way so it wouldn't get crushed.

When animals make repeat appearances in my life, I've learned to slow down and ponder over their messages. What characteristic does the praying mantis have that I need to also have at this time? Well, obviously, I need to pray constantly. I get that. I chuckle to myself as I envision a party in the cemetery to commemorate Mother's death one day, with much praying for *our* souls going on at the church below it. Nah, that's not it. I think back to the bottle garden. I wouldn't have even seen the creatures if I hadn't disturbed them with my weeding, as they were so still.

That feels right...*BE STILL, Amantha, and know that I am God. Wait on me. Be fully present in the moment. This moment. Breathe. Give thanks. Live every day as if it's a precious gift...because it is.*

I almost cry because I am so grateful for this message! I am relieved to be still and let God take over, because frankly, the situation with our church has left me so sad and depressed, and I've wondered what to do next. There's a hole in my heart, but I'm not quite ready to search for another church yet. With the pandemic, many churches aren't meeting in person anyway. Churches that are meeting and aren't taking Covid precautions do not interest me, as they are not loving their neighbors, pure and simple. So I choose to take this praying mantis's sign to heart. I will be still and let God lead. I will pray and read His Word and let the Son comfort me.

When I return home, I pack my bags for my hiking trip to Cashiers, North Carolina. It's just for four days, but I am excited to get away with my friends Sally and Kim. It worked out perfectly, too, because Matthew is taking a week's vacation while I am away, so he will be able to look in on Mother. He has a huge list of things he wants to accomplish around here, such as cleaning our decks and washing Mother's house. I am so glad to be married to someone with such a strong work ethic. I appreciate that trait. I do hope, however, that Matthew will rest some while I'm gone. He's always so tired, but the man doesn't seem to know how to slow down.

When I return, we plan to go to Salida, Virginia, to visit his family during an outdoor, socially distanced barbecue. I like his brothers and sisters and know that being around them will be good for my workaholic husband. We plan to wear masks, but we have to assume that his family will not, as that's just the way things are now.

This is the new reality in the United States right now. I know it sounds crazy, but if we're going to see others, we can't get angry. We have to take the necessary precautions for ourselves and try not to meddle with people who think differently. I have learned that my health suffers when I get angry, and it changes nothing anyway. If people haven't changed their behaviors by now, they're not going to.

We are not around other people much anyway. Everything that we normally do has already been cancelled—the family reunion, the church homecoming, picking parties, and apple-butter-making get-togethers. And Thanksgiving and Christmas are rapidly approaching. I place more X's on my calendar. In the meantime, I will go chasing rainbows and waterfalls.

PART THREE:
Fall in Line at the Polls

Nancy Mae

Monday

I crunch through the fallen, dead leaves as I make my way to the chicken coop to let the girls out. It seems like the leaves are just falling to the ground instead of changing colors. I guess it's still too early and warm for the rainbow of colors we are hoping for. I open the gate and scatter my food scraps along the bank before releasing the birds from their warm, cozy house. One by one, they fly down from their roost and race to be the first one to reach all the leftovers that had been accumulating in my refrigerator.

I look into the nests for any eggs, but there still aren't any. I know my son-in-law is impatiently waiting for a return on his investment, but as for me, I just enjoy the company of the chickens. Live creatures are surely a comfort to old hermits like me, and I pull up a chair to watch their morning antics. The younger white ones are still getting bullied by those mean black-and-white ones (Domineers?), who peck them when they try to get a bite in. I try to shoo them away, but they look like they might peck me, so I slowly exit and meander away.

I walk around the pet cemetery to the bottle garden and then walk on to the garden. The flowers seem to be more vibrant than ever, as if they know their time is short and must get one more dance in at the ball before midnight strikes. They sway and beckon to me in the morning light that streams in over Hickory Nut Mountain, lighting up our river valley like a beacon of hope. I reach for two ripe tomatoes and four ears of corn, which I plan to fix for our dinner, along with pinto beans, cornbread, and milk, of course. I'm almost out of milk and make a mental note to ask Matthew to get two gallons when he goes to town tomorrow. I tell everyone I'm like a baby because I just have to have milk. Sometimes for supper, I just crumble some cornbread into a glass and pour milk over it. So good!

I finish my walk at the tiny house, where I carefully make my way up the stairs and let myself in. My daughter Eileen, who recently stayed here, did a great job cleaning it, so there's really not much to do to get it ready for the next guest: my oldest son, Dan. I haven't seen him since last Christmas, and I get a lump in my throat just thinking about him. How I've missed my firstborn! There's just something truly special about your first child, and I so look forward to his visit even though he can only stay two nights.

Eileen was here a little longer, and it was so good to lay eyes on her, too. I made sure she was satisfied with my final exit plans, and I made sure I remembered which heirlooms she had claimed in my house. She is getting the cherished painting that my dear cousin Berthie painted of the homeplace, which I know she'll treasure. It shows me hauling water from the spring, Momma feeding her chickens, Sister Sadie rocking one of the twins on the porch, and Dad splitting wood in the yard. She's my oldest daughter, so I want to leave her something special.. I know she has no interest in the land. Eileen has never been drawn to these hills, not like Amantha.

The bugs just eat her up, too. How did that young'un ever survive growing up in Georgia? I tell her to eat lots of garlic. That's what I do, and they never bite me. Dan and Jay both asked me once if garlic would keep the snakes away (they have a thing about snakes), and I told them that it didn't seem to bother the black snake I found in my basement a few years back. No one has stayed in my basement since, though it's really nice now that Matthew has finished working on it. I never told them that the snake was actually upstairs in my bedroom—on the floor right next to me, in fact. It seemed to be watching TV with me as I lounged in bed. I had a time catching him with my blanket and felt a little guilty about evicting the poor creature.

I am brought back to the present by this thought, and I do a quick check under the bed, in the closet, and even behind the couch to make sure there are no slithering serpents in Bear Necessities.

It sure has come in handy this year. Amantha did her two-week quarantine here after her trip to "Hiwahyah," Eileen was able to socially distance here, and now Dan will be able to stay here and keep away from me, as well. I'd really prefer for him to stay in my house. There's so much I need to discuss with him. Plus, I just like hearing the creak of the wooden boards upstairs, a reminder that I am not alone. I want to show him my new will, which Amantha convinced me to have drawn up. After all, he will be inheriting my property. I know he already knows my desire for him to leave it to his children, as they love this place as much as he does.

I look out the window at the fishing rock, Dan's favorite spot. He likes to take his journal and sit cross-legged on the large rock (there used to be a concrete bench, but the river keeps reclaiming it), writing down his thoughts, clearing his mind. He's so very busy with his successful financial consulting business. I'm sure that these days his customers, and he, are worried sick. So many small businesses have gone under, but he's reassured me that his is still going strong. He meets with the clients who live close by in person and uses Zoom (whatever that is) with the ones who live farther away, as flying is still risky. I wonder if the airlines will ever recover from this pandemic.

I remove the sheets from the bed and take them with me to be washed. The tiny house does have a washer and dryer; I just don't know how to use them. I hate new contraptions! Why does everything new have to be so complicated? I despise my new vacuum cleaner and washing machine equally, but at least I finally figured out the washer.

I lock up and carefully make my way down the stairs again, stepping down onto the carpet of fallen leaves. Dan is supposed to come Friday (or is it Saturday?), so I have plenty of time to get ready. I know he'll want coleslaw. I wonder if that boy really likes it that much or if he just likes to aggravate his siblings by always eating more than his share? Either way, I'm glad Amantha will be back to make it, because I just can't do all that chopping anymore. I can fix the green beans, corn, and cornbread myself, and maybe I'll make his favorite dessert: banana pudding. But only if I'm not too tired. We'll see.

Right now, I'm needing my bed and a snack—maybe a glazed doughnut with another cup of coffee. Then I'll start the load of laundry. Matthew and I will eat together around 3:00 PM, so that gives me time to fix our vegetable dinner. That is about all I plan to do today, and that's enough.

I'm still sick and haven't gone back to the doctor, but I did have a telephone meeting with her. She tried to insist that I come in person, but I absolutely refused and convinced her to call in another two weeks of the antibiotic that treats my UTI...if that's even what's wrong with me. I just don't have much faith in doctors nowadays and wish I could find a good one. I asked around and tried several that my friends and family recommended, but as Matthew would say, they were "no account." I promised Eileen that I would go if I wasn't better, and that was two weeks ago, but as I tell Amantha, I have to make my own decisions. I'll finish taking this awful medicine (that's what's probably making me feel so bad), and then I'll decide what to do.

That's one thing I loved about my mother: she let each one of her children make their own decisions and seemed to know exactly what each kid needed. I needed independence, and that's what I got. She never once tried to stand in my way or talk me out of something, even if she knew it was something I would regret later. I was allowed to have my own successes and failures. I've tried to do the same for my children, and now that the roles are reversing, I sincerely hope that my children will allow me the same dignity.

I take my second breakfast to bed and am finishing it when the phone rings. I pick up and talk with Amy, my great-niece, for an eternity, it seems. She invites all of us to a birthday party for her grandmother Violet, which will be at their river property just down Mavie Road. I've been wanting to see the new place and am dying to get out, so I accept. It will be two weeks from now, so hopefully it won't be too cold, because of course, it will be held outdoors. *I can't take the cold anymore*, I think to myself as I bury deeper under the mountain of blankets. I thank her and say goodbye, then mark the date, October 9th, on my calendar.

I hope my brother RC will be at the party. We hardly ever talk or see each other anymore, and I suppose it's just as much my fault as his. I was fourteen when he was born, so we were never close. Momma sure doted on her youngest, and she sure would have been proud to see all that he's accomplished. He held the office of sheriff in Elk County four times and loved his job so much that even now that he's older, he continues to work as a constable.

I remember RC as a child, proudly carrying the bb gun that Dad gave him for Christmas one year, shooting every critter in sight. When he killed a squirrel, I refused to even try the squirrel gravy Momma proudly served up, but that was not unusual for me. I used to run up the mountain to hide when it was hog-killing time, and I cursed the preacher under my breath when he came a-calling after church for his fresh chicken dinner. I love all creatures and am pretty much a vegetarian.

I chuckle as I recall the time RC took Dan, my city-slicker ex-husband, hunting with him. I remember the angry shouting that echoed down the mountain as they returned empty-handed, though they didn't *exactly* return empty-handed. Dan had shot my youngest brother's favorite coon dog, Biscuit, and even though the poor hound miraculously didn't die, it never hunted again. RC never let my husband forget it, and he still talks about it to this very day even though Dan and I have been divorced for nearly fifty years. I never remarried, but he married two more times and still lives in Georgia.

I don't have much use for men anymore, except for Matthew. He sure does a lot for me, and I know I couldn't live in this isolated place if it weren't for him and Amantha. I hear him outside now, his ladder scraping in the gravel. I almost forgot that he's supposed to clean the outside of my house today. I guess I'd better start our dinner. I'm a little hungry now, so I fix half a ham sandwich. I need a little protein.

Nancy Mae

Sunday Morning

Amantha is back from her trip, and I am surprised that I missed her so much, but I did. Dan is leaving this morning after breakfast, which I'm fixing now—eggs, bacon, and granny bread. My granny Myrtle inspired the recipe for the bread. It is basically biscuits; you just don't have to cut them out, which suits me fine. Even though it's work, I love having them all here on Sunday mornings. It takes the edge off the loneliness.

I decide to bring up the birthday invitation to Amantha, and to my surprise she agrees to go with me next Friday.

"Do you suppose that any of them will be wearing masks?" Dan asks.

Matthew laughs and says, "Why no. That's probably why two of them have already had the virus. Do you all really think you should go?"

"Well, we went to your family's cookout on Friday, and none of them wore masks, either," Amantha points out.

I add my two cents, saying, "I'm going on ninety and am going to die anyway. This will be as good a way to go as any."

"We wore masks at Matthew's family's get-together, and we'll wear them to this one, right, Mom?" Amantha points at me and adds, "Besides, she needs the socialization."

I shake my head in agreement and say, "I do, I do. I've been cooped up in Mavie for too long. I want to see their new river place and see if it's as purty as our No Place. Now come and get it before Dan eats all the bacon."

Dan blesses the food after he inhales two pieces of bacon. He sits on the other side of the room even though I try to persuade him to sit with me at the table.

"Momma, you've got to take this virus seriously. Even POTUS has it now," he says as he settles into the "man-chair."

"Well, I say let Mother Nature take her course," I mutter, and my family looks at me incredulously. I add, "I guess there is a God, after all."

"Nancy, you don't care to say what's on your mind, now do you?" Matthew splutters as he chokes on his egg.

The big news broke last Thursday about POTUS getting sick, two days after his debacle of a debate with Job Bright. I couldn't stand to watch more than ten minutes of it and was really peeved that *Perry Mason* was not on. In all my years here on this Earth, I have never witnessed such rude behavior from a president. Poor Bright couldn't even get his points across because of the constant interruptions. I turned it off when the Democrat finally lost his cool and told POTUS to shut up. That Fox moderator tried over and over again to rein him in, but the president made a mockery of the whole thing, just as he's mocked the Coronavirus. And now he has it. I'm just being honest when I say he got what he deserved. Perhaps he will now feel some compassion for the two hundred thousand who have now died in our country.

They say he got it, along with ten others in the White House, during a Rose Garden event for that new Supreme Court judge he wants confirmed before the election—a judge who will tip the scale to the Republican side, six to three. She is anti-abortion, of course, and she also wants to overthrow Hopecare.

Hope Knocking

Hopecare is the health-care program started by President Hope, the first Black president of the US. He was probably the reason our current POTUS was elected. Whites just couldn't stand the thought of a Black man running our country, and thus POTUS, born with a silver spoon in his mouth, became the voice for the many poor, uneducated, disenfranchised whites who felt they were losing *their* country. POTUS even started a rumor that Hope was not born in the United States and was therefore ineligible to be Commander-in-chief. When this ridiculous theory was discredited, Hope mocked him in public, on national television, and POTUS never forgave him for that. In fact, he has tried to undo everything Hope started, therefore hurting the very people who put him in office. Poor, working people are the ones helped by Hopecare; twenty million Americans who had no insurance before are now covered by this program.

The most concerning thing of all is the upcoming election next month. If POTUS loses—and I'm not sure that he will—he hopes that the Conservative justices will side with him when he claims that the vote was fraudulent, then declare him the winner. *Can this really be happening in the United States of America?* We have never had a president who was unwilling to accept defeat. We've never had one who declared that the only way he could lose would be because of voter fraud.

We've also never had a president who held so much sway with his supporters. I remember that when he ran four years ago, he stated that he could kill somebody and his followers wouldn't blink an eye, and I think he was right! It's like they are brainwashed, and I just don't understand it. The majority of his supporters appear to be uneducated, poor whites, like most of the people around here. My people. *POTUS has done nothing for them, so what is it?* I think. Perhaps they think they are losing *their* country to immigrants who take jobs no one wants. Maybe they worry that non-whites are reproducing at a rate that will make them the majority, which is true, but who cares? (Jay, my demographer son, says that is inevitable.) Maybe there's nostalgia for the "good old days," when whites ruled and blacks knew their place.

I don't recall those days being good. I just remember being hungry all the time. We never knew any blacks around here, but if they had been here, I suppose we would have felt superior to them. Maybe being white was the only trump card we had, but I guess I never thought about it. Instinctively, I know I never would have been recruited to work for the FBI if I were Black, and getting that job saved my life.

My second job, working for Head Start in Georgia, was another steppingstone for me. It helped me land my teaching position years later. Thank God (okay, there *might* be one) those wonderful Black women didn't discriminate against me and chose to hire me! I was scared to death at first—after all, I had never known any blacks before—but before long I had made two of the best friends I'd ever known: Bertha and Mavis. I even marched with those sisters, arm in arm in Atlanta, trying to get the Equal Rights Amendment passed. Sadly, the amendment did not pass, and women are still fighting for equality, especially Black women. They were both beautiful women—tall, like me, with huge, impressive afros. My children played with their children at our homes, and I also took Amantha with me to work, where she played with all of my African American students.

"Amantha, do you remember when you were about four and I took you to work with me at Head Start? Do you remember playing with all those Black young'uns?"

She's at the sink now, running water over the huge pile of dishes stacked there, and I fuss at her, saying, "Now, you leave that. I'll do those dishes later."

She ignores me and says, "Oh yes, I most certainly remember that. That really impacted my life, Momma. I remember one time...I don't recall which swimming pool it was, but I'll *never* forget one very hot day in Georgia. We were all sweating profusely in the van, squirming excitedly with anticipation. We were going swimming, and the thought of plunging into that cool water brought such joy. When we got there, none of us noticed the white parents scrambling to get their children out of the water as we cannonballed into bliss. I remember surfacing from that icy cold water and hopping up onto the side of the pool, ready to head for the slide. One of those parents pulled me up by the arm and yelled at me to get out quickly. I gawked at her and asked her why.

"She pointed a finger at the other children and said, 'Because those'—she used the N-word—'are dirtying up *our* pool, and you might catch something from them.'

"I've never seen you move so fast, Momma! You grabbed that woman's shoulder and spun her around, demanding that she release me at once, and you told her she was a racist idiot. I had never heard the N-word or the word racist before, and I had no idea what either meant, but I remember crying the whole way back in the van. The other children were so quiet, and you know, I have never thought about *their* feelings. How devastated they must have felt! All they wanted to do was swim, escape that oppressive Georgia heat, and that fleeting happiness they felt as they jumped in that water vanished because of those thoughtless white parents. I wonder how their children felt. I feel sure they didn't understand, either. How could they? Children don't see color until it is pointed out to them by adults."

I say, "I don't remember any of that. Isn't that strange? I guess because racism was such a big part of our lives back then. That's just how ignorant people thought. Our next-door neighbors were just as bad. One time when they were at our house , Mavis dropped her children off for me to watch while she went somewhere. I introduced her to Mrs. Conway, and she turned to me and said, 'I didn't know you had a maid!' I was so embarrassed! Like you, I've never considered Mavis's feelings. I'm sure it made her mad as a hornet—since she was my *boss*—but she never let it show. I guess she was used to this sort of treatment."

Dan pipes up and says, "Do you remember when I played baseball in high school and I rode back and forth to practice with all the Black players? I got to be friends with all of them, though now I have no idea where they are or what has become of them. One time, we got pulled over by the police for no reason at all. The white officer kept us there for a long time, making us late for practice. I kept telling Maurice, who was in the bed of that pick-up truck, to ask the officer why we were being held, but he kept telling me to shut up. I had never seen him so scared before. Sweat was staining the armpits of his shirt, and we hadn't even started playing ball. The cop kept calling him 'boy,' and I didn't think anything of it because I thought we were boys. But then, just before he decided to let us go, that cop patted me on the arm as he was leaving and said, 'What's a nice young *man* like you doing with these yard monkeys?' I was so ashamed of my whiteness that day, so ashamed of my southern-ness."

Amantha finishes the dishes and continues the interesting conversation, saying, "You know, that's another thing that the Coronavirus has revealed. Racism is *everywhere* in this country, not just the South. I believe it's in the actual fabric of American society. We're a white supremacist nation and always have been. Even the Founding Fathers were slave owners. Now we are at a pivotal moment in our history. Are we going to finally admit to our racism and work to eradicate it, or are we at the brink of another civil war. If so, we will be fighting for equal rights for all, just like we did in the Civil War over one hundred years ago."

"I sometimes wonder, what *happened* to white men?" I question.

"Easy now, we're not all bad," Dan replies.

"But think about it," I say. "They killed off the Indians and took their land. They enslaved the Africans and kept them in bondage long after slavery was abolished. Now they persecute immigrants of color, caging their children and sterilizing their women. And women...Just look what they've done to women. Women are treated like property, sex objects, and still have to fight for control of their own bodies."

"I think it's all part of our genetic make-up," Dan says. "We had to possess the biggest, baddest cave in order to attract the prettiest cave chick so we could procreate...*survive*."

"But what is it about color?" Amantha interjects. "Why do we distrust, fear, *hate* people of color? Do you think blacks feel the same way? I think the time has come for all Americans to have these kinds of honest conversations about race. It's the only way we're going to survive and thrive. You know, I miss being around Black people. There are so few here in the mountains. I don't have any Black friends. I *want* to be part of the solution, part of the change, the healing. I'm doing a lot of reading and writing—my book, you know—but I need help. I need Black people and Brown people to show me how. Whites must listen now. This moment belongs to people of color, and we must honor them by empowering them, letting their wisdom lead us to a better place in history."

Dan stands up and claps his hands loudly. "Wow, baby sister, I'm impressed. I wish I could stay all day so we could solve the problems of the world, but I have a client waiting in Cleveland, so I'm outta here."

We hug and kiss from a distance, and he promises to come back for Christmas...if Santie Claus allows it.

Amantha

**Wednesday, November 4th
4:00 AM**

The polls got it wrong again; it will not be a landslide. POTUS has already declared victory, though we may not truly know for sure until Friday. He has also stated on Twitter that "they are trying to steal the election, and any votes not counted on Election Day should not be counted." The electoral vote now stands at 224 to 213, in favor of Bright, but there are many cliffhanger states—such as Wisconsin, Michigan, Pennsylvania, Arizona, Nevada, and my home state of Georgia—that are still waiting for all votes to be counted. POTUS could win; that much is clear now. The Democrats' hope lies with absentee ballots that were cast before Election Day, as Democrats overwhelmingly cast their votes that way due to Covid. Those votes are usually counted last, depending on the states, so there is still hope for Bright supporters, especially in the big cities.

The House and Senate, though, have been big disappointments for the Democrats. The Senate may still be controlled by Republicans, and the Democrats will be lucky to hold on to the House of Representatives. Even *if* Job Bright is declared the winner, it's likely going to be by so close a margin that POTUS will take it to the Supreme Court, which leans Republican now because he just added the new Conservative justice last week.

I am trying my best not to cry right now. I am trying my best to hang on to my faith that people are good and will do the right thing. I am trying to have faith, like a mustard seed, that God will not allow evil to win. He is not the author of confusion; therefore, Bright must win.

My brain is in a stupor at this early hour, even after three cups of very strong coffee, and I am transported back to 2016, when POTUS beat Hilda Kilgore even though she was winning at midnight and the polls had predicted her victory. The entire nation woke up to the nightmare of POTUS winning the Electoral College and Kilgore winning the popular vote.

I do not understand how a democracy can still, in the twenty-first century, allow a candidate to win an election when the *people* do not choose him. It is unacceptable and reprehensible to me! Democrats have won the popular vote six out of the last seven presidential elections, yet the antiquated electoral college persists. I guess because this is how Republicans won the presidency in 2000 and again in 2016. They know they need the College. But how can Americans explain this to the world and to themselves? I was asked about the constitutionality of the Electoral College during my stay in Chile, and I simply could not justify it. Whoever wins the presidency in this tumultuous year of 2020 will still be unable to change it due to the division that will still lie in Congress.

Whether Democrats win or not, Americans can still be proud of the record voter turnout in 2020. 66 percent is projected to break a century-old record.

There's so much at stake this year—the Coronavirus, climate change, police brutality and Black Lives Matter, health insurance, homelessness and poverty, and democracy itself. People on both sides feel strongly that their side is right, and the vote is showing that the division in our country will not go away when the last vote is counted, the winner announced. How will the next president address this chasm? The current methodology has been demonizing the other side, lying and spreading wild conspiracy theories, and enriching the elite 1 percent, and that has only served to enrage the people. Well, half of the people. The other half seem determined to continue riding this train. I'll be the first to admit that I *do not understand them*, but I *want* to. I have hope that with Bright, healing the division will be possible. I believe that he will listen to *all* the people and have compassion.

I really feel deep down in my bones that Bright will be like FDR: a president for *all* Americans. He is far from perfect—and let's face it, he's *old*—but maybe his wisdom and experience are what we so desperately need right now.

America needs to listen to the elders right now, not disparage them for their weaknesses. Yes, they may forget names and words for things that they easily recalled the year before. They may walk with a stoop and require a cane. They may require more assistance with basic tasks, especially during the pandemic. But these are human frailties that we will all face one day. Just because the elderly have these weaknesses, it doesn't mean we should just shut them away in nursing homes to die of loneliness. They have so much to offer us, especially now, and we must learn to seek their wisdom and give them the respect they certainly deserve.

Seeing my own mother begin to physically deteriorate has been an eye-opener for me. I have been guilty of treating her like an invalid, or something almost sub-human, and of invalidating her years of experience. The good news is, I am catching myself doing this, and I don't like my behavior. Therefore, I am *changing* my behavior. I can learn to gently remind her to don a mask without belittling her or starting an argument. I can give her the freedom to drive herself to Betsyville next Monday, because that independence means so much to her. I can listen to her political and religious beliefs that differ from mine without immediately discrediting and dismissing them. After all, her opinions also count. It can't be "my way or the highway." I don't always agree with her, but I am learning to *honor* her, to *listen* to her, and to *seek* out her opinions and advice.

That is what all humankind must learn to do: *coexist*. We have to do more than just tolerate our differences. We must validate them. *We must learn to see the humanity in each of us.*

I am choosing to take off my blinders so I can begin to compassionately see what lies beneath many Republican supporters—*fear*. It *must* be fear. Fear of losing one's identity: whiteness. Fear of losing all things American, like the National Anthem—hand over heart...stand up straight and remove your cap...don't you dare kneel...that's disrespectful. Fear of socialism, which gets wrapped up with Cuba, and communism, which is associated with the U.S.S.R. Good against evil: those baby-killing, abortion-loving liberals must be Satan worshippers. Fear of the dark: the brown immigrant coming over here to take our jobs, our women, and our land. The black "mob" rioting in the cities, looting and destroying, tearing down our statues of white men, our heritage. Fear of the foreigner: the Asians who started this pandemic and who are trying to take over the world; the Muslims who tore down our towers and don't dress like we do. *Fear of the unknown*. I must emphasize that I really do want to know why Republicans think the way they do. I think it's imperative to know in order for us, *all of us*, to move forward, to be better, and to truly be the *United* States of America.

I sigh, put my writing away for now, and dress for a hike on Beulah Bald. I am so happy to be with Sally, Kim, and Joanie and to just be in nature, surrounded by the sweet smell of fallen leaves and the big, blue sky. It feels good to sweat, to put one foot in front of the other, and to be rewarded by three-dimensional views at the top. None of us talk about the election, which is a great relief, because I for one have been glued to CNN, Fox, and any other news networks that can give me any clue about how it may all turn out. It has been a media overdose, and I am overjoyed to be removed from all of it. All of us have the same political affiliation and do note, on the way down the mountain, that we should stay away from social media and be careful what we say anywhere around here. You could cut the tension with a knife on Facebook right now, and many are lashing out. Most worrisome of all, we all fear that the far right will not accept a Bright victory. Lord help us all.

Amantha

Thursday, November 5th
4:00 AM

The cardinal has returned with a vengeance, and she seems to be seeking me out. She starts downstairs but then must realize where I am, and I see her banging against my bedroom window and looking in at me. *What is she trying to tell me?* I think. I go to the living room to do my workout, and there she is again, this time on the porch, chirping crazily and throwing herself against the French doors. *She's going to break*, I think, then realize that it's me who is broken. And perhaps our country is broken, as well. *Can Uncle Sam put himself together again? Can I?*

I forget my workout, forget that I've gained back five pounds, forget the fried chicken, fries, and four ice creams I inhaled yesterday, and forget about beating myself up again and again for not being enough. I guess I've felt this way for a very long time—not slim enough, not smart enough, not interesting enough, and not a good enough daughter, wife, sister, or Christian. The list could go on and on. I had planned on another fast today to try to get control of my diet, but it seems too exhausting to consider. I know what I need to do, so I get back in bed with my laptop and write.

I think, *How much of my soul should I bare? Is this book ever going to be read by people who might judge me, condemn me, persecute me? Do I care? Am I ready to be my true, authentic self, a being who is inherently loved by her Creator and therefore doesn't need external approval? Could this book possibly help others who are feeling like me? How many people go through life seeking constant approval from the world instead of reaching for their own goals and dreams?* I don't want that for myself. Life is too short. How sad it would be to reach the end of your life with such regrets! Most importantly, *is this book helping me?* I know *that I matter*, and I know *that writing most certainly helps my brokenness, so I do think it will help others who are broken, too.*

I pray before I write. "Lord, I know you accept me exactly the way I am, so I pray that I learn to accept myself, too. I pray for guidance in my healing, and in the healing of our country, too. Help us to reach out to one another. Help us to accept one another—ALL OF US. The blacks, whites, browns, Asians, Native Americans, immigrants, Democrats, Republicans, females, males, rich, poor, gay, drug-addicted, homeless, Christian, Muslim, Jewish, and Atheist. Let us have compassion for our brokenness. Let us move forward toward the light together. Amen."

How do we fix ourselves? How do I fix myself? Will that fix be , temporary, or will it be a more permanent one? Wait...I don't like that word, "fix." That implies that there is something inherently wrong, and if we are to accept ourselves, then we have to accept *all* parts of ourselves with loving compassion. Maybe the better word is "heal."

How do I heal the wounded cardinal within me? What does she really need in order to nourish herself? She craves food because she longs to be full, longs to keep those gnawing hunger pains at bay, longs to keep her demons away—the demons of loneliness, isolation, and self-hatred. Food became a balm for me a very long time ago, so it is now so very difficult to replace it with something else. It became a friend and companion to me when I felt ignored, unheard, unloved, unwanted, *not enough*. How do I convince that child that I really am enough? Food also became my punisher, my overly strict parent, disciplinarian, and executioner. How many times have I used food to inflict pain on myself, gorging on unhealthy foods as a punishment?

This is an American problem, too. Until we as a nation learn to confront our deep unhappiness, we will continue to numb ourselves with junk food, drugs, technology, the latest fashion, redecorated homes, bigger boobs, bigger lips, stomach reductions, and the latest exercise trends. We will continue to BUY, BUY, BUY.

Have you seen the latest home exercise equipment called The Mirror? How narcissistic have we become that we feel the need to critique our bodies constantly, fueling our self-hatred and self-doubts? The traditional female model is now expected to be a size *zero*. That's so telling, isn't it? Maybe if women shrink enough, they'll just disappear. Sometimes I feel like this is how the world still wants to depict women, and it is so infuriating that it makes me want to scream.

I feel anger at people who dismiss women who do not further their causes, feel threatened by women who take power from men, and hate women who scream, "NO MORE!" at the top of their lungs. I know other women also feel enraged about all of the injustices in our country, and they are probably now anxiously awaiting the results of the election. *We will be heard.*

I decide to turn on the TV to see if the votes have been counted, a winner declared, but first I put on my garden shoes and go out to the courtyard to fill up the empty bird feeders. Maybe the cardinal really is just hungry. After all, I always feed the winter birds and winter's practically here. I see the red bird nearby, and she seems to be happily broadcasting the news to all her feathered friends. Seeing all the birds pleases me, and I hope I will be as pleased by the news.

CNN is showing the recent tweet by POTUS; he is demanding they stop the count. He seems to think that only the votes that were counted on Election Day, which was Tuesday, should count. He knows that the absentee ballots and early votes are overwhelmingly Democrat. They will be counted last by many states, especially in the swing states of

Pennsylvania, North Carolina, Georgia, Arizona, and Nevada. POTUS sees Bright beginning to move ahead in these states. He uses dangerous talk about voter fraud and the socialist left stealing the election. He does not care what the people decide; he just wants to win. I worry that he will never admit defeat...if he is defeated. Most worrisome of all, though, is that his supporters seem to believe everything he is saying, and they are starting to protest outside voting centers where the votes are being tallied. They carry guns and American flags, but they wear no masks as they parrot the president, shouting angrily about "stopping the steal."

I can take no more of the media frenzy. I realize there will be no outcome today, so I gladly turn off the tube and just sit in silence for what seems like an eternity. Something seems a little off. It's almost too quiet. I then realize that the cardinal is silent, no longer chirping and throwing herself against the window. I see this as a good sign.

Amantha

Friday, November 6th

Mother and I have plans to visit a classmate of hers who lives in Betsyville, so I get dinner fixed. I roast a whole chicken with butter, garlic, olive oil, and thyme, then prepare mustard greens, Basque green beans, and sweet potatoes to complement the bird. I do my stretching/strengthening workout before we leave.

I barely have time to check the status of the election, but it doesn't take long, as nothing has changed except that Bright is edging closer and is predicted to *win*. POTUS is really going over the edge of sanity and wants to take the whole country over the precipice, too. He continues to say that he won the election already and that any other outcome will be unacceptable. There has never, in the short history of the United States, been a president like this—one who is refusing reality, one who is creating an alternate reality that makes him the winner, and one who does not consider the havoc he is wreaking on our country.

What will the fallout of this election be, I wonder? Where is my country headed? I reach for my Bible and search through the back, then go to 2 Thessalonians 2:11 and read, "And for this cause God shall send them strong delusion, that they should believe a lie."

Are Republicans willing to believe anything POTUS says, and if so, *why*? Are they completely loyal to this administration, and how far are they willing to go? I think about past authoritarian regimes and those condemned writers, scientists, artists, teachers—*anyone* who dared speak the *truth*. Those in Russia during the time of Stalin, those in Spain during the Inquisition and then again with Franco, the brainwashing of Germans during World War II, the scholars in Cambodia during the Khmer Rouge regime, the disappearance of thousands of Chilean dissenters during Pinochet, and the countless other human beings who have suffered at the hands of a tyrant. In reality, you didn't even have to oppose the tyrant; you only had to look and be different. How many Jews, Blacks, Romani, gays, poor, disabled, mentally ill, and women have been executed by the powers that be?

What is it about the acquisition of power that makes men commit genocide? I am reminded again of Hitler and the tactics he used to gain popularity and power. The very same ones used today. "Make Germany Great Again" (nationalism), talk of a revived economy, and convincing the masses of the threat of *them*—Communists, socialists, fascists, scientists, elitist scholars, Jews, and anyone who opposed the Reich. *America, WAKE UP!* It is not the Black Lives Matter protesters you should be afraid of. You will not get law and order with this president; you will only get more of the same: *chaos*.

I gladly turn off the TV, pack my guitar and songbook into Cielito Lindo, and drive down to the bottom to pick up Mother. It takes about thirty minutes to get to town, ten to pick up lunch for the three of us, and another ten to locate Mary Beth's home. She has dementia and did not remember our scheduled visit, but we don't mind that she's still in her pajamas. She's not wearing a mask, but Mother and I don ours until we eat, Mother and her friend at the kitchen table and me in the living room. I try to convince Mother to eat with me, but she understandably wants to spend some time with her friend. I surrender another Covid battle and hope that neither we nor Mary Beth have unknowingly been exposed to the deadly virus.

Truthfully, a part of me understands why so many people have just given up on trying to fight this enemy. It's so easy to mess up, and it can take only one mess-up for you to get it. I suppose it would be a lot easier to throw up your hands in defeat, deciding that we're all probably going to get it anyway, so why bother? The other, more compassionate part of me knows that if we all think this way, we are doomed to lose a record number of Americans this winter. We could lose *our* loved ones. We owe it to each other to try our best to protect each and every person. *Love thy neighbor as thyself.*

After we eat, I play several old songs that Mother and Mary Beth both know, and it amazes me to again witness the healing power of music. Playing at nursing and retirement homes for years has enabled me to see how familiar tunes can transport memory patients to a happier place in time. It has an amazing impact on their health, and the patients can recall the lyrics and sing along with me! They may not be able to tell you their own names at that moment, but they know every word of "Precious Memories."

The familiar songs also seem to impact Mary Beth in another way: she begins to recall stories of her childhood and her mother singing those same old hymns. Her face lights up as she and Momma recount stories from high school. I put down my guitar and just listen. *That's all she needs at this moment,* I think to myself, *just another human being to listen to her story and validate her existence.*

After two hours, I notice the fatigue on Mother's face, so we pack up to leave. Mary Beth begs us to stay all day and night, and this about breaks my heart. It is so obvious that the old lady is terribly lonely and isolated, and she even admitted to Mother that she should be in a facility. She claims that she sees no one all day, and I find this terrible considering she uses a walker and has dementia to boot. *Isn't anyone taking care of this old saint? Where are her children?*

Seeing Mary Beth, who is the same age as Mother, has really made me see that Mother, in comparison, is in terrific shape and is much more fortunate. I tell her this as we make our way back to Mavie, winding our way past the glimmering lake that looks like a cold, shining gray stone. She appreciates my compliment, but I can tell she is preoccupied and sad about Mary Beth.

"It's just so sad to see your friends like this, all alone in the world, ignored and neglected, life just passing them by. The outside world has sped up, while our world is confined to home, which can sometimes seem like a prison. I know I am so lucky. Luckier than most. I wish I could help her somehow."

I squeeze her hand reassuringly and say, "Maybe we could try to tell her son that she told us she was ready to sell her house and go to a nursing home. But, Mom, she may not even remember our conversation or our visit, and she may deny having said this. I'll bet her family has had that conversation with her many, many times. We don't know anything about them."

"That may very well be true, Amantha, but I have to do something. The thought of her body being found in that big old house, all alone, perhaps having lain there for days suffering...That thought will keep me up at night. I have to call her son. I dread it, but I must."

I see the tears well up in her beautiful blue eyes, and I feel so proud to be her daughter.

Amantha

Saturday, November 7th

I don't wish to put any energy into the election this morning. It's all so consuming, so I just lie in bed without turning on the TV. I turn inward, place my hands over my heart, and check in with myself. I make a conscious decision to focus on *love*. Love for myself first of all. I know I still have unresolved hurt and anger from my past that is getting in the way of my recovery, so I send *compassion* to myself from God, from the universe, and from the angels. I direct that love-light to all parts of my body and pray for healing and forgiveness.

How I need to forgive those who have hurt me in the past! *To forgive them, is it necessary to confront them?* I have found my voice this year, for sure, and have stood up for myself like never before, but not with the people who have hurt me the most. To do so seems a little scary. Plus, I worry about hurting *them*. They probably have no idea I feel this way, and they would probably be defensive and full of denial, which in turn would make me angrier. *Can I forgive them without confronting them? Can I trust them enough with my innermost feelings to confide in them? If they betray that trust, will I be able to forgive myself for making that leap of faith?*

Trust is everything to me. I decide to trust myself to do the right thing at the right time. If I do decide to open this can of festering worms, I will trust myself to be gentle with myself and others. If I mess up—no, *when* I mess up—I will choose compassion, forgiveness, and enlightenment. *What did I learn, and how will I try to react the next time?*

We are all here to learn from each other. We are supposed to be both guide and guided along the pathway of life, striving for wholeness yet never quite achieving that goal...until death, perhaps. Do we attain it in the moment of death, gaining that peace, knowledge, and acceptance we've craved our entire lives, or is it possible to achieve total enlightenment in the here and now? I think we all crave wholeness, and some of us use different methods to try to achieve it, such as power, wealth, beauty, creativity, and soul-searching.

Dictators, for example, have obviously used power to try to fill that emptiness, but it will never be enough. I guess they did this because they have never felt like enough. It is difficult for me to do, but I now visualize those who have hurt me as small, helpless children and send each of them bright, shining rays of compassion. I want them to feel the compassion they must not have received as children. I want our leaders to feel compassion, too, for the state of our country, the state of the world. People are suffering so much right now, with illness, hunger, unemployment, depression, and loss, and the leaders are in positions of power. They can help, if they only chose to.

I get out of bed and turn on the TV, not to watch the news, but to listen to the soothing New Age sounds of *Aura*. Just recently, I have begun dancing to get and give energy. I love starting the day this way! There's no self-judgement. I just dance what I feel, be it joy or sadness. I close my eyes and allow my body to decide the moves, and it knows instinctively how to move to receive and release love into the universe. This is an area I want to explore once Covid has passed: sacred dance. Matthew tells me that King David danced for God, so I, too, allow myself this supreme pleasure. Just ten or fifteen minutes is all it takes to fill me with hope for the day, this election, our country, and our planet. Hope for enlightenment.

I turn my attention to the kitchen now, as I am reminded of the potato salad I am supposed to take to the funeral dinner for Joy's sister this afternoon. She was in the nursing home in Cerro City, where she contracted the virus and died.

The number of deaths in the US has now risen to nearly two hundred and fifty thousand, and there are over a million worldwide. Are we becoming numb to these staggering statistics? How many will there be by Christmas? How many more will die before everyone begins to take this pandemic seriously and wear masks, socially distance, and stay at home? One has to assume that, around here at least, there exists an alternate universe in which Covid plays no part whatsoever. Mother and I attended Violet's birthday party at the river last month, and as expected, we were the only ones wearing masks. I took some used clothing up to the center last week, and all of the elderly patrons were seemingly oblivious to the reality of the virus wreaking havoc on our community. No masks, no distancing. Life was going on as if it were 2019, not 2020. In fact, the center never even closed down at all! I'm so thankful my mother is *smart*; she no longer attends.

I finish the salad, get dressed for the graveyard service, and find a mask that will be appropriate for a funeral: a black one. *Surely, people will be wearing them at a funeral*, I think to myself as I drive down the driveway. As I pass by the five cemeteries that are on the way to my destination, I count three funeral tents that are awaiting grieving families. I can personally count seven dear souls I have known who have died from Covid since March. These are truly sad times, and the saddest of all is the knowledge that many of these people did not have to die.

I arrive to the church alongside the lake. I park Cielito Lindo in the shade since it is already unseasonably *hot* for November. I put my mask in place over my nose and mouth, and I take my potato offering to the fellowship hall. My dear friend Cheryl hears me and exits the kitchen. I so want to give her a huge hug, but I don't, of course. Her husband, Doug, died just three months ago, and I know how difficult every day must be for her. I was asked to sing at his funeral, so I wrote this song to commemorate a life well lived:

"Up There in Heaven"

Oh, my sister, I want you to know
I'm praying for you right now at God's throne
I know you miss him each day and night,
When it's dark and dreary and when the sun shines bright

CHORUS
But up there in heaven, he hurts no more
He's waiting for you by that peaceful shore
I can just see him with a smile on his face,
For he's with Jesus and His amazing grace
This time of sorrow, troubles at our door
Sickness surrounds us, rumors of war
When the storms arise, cling to the Rock
He stills the wind, watches o'er His flock

CHORUS
Up there in heaven, we'll hurt no more
He's waiting for us by that peaceful shore
I can just see Him with a smile on His face,
For He is Jesus, my amazing grace

I walk up the hill to the graveyard tent and see Joy under it, looking in at her sister lying in the casket. I sign the guest book and start to stand in the small line to offer my condolences to the family, but a preacher approaches me first. He whispers conspiratorially to me that masks are optional, so I can take mine off if I choose. I stare unbelievingly at this man who should be concerned about the well-being of his flock instead of making a political statement, but I say nothing. Mask still in place, I move on through the line, greeting the family until I am in front of Joy. Our eyes meet, and I see the tears well up in hers. I so want to hug her, or at least hold her hand, but instead I try to choose the appropriate words to comfort my friend. Words are not sufficient, but they, along with my tater salad, a sympathy card, and my presence, are all that I can offer right now.

She inquires about Matthew and Mom, we promise to talk more later, and I move on through the line and exit the tent. I find a spot on the green grass to plant myself and look for any familiar faces in the small gathering. About half are wearing masks, I notice. The same preacher approaches me again and asks my name but doesn't offer his. He tells me again that I can remove my mask if I choose, and I am relieved to see *my* preacher (I wonder how long I will continue to refer to him this way) heading my way. We make small talk for a while, and he then enters the burial tent, leaving me alone in the growing heat of the sad day. I see just four more people from our church, but none of them greet me. I wish the funeral would begin, and I find myself wishing I had not come at all. Surely, it won't be a long service. Usually graveyard services are kept short.

Finally, that same preacher begins the service, and he has the audacity to tell the gathering of mourners that masks are optional, so many masked attendees remove theirs now. I find myself getting literally hot under the collar, both from his ridiculousness and my winter attire. I count the minutes, prayers, songs, and eulogy until finally the service is concluded. I quickly make my escape down the grassy hill, but I am intercepted by Melissa and Dot, two dear friends from church. They tell me how much Matthew and I are missed, and then Dot grabs me, giving me a bear hug. I don't resist and pretty much melt in her arms, feeling the tears soaking my mask. I assure them both that we feel the same way and ask them to continue praying for God's will to be done.

We say our goodbyes, and I start to leave in Cielito Lindo but decide to first check my phone for any recent texts from Eileen. My sister and I have been constantly keeping each other informed about any new election results since Tuesday, and I've enjoyed the camaraderie. I stare at the all-caps message and cannot believe what I'm seeing: *BRIGHT DID IT! HE'S BEEN DECLARED THE WINNER!* I want to roll down my car window and scream the wonderful news to everyone, but of course, I realize that there is probably not one soul there who would share my extreme excitement, so I drive home instead, shouting praises to God and sobbing uncontrollably. I cannot begin to explain the joy I'm feeling! It's as if a huge burden has been lifted from the whole world, and I feel like it's all going to be okay now. Good has indeed overcome evil again. God has kept His promise, and I am so grateful.

With Bright, I sense hope knocking. Our country can begin to come together again, healing the virus and the awful fear, distrust, and hate that has been dividing Americans. *It is so good to feel hope again*, I think as I fly down the winding country road, drive down the steep driveway into No Place, and pull into Mother's driveway. I simply cannot *wait* to tell her the news. I run up the stairs and bang on her door until I see her worried face exit her bedroom.

"WHAT ON EARTH IS WRONG?" She finally lets me in, and I burst inside, grabbing her and jumping up and down with glee.

"Absolutely nothing is wrong, my dear mother. Not anymore. Bright will be president of the United States!"

"Really? Are you sure?" She sits down in the "man-chair" as if she's had the wind punched out of her and says, "Maybe there is a God."

Amantha

The Day Before Thanksgiving

2 Chronicles 30:9:
"For if ye turn again unto the Lord, your brethren and your children shall find compassion before them that lead them captive, so that they should come again unto this land: for the Lord your God is gracious and merciful, and will not turn away His face from you, if ye return unto Him."

It has been three turbulent weeks since the election, and the present POTUS still does not concede. He has even gone as far as asking Republicans on the board of elections in swing states to outright overturn the vote. He wants them to *overturn the will of the people of the United States*. It is so surreal to be a witness to such authoritarianism in my country. It's as if we have become another Banana Republic.

The entire world watches in disbelief as its leaders come forth one by one to congratulate Bright, while only a handful of our own duly elected Republican senators do so. They seem terrified of the present POTUS and his infantile temper tantrums and do not seem to realize the real harm they are doing to the fabric of our democracy.

It has become so obvious how fragile a democracy is, like one of the eggs in our henhouse. If one of the hens is uncaring or too rough, she could break it or, even worse, eat it. The present POTUS is obsessed only with remaining in power. He does not care one iota about democracy. This is becoming all so apparent now.

POTUS also does not appear to even remember that the pandemic has reached an all-time high—thirty-eight states are now in the red, meaning *danger*, with hospitals running out of ICU beds, especially in the rural areas. Doctors say that if this course continues, they will be forced to decide who gets treatment and who does not, an unimaginable decision for these stressed-out, overworked, and exhausted healthcare heroes. I cannot fathom how they must feel after working all day, and sometimes all night. Then, on their way home, they have to witness huge gatherings of unmasked people in restaurants and bars, out trick-or-treating, at weddings and football games, etcetera. It has got to be like a slap in the face! So demoralizing! But people will continue to gather, and they will travel to be with their loved ones tomorrow for Thanksgiving.

Thanksgiving has always been my favorite holiday. I love its simplicity and think it is important to pause and consider each and every blessing the year has given. This year, I can be grateful for every day that I wake up healthy. I am thankful for my pension and Matthew's job, which keep food on the table, the power on, and a roof over our heads. I'm grateful that so far we have been spared by Covid-19. I'm grateful to have the privilege of living next door to the person who has probably influenced me the most: Mother. I'm grateful to have both of my parents and all of my siblings alive and well in this world. I'm grateful to live here, on the banks of the Diamond, cradled by Hickory Nut Mountain, surrounded by God's beauty. 2020 is teaching me to be grateful.

We all learned in elementary school that the pilgrims, with the help of Squanto and other Native Americans, ushered in the first Thanksgiving in the year 1620. They were in a lonely, frigid place the pilgrims called Plymouth, named after the same English port from which they set sail. They left too late in the year to plant crops and would have starved to death had it not been for the Wampanoag Indians, who took pity on the ill-prepared travelers and shared their food with them. I wonder how long it took Squanto, who had just been returned from England after being taken away from his native soil and held as prisoner, to convince the others to help these English trespassers? After all, previous Europeans had only brought death in the form of smallpox, which had killed thousands. *Why would Squanto want to help them?* If they could have foreseen the misery my ancestors would inflict upon all American tribes, I'm sure they would have killed them right then and there and would have been justified in doing so.

The plight of the Cherokee and the other native tribes in the southeastern US, displaced by our government and forced to walk the Trail of Tears in the years 1838 and 1839, indeed put a dark stain in American history. The most vulnerable died of exposure and disease along the way. More than a thousand. My song *"Trail of Tears"* was written to honor their memory. May we not forget our past so that we do not repeat our mistakes.

"Trail of Tears"

My story is old, but it must be told
Oh, the pain and sorrow that came
The red Georgia clay washes and flows,
Like my children's blood in the rain

For thousands of years, my beloved Cherokee
Nursed from the waters of the Hiwassee,
Where the elk and red wolf roamed
On the land that no one owned

CHORUS
Trail of Tears, bitter tears will flow
Across the Great River, where the buffalo did go
Thousands will perish walking in the snow
How will my people find their way in Oklahoma?

White Man came from distant shores,
Seeking food and shelter from the cold
Filled with beans and maize, yet more he craved
The timber, furs, and gold

Trying to adapt, trying to survive,
Red Man changed his moccasins for coats and ties
But like the forest felled and wolves shot on sight,
My people were removed from paradise

CHORUS
Trail of Tears, twelve hundred miles long
There's no way to right this wrong
One babe at my breast, the other in the ground,
Never will our home be found in Oklahoma
My story is old, but it must be told; the exodus of Cherokee and Creek
One day, we shall rise and fly like the phoenix back to the Hiwassee

It makes me sad to think that our first settlers twisted the Word of God to get what they saw as *theirs*. Manifest destiny. How convenient for them to think that this new continent was given to them by God! After their own religious persecution by the Church of England, the harrowing journey across the Atlantic, and encountering an unforgiving wilderness full of strange beasts and strange men, they must have needed to believe that *they* were God's chosen people. In fact, their belief that Native Americans were animals, not men, surely eased their consciences as they began to eradicate them from all the Americas. This same justification would be used later with African slaves.

I guess the colonization of our country was inevitable. If it had not been the English, it would have been the Spanish, the French, or the Dutch, and their tactics would have been the same—seize lands from "uncivilized savages," then enslave them and force them to grow food, cut down forests, build roads and railroads, mine minerals and metals, and so on. All the while claiming to *help* them become "civilized" by indoctrinating them and educating them in our languages and religions, forbidding their own.

These tactics have been used all over the world. By the British in India, the French in Vietnam, the Spanish throughout Latin America. By people who get a taste of power and do anything to hold on to it. *I wonder, who are the civilized ones?* When will humankind finally realize that happiness lies within and cannot be bought, stolen, or consumed?

When will we realize that it is not sustainable for us to keep consuming this way? There is not an infinite number of natural resources on Earth, and we are greedily consuming all, causing irreversible harm and destruction to other species and to the Earth itself. Is it too late to reverse our course of self-destruction? Can capitalism continue, or must we choose a new way to live? I simply cannot fathom real sustainability coexisting with Black Friday, Cyber Monday, supersized Big Gulps, plastic-wrapped items, and McMansions. But perhaps I lack imagination.

Am I proposing scrapping capitalism for socialism? I can just hear those Republicans' teeth gnashing as they condemn and accuse me of being a Communist, socialist, unpatriotic, ungrateful traitor. Whatever. I don't have the answers, but I do know, as many others also know, that *we must change.*

Perhaps it is time for us to realize that there is an infinite supply of love and compassion in the universe, enough for every living thing.

We must stop thinking that the world consists of us versus them. WE ARE ALL US. *All life forms on Earth are connected.* We will have to work together to solve these seemingly insurmountable problems, or we will perish together. We must believe it is possible; we have to hope and dream big for our children, for their children, and for the offspring of every living creature. It is time to turn back to God, to stop holding ourselves and this Earth captive, and to be willing to see everyone as His children. Are we finally ready to reach our full potential as children of God?

Nancy Mae

Thanksgiving Day

I feel the dark holiday cloud brooding in my spirit as I stir awake, and I find myself wishing that today, Christmas, and the New Year were already behind me so I could be left alone. Jay is not coming, and I am so disappointed, but of course I understand that it's because of the virus. *This damned virus!* I am so ready for it to be over. Will it ever be over?

Just a few days after the election, the world rejoiced at the news that a vaccine had been found, and they say it is over 90 percent effective. 95 percent, I think. This news, along with Bright's win, does indeed provide a beacon of hope for a suffering humanity. But...I have my doubts. *Will these morons take the damned thing? Will I?* I never even get the flu vaccine, though everyone nags at me to do it, especially Amantha. She says she and Matthew will run to the front of the line to get the Covid vaccine, but I tell them they may not have to. According to the latest polls, only a little more than 50 percent of Americans say they plan to take it.

Not surprisingly, only about 30 percent of African Americans and other people of color trust it. I say that because I remember what happened in Tuskegee, Alabama, back in the thirties. Poor, Black sharecroppers who suffered from syphilis were studied but left untreated until the 1970s! They weren't even told they had syphilis. Instead, they were told they had a disease of the blood. Penicillin, which became available during the study, was not given to them to cure the disease, and many died or passed it to other people. It took one whistleblower to finally bring this atrocity to the national spotlight in the *seventies*, which was forty years later. How could a government do this to its own people? No wonder they have their doubts about the Covid-19 vaccine.

Furthermore, many citizens worry that the soon-to-be former POTUS pressured the scientists to develop the vaccine too quickly. He wanted it done before the election, as he was hoping to give himself an edge with voters. The scientists have tried their best to reassure the public that all precautions were taken and that adequate test trials show that the vaccine is indeed safe and effective, but people just don't trust the government. People may have good reasons for not trusting the government. After all, *all* governments have lied to the masses to maintain control.

Mountain people seem to be especially distrustful. This is probably what drove them to the remote mountains to begin with—to be left alone. Therefore, most vote Republican since the GOP has traditionally believed in a hands-off style of governing. Now, however, this doesn't make sense, as so many mountain people are now dependent on the government welfare and disability checks they receive, and they receive them because of the Democrats who started these programs. Yet overwhelmingly, mountain people continue to vote Republican. I guess it's hard to switch teams.

Some American citizens have swallowed nonsense about the vaccine being the sign of the beast, saying that it contains a chip with 666 that can also track you. Where do they get this malarkey? I thought we were better than this.

There's a group of the current POTUS's supporters—they call themselves Q something—who say he's God's chosen one, put in Washington to stop the evil liberals from drinking the blood of unborn babies and engaging in pedophilic acts. My dear Lord, where on Earth do they get this crap? A better question may be, how on Earth did Americans get *so stupid?*

I blame it all on religion. From everything that I've read and seen in my long life, religion has caused much more harm than good. Look at all the wars fought in the name of Christianity, like the Crusades. Even branches of Christianity fight amongst themselves, like the Protestants fighting the Catholics in Ireland. Extreme sects of Islam, in the name of Allah, tearing into those towers on 9/11, ISIS recruiting our young people to kill fellow Americans, Jim Jones convincing his followers to drink cyanide-laced Kool-Aid, the Inquisition, and the Salem Witch Burnings. The list is never-ending. If there is a God, He must be a bloodthirsty one—one who demands sacrifice and retribution. Or maybe He's as helpless as I feel now and is sobbing up in heaven, unable to rein in his Frankenstein's Monster: humankind.

If there's *not* a God, then religion is the biggest con that we have fallen for, and it continues to brainwash and numb the masses around the globe, causing far more harm than good, at least as far as I can see.

I used to believe...a long, long time ago. Dad took us to church up at Birch Springs Baptist Church, where his family had gone forever, and I even got baptized in Birch Creek one hot summer day, along with my best friends, Dollie and Mattie. Mom didn't go. She was too busy, she'd say, fixing Sunday dinner, which was a huge undertaking in those days. She'd have to keep the fire going in the wood cookstove after having fixed biscuits and mush for breakfast, then kill one of my pet chickens to fry up with taters, slaw, and green beans. She'd wait until I'd left for church to start, as she knew I'd try to hide the chickens down by the spring, enticing them with dried corn in order to delay the inevitable.

I never really knew if Pennie, my mother, believed in God or not, but when she died, I never forgave the preacher who made an example of her at her own funeral. I'll never forget the coldness that entered my heart as I sat with Dan in that stifling-hot church, listening to that man give God's cruel eulogy. He begged people to "repent for their sins instead of living a godless life like Penelope, who did not attend church." I tuned out the rest, but I do recall never stepping inside that church again. Shortly after Mom's funeral, and after Dan and I had returned home to Mississippi, I stopped going to church with him and the kids. I guess I've blamed God all these years. After all, if He were such an all-powerful God, why couldn't he stop that preacher man from tarnishing the memory of the kindest person I've ever known?

Pennie sacrificed all for her family and was always the first person in Mavie to reach out to a neighbor in need, sharing food, tools, a kind word. Whatever was needed and more. I wonder if that preacher knows the lasting effects of his words that day? Does he know that instead of encouraging me to draw closer to God, I rejected everything about religion? When he died and entered those pearly gates, was he surprised to see Pennie standing there welcoming him home?

Is there a heaven? Oh, Momma, if there is, I just know you're there. Will I find a home there with you?

I come back to Earth and try to think good thoughts. I am alive right now. I have what's left of my mind and a good, strong body. I know we are more fortunate than most these days. We are all healthy and live surrounded by beauty. We have money to pay our bills and buy food. Amantha and I can stay at home.

But I do worry about Matthew, who sometimes works six days a week. I worry he'll bring the virus home and that one of us will get sick and have to go to the hospital, which is already overrun with Covid and quickly running out of beds. I worry about Bart, who hasn't called me in a long time. I hope he's not sick or in trouble. My other nephew, TJ, who's coming to our dinner today, is another one I worry about. He's all alone in the world now that his mother, my sister Madge, is gone. And he just recently left his wife of twenty years and is barely hanging on. I don't even know where he's staying these days, but he'll be here at 2:00 PM. Amantha has insisted that we eat on the porch of Bear Necessities , all socially distanced, all of us wearing masks. I fought her on this for a while, but I finally gave up and don't even care anymore. I just want it all to be over. *I'm so sick of worrying about it all!*

I roll out of bed, fix my coffee a little stronger than usual, and make it back to bed just as the phone rings. It's Amantha telling me to come up to her house at noon to do a Zoom chat with all of my children. I complain bitterly that I don't know how to do it. I don't even know what Zoom is. Besides, we have to cook and haul all the food down to the Tiny House before 2:00 PM. She convinces me that she and Matthew will take care of the food and that everyone wants to see me, so I should wear something pretty. I grumble but agree. I don't have the energy to put up much of a fight. I finish my coffee and find something in the closet to put on my old body. I lay the purple dress and scarf that Amantha gave me on the bed. It has a picture of a hunched-back figure on it—some kind of Native American symbol, I guess.

I feel like that old hunched-back figure today, I think, then turn to scrutinize myself in the mirror. *How can I be that wrinkled old crone in the glass when I still feel like the same curious girl of ten?* I stick out my tongue at myself, laugh, and then hug myself until I feel ridiculous.

I slowly and carefully go to the kitchen, careful not to trip over the rug in the hallway. I make the cornbread dressing that my family loves, with extra celery and onions, and put it in the oven to bake, along with the precooked spiral ham. I get dressed and add a few extra layers since we'll be eating outside, though it's supposed to be sunny and over sixty degrees today. I am cold all the time now, even in the summer, and summer's long gone.

I find a hat and gloves and sit on the couch, waiting for the timer to go off in the kitchen. I admire the mantle with its newly decorated Christmas garlands, along with the metal tree and the ornaments reflecting the sun in the window. I hadn't wanted to decorate, but Amantha insisted it would cheer me up. It does all look pretty, but I'm not sure it did the trick. I still sense the dark cloud trying to descend on me, and to tell you the truth, I'm not really fighting it at all.

I move toward the window because something has caught my eye, and to my pure delight, I see four small raccoons staring in at me! Not only are they staring, but they are also pawing at the screen as if they want in! Their intentions do not seem malevolent. They seem to want to play, to eat, to be petted, to be loved. Maybe they have come to offer me the gift of joy, a gift I am surely needing today. I'm certain that is it. Of course, I don't let them in, as they would surely wreck my house, but I take their timely gift into my heart. In the time it takes for a smile to replace my scowl, the four visitors have disappeared into the morning sun.

When the food is ready, I hear Matthew driving up my driveway in his red truck, coming to fetch me for the Zoom meeting. I greet him warmly and wish him a happy Thanksgiving, and he tells me how pretty I look. He helps me with my coat and helps me down the stairs, and I tell him about my morning guests. He laughs and says that they are certainly making their rounds in Mavie, as Amantha had just seen them yesterday on their back deck. And he saw them crossing the road a few days ago.

"I sure hope they don't get run over up there on that mean road," I declare as we climb their steep drive, "'cause they are so cute."

"One of these days, we're going to find out that you've taken some coon, or chicken, in as a pet, Nancy Mae." He chuckles.

"Do you think they can be potty-trained?" I smile and laugh as we get out and climb the steps to the Treehouse.

Amantha smiles as she opens the door and gives me a big hug, which I return. She has her laptop open on the massage table, three chairs in front of it, and there on the screen are my three other children: Jay, Dan, and Eileen. I feel my heart lurch, and I bite my lip to keep it from quivering. I never realized that seeing them, even on a stupid computer, would invoke these feelings...of what? Love? Loneliness? Sorrow? Pride?

I think perhaps each of these feelings are battling for control, and I think to myself, *That's okay. At least you're feeling. You're alive on this imperfect Thanksgiving Day. Your heart is beating, and you're in the presence of your loved ones. This is enough for right now.*

After the excruciatingly long Zoom meeting, we pack all the dishes into our vehicles and drive down to the tiny house, where we find TJ and his granddaughter Tabby waiting for us on the porch, masks in place. I can tell, even with the masks on, that they are smiling, and it is good to share a meal with them. I take the girl to the chicken house after dinner so we can feed the scraps to the other "girls." Tabby places her hand in mine as we walk past the brown flower garden and the scarlet blueberry bushes. She seems happy just to be here, and I wonder if her home life is good. TJ catches up with us and tells Tabby not to hold my hand because of the virus. She reluctantly releases my hand, but I take hers again.

I say, "Now, TJ, don't scold the girl. I can wash my hands later. Let's not worry about that virus right now. Let's enjoy this beautiful day together. We don't know what tomorrow will bring."

I look over my shoulder as the sun slides behind Hickory Nut Mountain, then lift my face to catch the last of the warm rays it offers. It feels good to be in my body, and I feel alive. Darkness will soon spread its velvety blanket across our river valley, but I now feel none of the gloomy foreboding that dawn had brought. Peace and serenity fill my heart, and I am grateful.

Matthew

December 1st
4:00 AM

As always, I wake up before the alarm clock buzzes, roll onto my side to see what time it is, and then snuggle into the warmth of Amantha's soft body before getting up. She's snoring, not softly, either, but I feel her body start to stir, and she wraps a leg around me, pinning me in the bed.

She raises up to look out the wall of windows and exclaims gleefully, "Oh, look at the snow! It looks like three inches, maybe more."

I am transported back to her teaching days, when she would actually do a snow dance at the first mention of the white stuff. And if she got a snow day, which was usually guaranteed even with just a bare covering on the roads here in the Appalachian Mountains of Tennessee, she would shout with joy before snuggling back into the warm blankets.

I grumble, give her one more hug before wriggling out of her leg lock, and say, "I dread driving down Slump Hill. Of course, the roads won't be plowed at this hour. I am so glad I had those new tires put on last week."

"Will you call me to let me know you got there, sweetie pie?"

Hope Knocking

I start to tell her not to worry about such a small snow, but instead I promise to call her as soon as I've made the hour-long drive into Betsyville.

I get up and get ready to leave in fifteen minutes, lunch pail and flashlight in hand as I exit the warm house and head into a winter wonderland. I carefully make my way down the snowy steps and then warm up Big Red as I scrape the ice and snow from the truck. He's ready to roll, and I head down the driveway, but then detour around the steep hill and take the bottom way out to Mavie Road. Our neighbors gave us permission to use their right-of-way during the winter years ago, right after their grandson flipped and totaled his truck on ours during a blizzard. *Luckily, the boy wasn't hurt too bad*, I think as I carefully make my way along the bumpy dirt path up to the road, which, of course, has not been touched. It looks like I'm the first person out this morning, but I don't mind.

This has always been my second favorite time of day: the quietness of morning. My favorite time of day is when I get to the Treehouse in the afternoon. I love opening up the door to the smell of dinner cooking, the smell of lavender and other oils that Amantha wears, and the smell of her. She always smells fresh, like the woods or something earthy. This time, however, at this lonely, dark hour of the morning, is my time with God, and I cherish it so much. The day seems so full of possibility and promise at this hour, and I pray for a good day at work. I pray that God will give me lovingkindness and compassion for my fellow man at ClothTreat, which I so desperately need every moment of each workday.

I admit to myself and my Creator that I dread going to work , mainly because of my ignorant co-workers. They are all supporters of the current POTUS and believe all the crazy conspiracy theories spreading like wildfire these days. They hate the fact that Bright won. Well, they actually won't even admit that he *did* win. But what really makes them froth and snarl is that a woman will be vice president. I believe they hate women more than blacks...if that is possible. I just keep my mouth shut and try to stay away from them all, especially since the majority of them don't bother to wear a mask. I just show up every day and do my job.

Even my best friend, Tim, seems to be under the spell of POTUS, and he is smart. *Really* smart. The man can do and fix anything and has saved us hundreds of dollars by fixing our dryer, refrigerator, water heater, and vehicles. He even surveyed Nancy Mae's property a couple of years ago. He won't let us pay him, either. Amantha and Nancy are all the time baking cakes and cookies for him because the man does like to eat. I always help him in his garage or on his farm whenever he asks. To his credit, he doesn't talk politics with me at all, but at work he acts like a different person and joins right in on the stupid talk. Talk about the vaccine containing dead fetuses and the mark of the beast. I constantly have to bite my tongue. They talk about the "Dems" stealing the election and discuss how we better all go buy more guns because Bright will try to take them away. They talk about a race war coming, and I think they would welcome that. Tim must have two hundred guns already, and he's buying more. How many guns does one person need?

Amantha thinks it's an ingrained fear of the government that has caused the poor, white, mountain men to wholeheartedly support the current POTUS, who is seen as a Washington outsider and a successful businessman. I wouldn't call him successful, as his rich daddy gave him anything he wanted. He's just another elite 1 percent born with a silver spoon in his mouth. What has he done for the working poor? Nothing, that's what. He doesn't care about anybody but himself, and it doesn't take a genius to see that.

I am not an educated man. I didn't even finish high school. I had to quit at the age of sixteen and go work at the textile mill to support my family after my dad died, and I've been working ever since. Well, I actually started way before then, I guess around the age of twelve, growing tobacco, farming, and trapping and selling the skins of coons, mink, foxes, and beavers. I did whatever I could to bring in cash so that we could buy whatever we couldn't raise. I even helped Momma can green beans, corn, potatoes, and tomatoes. Anything and everything. The only things we really had to buy were flour, coffee, sugar, and mill.

Sometimes if we didn't have money, we'd trade eggs, a chicken, or even a whole hog if we had to. They'd let you do that back then, especially at Mack's General Store, which is long gone nowadays. All the old mom-and-pop stores have just about disappeared. And with this virus, all small businesses are hurting really badly, and many have had to close down. They probably won't be coming back, either. Everybody shops online at the big stores now. You can have things shipped to you, or you can go to the store and have it delivered to your car. Even grocery stores are now providing this service. I know lots of people, including Amantha, appreciate these conveniences, but I for one long for the good old days.

I know the good old days won't be coming back, and I know that I'm an old, backwards hillbilly, but I have no use for all this change. Especially technology. It burns me up when those young fellows at work are on their blasted cell phones! They hardly work at all because their faces are stuck inside those phones, and the supervisors don't say anything to them, because they are just as bad. In fact, I don't know of anyone other than me who doesn't have a cell phone. I don't want one, and I think they are a complete waste of time. Nancy Mae doesn't have one, either, but Amantha does. She keeps up with technology, but she's not addicted to it, at least not yet.

I do admit phones come in handy sometimes, like two weeks ago, when the old beat-up pick-up truck at work broke down on me. I had to park on the side of the highway for at least two hours before Tim finally came looking for me. I asked my supervisor if the company would buy me a cell phone, and they agreed. I can't believe *I* will have one, but I will only use it at work, and Tim will have to show me how to use the thing.

My thoughts have wandered, and I'm blasted back to the present when I pass what Amantha calls Hillbilly Holler, an unofficial campground on the lake. I notice lots of tents still set up—more than I've ever seen in years past—and I wonder if these people are homeless. So many people are hurting now, and I try to imagine what suffering they are enduring this morning in this extreme cold and snow. I pull off to the side of the highway at the overlook, put Big Red in park, and bow my head to pray.

"Oh, Father, I thank you for this day and the opportunity to work. I pray that your love shines through me so that those who don't know you might see a glimpse of you in me. Help me to do your will, not mine, and please forgive me when I fail you, Lord. Oh God! Help those in need of shelter, food, work, healing, and compassion. Help us all, dear Lord, get through these dark days. Help us to love one another and help each other. Thank you for helping me every day and for protecting Amantha and Nancy Mae from this virus. I love you, Jesus, and I pray that you help me to love myself, too. Amen."

Amantha

Monday, December 14th

This day brings our country hope that there is a way out of all the Covid misery. First and foremost, the vaccine, which was recently approved by the FDA, is currently being packaged in dry ice and shipped to cities all over the US. England was actually the first country in the world to administer the vaccine last week. They gave it to an elderly woman in her nineties, and it was *not* the Queen. Here, the first person to receive it was a female, African American health-care worker. After all health-care workers get the vaccine, people living in retirement and nursing homes will be next in line. I hope Mother can get hers sometime this winter, and then older essential workers like Matthew may become eligible. People my age who are no longer working will probably not be able to get the shot until springtime, or even summer.

The experts also warn us that we will have to continue wearing masks and social distancing until herd immunity is acquired, even if we've been vaccinated. Nobody is happy about that, and I suspect there will be much resistance. Of course, there are so many people who have never donned masks and will not be doing so *ever*. There are also many who will not get the vaccine at all. I just hope that *enough* people take it so that herd immunity can be achieved.

There is so much that science still doesn't know about the Coronavirus. For example, it is possible that even with the vaccine you will still contract the virus and infect others; you just won't get a severe case. Also, if you've already had Covid, should you get the vaccine? What if you don't know if you've had it? (I still wonder if I had it last winter after flying up to Canada. I've never been so sick for so long. I was sick practically all winter. I missed Thanksgiving, Christmas, and New Year's!) Finally, how long will immunity last? Will we have to get a yearly booster? There is already a new strain of the virus on the horizon somewhere in Europe, so I'm thinking that yes, new vaccines will constantly have to be developed to keep ahead of this menace.

Still, this vaccine gives the whole world hope, which we so desperately need as we head into a dark winter. Over three thousand Americans are dying *every day* now. That's more than the amount of people who died on 9/11/01. There are over three hundred thousand dead in our country! Hospitals in Los Angeles have run out of ICU beds!

The virus has spread throughout rural areas now, too, including Mavie. Jewell's son, Eddie—one of the mask-less multitude—contracted it at the store where he hangs out, which is right down the road. He lives next door! So far, Jewell and Ernie are not sick, but we all know now that that doesn't mean you don't have it. Many people are symptomless but are spreaders. They'll never know because none of them plan to get tested.

At least three people at ClothTreat have it, so they are shutting down the week of Christmas and are not even going to pay the workers. I think this is so unfair, as the factory did not properly care for its employees. They didn't do temperature checks until recently, and then they only did it for one week. They never had a strict mask mandate and only started sanitizing surfaces two weeks ago. Nevertheless, I am happy that Matthew will be home, away from that Petri dish of germs.

The other reason I feel hopeful today is because the outcome of the election has *finally* been made official by the Electoral College. Each state is casting its official votes today, something that in previous years never even made headlines. 2020 has proved to be a year of exceptions. The people voted, and the election is *over*. It *was* a free and fair election, and there has been *no* evidence of voter fraud. The Democrats won the popular vote by more than seventy million, and Bright has the same number of electoral votes that the current POTUS had in 2016: 306.

Even the new Supreme Court Justice, who was appointed by the current POTUS in late October, sided with all the other justices who shot down POTUS's case yesterday. I'll bet he really thought he had her in his pocket! To tell you the truth, I held my breath, not entirely trusting the high court to uphold the Constitution and the will of the people. The current POTUS has gotten away with so much these last four years, somehow bending seemingly intelligent people to his every whim. Few Republicans have acknowledged Bright's win over a month ago, but maybe after today they will find the decency to congratulate the president-elect. They seem to be more afraid of losing their jobs than losing a democracy.

The current POTUS will soon disappear, at least from the White House, even if he has to be escorted. Can you imagine that? He's such a sore loser that he probably won't attend Bright's inauguration! I don't think that has *ever* occurred in the history of the United States. This will be part of his failed legacy and, I hope, a failed Republican party. In my opinion, it deserves to go down with him.

Bright *will* be inaugurated as the forty-sixth president, and I am so happy about this. I am *so ready* to be bored with politics again, not consumed and enraged by it. I try not to think about what will happen in four more years. Will the current POTUS run for president again? Or even worse, will he continue to control the Republicans in Congress from afar during Bright's presidency? *Do not go there, Amantha. Celebrate today's sweet victory,* I remind myself. *Be grateful that you get to witness the dawning of a new age.*

I find the remote hidden under the flannel sheets and switch the TV from CNN to my go-to music channel this year: Aura. I let the healing new-age sounds wash over me as I watch for the first rays of light to appear outside the Treehouse. I breathe in slowly and fully from my belly, hold my breath, and then release it. I do this several times at each of the four cardinal points, starting with the east and ending with the west. I visualize rays of healing light pouring through me, filling me with love, and I then focus this energy outward into the world, sending it to people I know who need it so desperately now.

I use sacred dance as another form of prayer. I dance to celebrate life, moving my body however it pleases, prancing and leaping around the living room, much to the amusement of Little Bit, who is curled up on the couch. It feels good to be fully present in my body, and I dance into the bedroom so I can gaze at myself in the mirror. I smile at my reflection and truly love the person I see there. I don't judge my body today. No, I don't find fault with it at all. This fills me with a sense of relief that relaxes me to the core, and I instantly realize how hard I have been on myself my entire life. So, instead of berating myself in my normal way, I thank my body for supporting me and keeping me well this year. I tell that beautiful, happy, smiling woman in the mirror that I accept and love her exactly the way she is at this very moment. This inspires a much-needed hug, and then I prance into the living room again, laughing with delight.

This is going to be an amazing day, I decide.

The world has been in a temporary state of despair but will surely right itself again in the upcoming year: 2021. Maybe I can plan a new adventure to a faraway land, like Bali, Iceland, or Crete. Hopefully, I will find a new church where I can lay my musical talents at the altar. I hope to volunteer more, doing something like delivering meals to seniors in our area, and maybe Mother will accompany me, which will ease her isolation. I want to be more involved with the Black White group in Junction City, helping to understand and heal racism in our country. I want to help immigrants and use my Spanish to teach and empower them somehow. There is so much work to be done, and in the light of a new dawn, I feel like anything is possible.

Nancy Mae

Tuesday, December 15th

Shades of green draw my eye toward the moss as I mosey along the river's edge. It's funny...I don't think I've ever paid it much attention before. I bend over, with the help of the cane, to examine it close up. It's so soft, like velvet!

I vaguely recall a hat of the same color and texture. I saw it in an old photograph that I pulled out of my picture box the other day. I was looking for some pictures to put in Amantha's stocking for Christmas and found this picture. The photograph was black and white, but I remember that hat well. It was the softest thing I'd ever touched, and it even had lace covering the front! It arrived around Christmastime, too, so I paired it with a red scarf that Aunt Oda had given me a few years before, and I felt as pretty as a shiny ornament when I wore them.

Momma got the hat in one of her packages from Ohio—Pennie's Packages, we called them. Sometimes there were just scraps of cloth, which she used to sew our clothing or to add to quilts, but other times there were treasures inside. Beautiful brooches sister Sadie and I proudly pinned to our worn, faded clothing. Pants for my brothers. Once, there were even salt and pepper shakers, but Momma kept those for herself.

Hope Knocking

Amantha has a song that best tells the story of how Momma got the idea to write to those rich women in Ohio. She told them about her rugs, hoping that they would send her whatever castoffs they had in exchange for her beautiful hand-hooked rugs.

"Pennie's Packages"

It was right before Christmas in 1935
It was a real hard year; we were barely getting by
To buy us each a store-bought toy from our mother,
Pennie saved up her pennies selling eggs and butter

"Christmas is just another day to poor folk,"
Aunt Oda declared as Mama dropped us off
Uncle John drove her down The Nowhere to Betsyville
Since Dad was in Carolina cutting timber down

She looked in Woolworths and was sad to see,
No toy could she buy for Sadie or me
Shivering in the cold in her thin, worn coat,
Mama walked back to the car with our gift of chocolate drops

There by the curb, a-blowing in the wind,
Was a Cincinnati paper; she picked it up and got in
She read about rich ladies from high society
When she got home, she wrote them to ease our poverty

CHORUS
Maybe you'd like a pretty hooked rug?
Take a look at these samples at your next tea or brunch
I'll only take your hand-me-downs
To make clothing for my children; signed Pennie Harmon

The orders came in, more than she could fill
She enlisted her neighbors from Mavie and Diamond Mills
The rugs were rolled and wrapped in brown paper and burlap
And mailed off to Ohio in the spring of '36

The neighbors came a-running as the mail came up the road,
Hauling Pennie's packages, two or three a week, I'm told
All seven children were clothed in this way
Imagine her surprise; one hot day in July,
Came a lady from Ohio with a carload of Pennie's packages

My family got first dibs on those boxes, and then Mom would pass them on to the neighbors who had helped her make the rugs.

I recall how years later, some of my classmates admitted to me how envious they were of those treasures that we wore proudly to school. If I was feeling kindly toward one of them, I might let her wear a piece of jewelry at school, but as soon as that bell rang at the end of the day, I would demand it right back. I *never* let anyone else wear the green velvet hat, though. That was too precious to share.

I am still walking along the river's edge, looking at the carpet of moss that has transported me back in time, when my daughter surprises me, saying, "I can just imagine it being a nice, soft bed for some lucky fairy, don't you think?"

I jump, and she steadies me as I wobble forward slightly. We walk arm in arm and point out the lush, verdant cushions growing everywhere—on the rock wall, over bird houses, and on tree trunks, roots, statues, and wreaths. She tells me she's begun planting gnomes among mossy banks and stumps on the trails she hikes.

"I guess it's a way to give other hikers joy. That's about all there is to it," Amantha explains.

"There is a shortage of joy this year, that's for sure. Keep on planting as much of it as you can." I add, "Just as nature has surely added this collage of green to give beauty to us."

We head up to my house, where I decide it's time for me to start another rug. One that I want to design all by myself. One that reminds me of Pennie and her packages, which brought so many people joy. It's got to have flowers on it. Roses were Mom's favorites, and she had the prettiest ones in Mavie. In her designs, she always included trailing vines that encircled her flowers, but maybe I could add some velvety green moss to the background, too.

I carefully make my way down the basement stairs and look for the rug frame that Matthew made me years ago. It takes me a while, but I finally locate it behind the bathroom door, propped up behind the ironing board and the roll of burlap. *Now, why on Earth did I put them here?* I wonder about my organizational skills, or lack of.

Amantha and I are so different that way. My method has always been a bit chaotic, whereas hers is one of *order*. She has a place for everything and never loses things, while I seem to operate on the fly and am constantly misplacing stuff.

I think our approach to people, and life, is similar, though. I tend to enjoy floating like a feather in the wind through my days and assume that others should be granted that same freedom. In fact, I remember telling one of my psychology professors that I raised my children with "studied indifference." He liked that term so much that he included it in his lectures about early childhood development. Give children the freedom to explore the world as they choose, but keep them out of harm's way.

I remove the clutter from the table, place the frame onto it, and stretch the burlap tightly onto it so it doesn't have any give. This simple action reminds me of my youngest, and I worry that she approaches life this way: trying to control every outcome instead of letting it be. Most times, I think life takes care of itself, and we humans just need to step aside and allow the universe to right itself. After all, look at everything we've messed up on this planet while trying to *control* other people, other creatures, the earth itself. We don't exactly have a very good record.

Perhaps a better way is my method of studied indifference, believing that people will do the best they can at any given moment. HAVE FAITH THAT GOOD WILL PREVAIL. *My goodness, did I just think that? It sounds kind of biblical.*

I can almost see Pennie smiling at me from across the great divide as she guides the marker in my hand, beginning to draw a design—*her* design. I allow creativity to flow without any censorship and then step back and admire her work: five soft roses connected by tendrils that support but do not hinder their beauty. *Thank you, Momma.*

I slowly drop to my knees and fold my hands in prayer. "Lord, I know you haven't heard from me in years, but I hope you are listening now. Please let 2021 be a better year. A year in which *your* goodness will prevail, and therefore *our* goodness. You see, I think you also raised *your* young'uns with studied indifference, giving us the freedom to choose our future. May we choose good. Help your children—help *my* children—to let go and let God. Oh, and give Momma a big hug."

Part Four:
Emerging from Darkness into Light

Amantha

December 21st

Isaiah 42:16: "And I will bring the blind by a way that they knew not; I will lead them in paths that they have not known: I will make darkness light before them, and crooked things straight. These things will I do unto them, and not forsake them."

I see snow in the woods on the mountains ahead of us, just a glimpse every now and then as Caleb and I drive up the mountain road toward our destination: Beulah Bald. We have come to witness the Great Conjunction of 2020, or as others are calling it, the Christmas Star. Since I first heard about the two planets of Jupiter and Saturn coming together for the first time in nearly eight hundred years, I knew I *had* to experience it up on Beulah Bald, with its three-dimensional views and access road.

My hiking friends at first seemed interested, but then it was announced that the National Forest Service had already closed the road, which would mean we would have to hike up the Appalachian Trail to the top, then return in the darkness after sunset. This didn't deter me since I have a headlamp, but none of the other women wanted to hike down the steep trail at night. I didn't want to go alone, and Matthew wasn't interested, either. Luckily, Sally's nephew Caleb *loves* night hiking, so here we are, pulling into the parking lot at Gentle Girl Gap. There are several cars here, and one elderly man warns us about the threat of snow that is forecast to begin around 8:00 PM. This only adds to the adventure, but we promise him we'll be back before the snow begins to fall, *if* it falls at all. Here in the mountains of Tennessee, the weather seems to have a mind of its own, much to the frustration of local meteorologists.

We begin our climb at 3:45 PM, hoping to time our summit with the sunset at 5:30 PM. As we hike, I begin to sweat and peel off one layer of clothing at a time. I feel my miniature gnome in one pocket and spot a perfect place for his new dwelling: the base of a moss-covered hemlock in-between a root and a quartz. I place him there and hurry to catch up with Caleb, noting that snow is now showing up in the woods beside the trail. He is waiting for me at the power line, looking westward toward the approaching sunset. He shows me an app on his phone that shows all the planets and constellations, and points out the exact location of the two planets.

"Right here, in-between the half moon and the sunset, is where they will come together. I read that it should be the most visible right after sunset, when it gets completely dark, and then will continue to move down the horizon and will be hard to see later on. I think we're timing it just right. We only have another mile to go, right?"

I nod my head and tell him that the last mile will be the steepest, right after we pass the road. He pulls off another layer of fleece in preparation and hands me a piece of his homemade "sea glass" candy. We pause to drink water and enjoy the lime-flavored treat, along with the fiery colors beginning to spread across the clear western sky.

I share my thoughts about the Christmas Star. "You know, I feel like this star is a sign of hope for 2021, a sign of light amidst all the darkness and death of 2020. Thank you for coming with me. I just *had* to see it, and I would have been too afraid to go it alone."

Caleb had night hiked often during the AT section he had completed three years ago, and he says he actually prefers it.

He questions me about my fears of the darkness, and I reply, "Well, it's not the darkness I fear. I guess it's other people, you know, being a woman and all. Fear is a terrible thing. I remember being a child and swimming way out in the Atlantic Ocean at Hilton Head Island, where my grandparents lived. We'd spend every summer there, and I was fearless in the water. I was a very strong swimmer. My parents would have to constantly remind me not to go so far out. Then came the movie *Jaws* when I was in high school, and I was never the same. I can't relax in the ocean now and hardly ever go past the breakers for fear of sharks."

He agrees with me and says he has the same phobias because of that film, but then he asks, "So I understand about fear of sharks, but why are you afraid of people? You shouldn't let that deter you from hiking alone."

"Well, you're *a guy*, Caleb. Women learn to be afraid—especially of men—because life has taught us that's how to survive."

I don't offer more explanation, and we continue up the trail, which is becoming more snow-covered. I take a few good photos of the snow blanketing moss, which gives me a chance to catch my breath. I think about my fears and ponder over how lucky men are that they don't have to worry about the things women do. *What a freedom!* I think with envy. The many times I've traveled, both in and out of the US, I've constantly had to watch my back for male predators.

I begin to tell Caleb of one scary encounter as we continue our climb. "When I was just seventeen years old, I was an exchange student in Madrid, Spain, my senior year of high school, and one night my friend Tomás couldn't take me home on his motor scooter because it broke down. I didn't think twice about hailing a taxi. I gave the driver the address of my host family and didn't say anything more to him. We arrived, and I paid him." I struggle to catch my breath, stop, and take off my pack to retrieve my water bottle.

Caleb, who has also stopped, does the same, and we both drink deeply. He looks at me hesitantly and says, "You don't have to tell me if you don't want to."

"I want you to tell you. I want you to understand. Are you okay with me continuing?" I search his eyes for the answer.

He nods his head affirmatively and says, "Yeah. I think I need to know what women go through. Let's keep walking though. It's getting colder."

We carefully make our way up the slippery trail and I continue, "As I struggled with the lock on the outside gate, he suddenly appeared and opened it for me. As he handed me back the key, he lunged at me, tearing at my clothes and hitting me. I fought back, of course, and recalled the words of Momma's friend Connie *"Kick him where it hurt,s and make it good!"* I followed her advice, and my actions stopped the assailant. He left, and I and went upstairs to the apartment I shared with my host family. Long story short, I told my host mother, Patricia, and she blamed me for the attack. I couldn't believe a woman could do this to another! I was so hurt! Anyway, I just buried the whole incident deep inside. Ever since that happened, when I've had to hail a cab, the same fear surfaces, and I get PTSD. I'm sure this fear will be with me the rest of my life."

I quit speaking, finally, and just hear our boots and breath. Caleb breaks the silence.

"Well, I completely get why you don't hike alone now. Wow! I never even thought about it. That must be awful to go through life that way, always looking over your shoulder. I'm really sorry that happened, Amantha. It had to be hard telling me."

"Thank you for letting me tell you, Caleb. I just wanted you to see that life is very different for woman."

Sadly, I feel sure that this happens all too often to women all over the world. The #METOO movement that began this year in our country has given a courageous voice to all of us who have felt so unsafe and disempowered right here in the good ole USA, *our own country*. The movement began when the current POTUS nominated a man as a Supreme Court justice who had assaulted a woman when he was younger. Long story short, he was appointed in spite of her heartfelt, truthful account of the assault, giving rise to the movement as women all over the world poured out their support and outrage. At least women are now supporting instead of blaming one another when we are attacked. We are finally finding our voices and are uniting.

I recall a second time I was threatened. It happened during my yearlong stay in Chile when I was forty. This time, I was on a bus, coming back from a weekend on Chiloé Island. I noticed a man staring predatorily at me as I waited to board. He boarded when I did and kept turning around to look at me on the bus, and when I transferred busses, he did too. I was angry, so right before I got to my stop, I walked up to the driver and told him what was happening. He told me not to worry and to go ahead and get off. After I got off, that saintly driver stood up to prevent the man from following me, and the other passengers held him back, too. I was so thankful to that good man and those other strangers! Moreover, I was thankful to my older, wiser self for taking care of me.

Men really have no idea what women must endure in this world! I have not let these scary experiences keep me from traveling, as I *love* exploring our beautiful, fascinating world, but I don't believe I'll ever feel safe enough to do the things that Caleb does, like hike alone in the day *or* night.

The sound of my boots crunching snow brings me back to the present, and I feel grateful to be here, grateful to be *alive*. I breathe in the fresh air and feel sweat dampening my collar as we begin the last ascent up to the top of the mountain. There are clouds quickly moving in from the east, threatening our view of the historic planetary event, but in the western sky all is clear, and magnificent colors are lighting it up like a beacon of hope. I feel like all of humanity is desperately clinging to hope for 2021, and this star is its representation. I know that the pandemic will not magically disappear after the dropping of the ball in Times Square, and in reality the worst is yet to come.

Tennessee now has the worst infection rate *in the world*, and I know this is due to people's obstinate denial of reality. It makes me so sad and anxious to see all the death hovering nearby. In the last month, four more cousins have contracted the deadly virus, leaving two of them dead and one with lingering breathing problems. None of their families wore masks or socially distanced. They thought that the Coronavirus was nothing to worry about. One-in-thirteen people in our area now has the virus.

The sound of a woodpecker brings me back to the present, and I see Caleb pausing near the summit, looking toward the sunset. "Look, a pileated woodpecker!" he exclaims, pointing to the large redhead pecking away at a dead Frazier fir.

I catch up with my friend quickly, eager to see the bird. It pauses its noisy message and seems to glance my way just as I spot it. It seems to be pecking at my heart, telling me to focus on *hope*, not despair. 2021, *not* 2020. One of my grandmother Pennie's sayings comes to mind: "Make the most of all that comes and the least of all that goes." I smile as I picture her grinning at me across the great divide, and I imagine that her spirit and the pileated woodpecker have become one in this magical moment. *Hope Knocking.* I breathe in gratitude for this timely message, and Caleb and I turn our attention once again to the trail.

We hoot and holler with joy as we make it up to the top, marveling at the beautiful light that is shining on the last of the trees and the swirling clouds overhead. It is *cold* now, and the wind is screaming, but our hearts are filled with a calm serenity. We look around for the perfect place to wait for the celestial event, and see a young couple with their dog approaching us. All the other people who were parked below were day hikers, apparently, and have already passed us on their way back down the trail. The shivering pair tells us they are going back down since the wind is so brutal, so it is just Caleb and I left on the mountain.

I unpack the hot herbal tea I made this morning, along with two huge slices of zucchini bread I made last summer.

I settle down onto my rain jacket, but Caleb remains standing, taking in the full force of the gale winds. I offer him the hot tea and bread, and he gratefully consumes them. I take videos of the outstanding sunset, and my gloves almost blow away into the approaching night, but I manage to capture them and put them back on my frozen fingers. I curl up in a fetal position to try to ward off the cold as we wait for the dark sky to reveal its secrets.

Finally, darkness is complete, and we see it! To the right of the moon, toward the sunset, are the two planets Jupiter and Saturn. They are so close together that you can barely distinguish them at first, but with the nighttime comes our improved vision. I take some pictures but know they'll never be able to capture what I'm seeing, and especially what I'm feeling.

I think that perhaps humanity has had to go into the darkness of 2020 in order to find *enlightenment* in 2021. We have arrived, and it is now time to allow the light to guide us.

Thank you, Lord, for Your light.

Caleb and I agree that we have endured enough of the cold wind and decide to begin our descent. We have headlamps but think that the half moon, along with the bright Christmas Star, will provide enough light for us to see the trail, so we carefully make our way down. The star is directly in front of us, leading us to safety, while the moon shines brightly to our left. About halfway down, we hear a huge crash to our left and realize that a tree has come down nearby. This quickens our pace, and before we know it we are at the sharp curve just past the power line, right where I hid the gnome. I tell Caleb to try to spot it, and after the third big tree on the right, he shines his flashlight on the tiny, smiling man. This makes us both laugh uncontrollably for some reason, and I think to myself, *My God, it has been so long since I've heard my own laughter!*

I make an early New Year's resolution right then and there, beneath that big poplar with the laughing gnome, that I will laugh more in 2021. I will find joy in the light. I choose happiness now, for God has not forsaken us. He is leading us home.

Matthew

January 6th, 2021

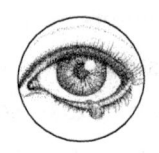

I drive back to ClothTreat after picking up several machine parts around town. I'm listening to the Patty Loveless CD that Amantha (or was it Santa?) put in my stocking at Christmas.

I can't believe that 2020 is finally behind us, and I say, "Good riddance!" *Surely, this new year will be better than the last,* I think as I try to drown out the loud backfiring of the "company truck"—a piece of *junk* that needs to be junked—with the soothing sounds of the Kentucky singer's mountain voice. Amantha and I saw her live in Junction City years ago, back when you could go see live music. *Man, I miss that!*

Hopefully, with this new vaccine that is slowly becoming available—first to front-line workers, like nurses, doctors, and EMTs, and then to the elderly living in nursing homes—life will return to normal sometime this year. Hopefully, Nancy Mae can get it soon. She is next in line and is already on the list. She said it took all day to get signed up by phone, and she still does not have a date or a time to get the first shot. Hopefully, the second one won't take so long. Surely, they'll have the bugs worked out of the system by then. It is unclear when other essential workers, like me, can get the vaccine. Soon, I pray.

Amantha and I worry so much about me getting Covid at work and giving it to her, then to her mother. Nancy Mae has suddenly become *so frail!* I honestly don't think she would survive it, and I couldn't live with that. I know that my wife would be destroyed.

Amantha's anxiety level is already at an all-time high. On Christmas Eve, she was so sad. I held her in my arms and just let her cry. She told me she felt so much *sorrow* over all the deaths. There are now over 370,000 just in the United States. Tennessee has one of the highest infection rates *in the world!* I think it's because of all the ignorance and selfishness of part of our citizens. It makes me so furious that many people still refuse to wear masks, and so many across the country got on airplanes and flew to see family over the holidays, spreading this deadly virus even more.

Amantha, Nancy Mae, and I spent Christmas and New Year's Day together, masks in place, and made sure we ate apart. If we can make these small concessions, then surely everybody else can, too. It's not that hard to do the right thing.

It is all too obvious that most non-maskers are Republicans and seem to be making some sort of political statement by refusing to comply. They talk about it being their personal choice, their *freedom,* to go mask-less. *What is wrong with people? Can't they see that they are* killing *others?*

Last Saturday, we decided to go to the auction over in Jordan County so we could find a rooster for our hens. The last rooster we had, Rojo, seemed to protect the hens from predators, clucking and crowing loudly to them when he spotted any possible danger. We've lost about six chickens since summer—two to a fox, one to a weasel, and three recently to a hawk. I also ordered some netting to attach to the top of their pen, so hopefully this will stop the killing.

Amantha and I arrived in Jordan County to what appeared to be a Covid party. Everyone was crowded inside together, no social distancing and no masks. We tried to buy a rooster out in the parking lot, but most of them had already been taken inside. We didn't stay long. I felt uncomfortable, and Amantha was downright disgusted. People were staring at our masked faces like something was wrong with *us*.

On the way back home, she called our friend Sally, who has a friend in Betsyville who happened to have two available roosters. We got our rooster on Monday, and we named him El Camino because I like the saying, "the cock of the walk," and Amantha always likes to give our roosters Spanish names. He seems a little skittish around us but immediately took a liking to our twenty-three remaining hens, and most of them seem to approve of the handsome bird.

I remind myself to buy more feed for them as I pull into the parking lot, backfiring and sputtering my way into a space by the garage door. I get out, pull my mask up, and notice that several of the younger men inside have their phones out and are not working. No real surprise. They are talking excitedly about something.

One newly-hired young man with tattoos all over his arms sees me come in, and with spit flying out of his unmasked mouth, he shouts, "Hey, Matthew! Temp's about to take out those f**king traitors in DC. I hope they kill them all for stealing the vote, including the vice president!"

I don't even make eye contact. I feel sick to my stomach as I go inside. I look up at the clock and see that it's 2:30 PM, about time to go home anyway, thank God. I take the parts to the office, along with the receipts, and wait for the secretary to get off her cell phone. *God, I hate those things.*

I hear her say, "He said he would drain the swamp, didn't he? That'll teach those disgusting Democrats! I hope they hang that woman speaker! Who does she think she is?"

I realize she is talking to me, and I tell her I don't know what on Earth she's talking about. She points to the television on the wall and back at her phone, then says that I really need a cell phone. I hand her the purchases without bothering to respond, as I am speechless. On the

Hope Knocking

TV, I see a mob climbing the steps outside our Capitol, dressed in all kinds of ridiculous outfits. One is clad in fur and a helmet with horns, and he has paint all over his nearly naked body. Some are dressed in military combat, waving Temp, American, and Confederate flags, all trying to push past the policemen, who are greatly outnumbered. Practically all of them are wearing the red "Make America Great Again" caps, and they are scaling the walls, breaking out the windows, and breaking doors down to get inside the building, where the lawmakers are recognizing the official count of electoral votes and will therefore declare that Bright is the next president of the United States.

In previous years, this ceremony has largely been ignored, but not this year. A small group of Republican senators and representatives have agreed to do the current POTUS's evil bidding and contest the outcome of the election. Everyone knew it would do no good, as Bright has already won, but they wanted to put on a show, and now we have this. The current POTUS went on Twitter and asked his base to come to DC several days ago, so they should have known. *WHERE IS THE LAW? HOW COULD THEY BE SO UNPREPARED?*

I feel my heart pounding. My hands begin to tremble, and I feel the bile coming up in my throat. *I have to get out of here*, I think. I leave the office and clock out; it's the first time I've ever clocked out early without telling anyone. I exit through a side door that nobody ever uses so I don't have to see anyone else. I crunch through the gravel and get to Big Red. Before I get in, I hold on to the door handle and retch, ridding myself of the ham sandwich I had gobbled down just an hour or so ago. I get in, take a drink of Mountain Dew to clear my mouth of the nasty taste, and look at myself in the rearview mirror. *My God, what is happening to our country?*

I leave work, get on the highway leading home, and turn on NPR to hear the news. The current POTUS is speaking to his mob, telling them that he hopes Vice President Price will do the "right thing for our country" and overturn the "fraudulent election," declaring him the president. Someone then whispers something in his ear, no doubt giving him the news that Price did *not* do this. In fact, he stated that he did not have the constitutional power to do anything other than read the electoral count, and he said that he was going to uphold the Constitution of the United States, which he swore to do under oath. The current POTUS then tells the mob that "we will march down to the Capitol and take back our country with force." The mob is doing just that, and he goes to hide inside the White House. The last thing the coward tells his enraged supporters is this: "You will not take it back with weakness, so be strong."

I try to focus on my breathing, as Amantha has told me to do when I feel an anxiety attack coming on. I breathe in deeply from my belly, hold it, and slowly release it. Repeat, repeat, repeat. As I drive next to the lake, I notice, perhaps for the first time, all the Confederate and Temp flags flying in front of people's homes. This saddens and angers me even more, and I think, *He must be removed from office for this. He's just got to. Surely, these people will finally see the evil inside this man. He has done so much harm to our country in just four years.*

Part of me fears, however, that this uprising is just what some people seem to want. The white supremacists *want* a race war. They *want* to overthrow the government. They are filled with *hate*, and they *love* the current POTUS. I don't allow these fears to surface, though, and try to refocus on my breath. *In and out, Matthew. In and out.*

I turn off the horrible news and think of the Scripture that has always led me out of darkness. *God, help me right now. I need you, Lord.* Psalm 27:14 comes to mind: "Wait on the Lord: be of good courage and He shall strengthen thine heart." Psalm 27:5: "For in the time of trouble, he shall hide me in His pavilion: in the secret of His tabernacle, He shall hide me; He shall set me upon a rock."

I pull off the road at the scenic overlook because I can no longer see the road through my tears. I sob uncontrollably for several minutes, and then I stare at the steely, cold gray waters of the lake. I take a deep

Hope Knocking

Then she says, "Momma, I *have* to watch the news. I just have to know what is happening. Do you want to watch it with me?"

I reluctantly agree, and we head back into my bedroom and huddle close together in my bed, watching the madness unfold. I find it almost unbearable to see the destruction happening in the city that gave me so much.

"You know, I never felt afraid in DC the whole time I worked for the FBI, and I walked home at midnight, all by myself, after taking the streetcar from my late-night shift. It was so hot in the summertime that I'd see poor people sleeping outside. That was before air conditioning. No one ever bothered me, though. The city was so intimidating to me at first, so *big* and *bright*, lit up like a Christmas tree all the time. But I found it to be magical, like Oz, and thought that nothing bad could ever happen there. We felt protected. It should be the safest place in our country, but look now! Where are all the troops? Where are the police?"

Amantha squeezes my hand, and we continue our vigil for another hour until we hear Matthew drive up. I let him in, and I can see by his face that he, too, is worried sick. He says nothing, though, and goes into my bedroom, where Amantha is. I see them embrace, clinging to each other like survivors in a lifeboat. We all go into the living room and settle into our respective chairs—Matthew in the "man-chair," Amantha on the couch, and me in my rocker.

One thing I hate about masks is that you can't really see how people are feeling because you can't see their mouths. "A heart is in one's mouth," I think the old saying goes. I know some people claim that the eyes are the portal to the soul, but I beg to differ. I need to see the lips or hear the voice to decipher mood. At the present moment, I am clueless because the two of them are as silent as church mice.

I decide to break the uncomfortable quietness, saying, "How on Earth is it possible that this madman has not been arrested? Why, he is probably just sitting comfortably in the White House, watching all this unfold. He's not calling for help, not calling off these crazies, not doing anything to stop this *coup* that *he* caused."

Matthew says that he heard on the radio that many Republicans who support the current POTUS have been calling him on his cell, begging him to do something. They want him to call in the National Guard, call off the mob, *help* them. They all fear for their lives. Even his own party can't really believe that a president of the United States could do this treasonous thing. The current POTUS is not answering their cries for help. He is doing *nothing* at all to help anyone, even those most loyal to him.

None of us can eat a thing, and soon Amantha and Matthew decide to go home. I try to encourage them, but my words ring false as I say, "Try not to worry. We'll get through this."

I close the door on the world and see my notebook on the floor, right where I'd dropped it earlier. I decide to write a few sorrowful words to commemorate this terrible day. I settle into the rocker, where I can look out at the gray day. The pen seems to move of its own accord, and I write "Homeland."

Homeland unraveling, coming apart at the seams
No longer a vibrant quilt that many immigrants built
Patchwork divided, boundaries drawn
No longer safe on your lawn
Feeling helpless as a fawn
Where did we go wrong?

I get the whole bag of chocolates from the kitchen and immediately return to my bed, where I watch the horror continue to unfold. Now there's a video of the current POTUS, nearly two hours after the terrorists invaded the Capitol, finally telling his followers to go home. He tells them that they're *special* and that he *loves* them. None of this seems real! Around 6:00 PM, National Guard units from around the country finally get a handle on the unruly mob, and they are ushered out of the building *without even being arrested.*

I think to myself, *Hmmm, if this had been a BLM crowd, I don't think the police would be so cordial to these criminals.* I know there would have been a lot of Black blood shed. Yes, if this had been a Black Lives Matter protest, the current POTUS would have sent out the cavalry in preparation of violence, but instead these white supremacist insurrectionists get help walking down the steps. The officers are even asking them to *please* exit the building. I realize right here and now, in my bed while eating dark chocolate Dove candies, that there are certainly two different kinds of policing in America: policing for people of color and policing for people that look like me.

By 8:00 PM, all the terrorists are gone, and Congress members finalize the electoral votes, officially making Bright the forty-sixth president. Unbelievably, some of the Republicans *still* try to contest the outcome, even after the *coup* that their leader attempted. *Democracy has won for now,* I think. *But can we keep it?* I know that someone famous said those words, but I cannot remember who. Washington? Franklin? Lincoln? MLK? I suppose it doesn't matter now, as he is dead, but the person's words still live and sure ring true today. Now, if we can just get through the inauguration on the 20th.

Amantha

January 18th
Martin Luther King Jr. Day

"I believe that unarmed truth and unconditional love will have the final word in reality." The slain civil rights leader's words give me assurance today, despite the fact that Americans of color have yet to achieve full equality and racism is alive and well in the United States of America. It is time to eradicate this virus from our society. In spite of the fact that the Civil Rights, as well as the Voters Rights and Fair Housing Acts, passed nearly sixty years ago, white supremacists and other extremist groups stormed the Capitol, trying to "take back" a country that has still refused to acknowledge the real problems: Hate and fear.

The temptation to label the rioters as thugs, racists, and crazies—although it might temporarily make me feel better, because I am *so angered* by what occurred on January 6th—is not helpful. *Enough already.* We have got to *stop* dehumanizing one another.

Many Christians and other faiths, especially their leaders, can play a huge role in teaching their flock to *love one another*, as Christ taught us to do. Stop preaching hate. Stop hijacking the Bible for your own purposes. *You have done enough harm.* Choose to be part of the solution now. I have personally witnessed the dehumanization of Democrats, gays, women, and people of color by men in the pulpit. *How shameful!* Well-meaning Christians were part of that mob in D.C., people who look just like me and could have been my neighbors.

Even after all that transpired, these misguided, good people insist that the people who committed these atrocities were not the current POTUS's supporters, but were members of the far-left Antifa movement. WHAT? *Where do they get this stuff? Why do people refuse to believe what's right in front of them?*

Many Republicans still believe that the current POTUS won the election. They so quickly gobble up lies. I believe part of the problem is that Republicans in office are reluctant to overwhelmingly reject him and his lies. The current POTUS has been impeached a second time by the House—the first president in US history to have this undesirable claim to fame—but only ten Republican representatives voted to do so. Price refused to invoke the twenty-fifth amendment, which could have removed the current POTUS immediately after the coup. So now, *unbelievably*, he still sits in the White House, fuming with humiliation but still in office, *still holder of the nuclear codes.*

What is wrong with this picture?

He is also being allowed to have a sending-off ceremony with gun and cannon salutes, though he will be the first president to not be present at his successor's inauguration on Wednesday. His approval rating has now dropped to the lowest in history: 34 percent. How could *anyone* still support this man?

I asked this very question on Facebook on January 7th, and one middle school teacher in Jordan County, who I barely knew, attacked my character and reputation. She even went as far as calling me a "fake Christian." *Whatever.* Okay, I admit that at first I was *so* hurt and angry. *How dare she!* She doesn't even know me, and the things she posted on my page were mean, spiteful lies. After I cried a little, I deleted her post, blocked her, and unfriended her. Why on Earth did I add her as a friend to begin with? I began to see how very angry these current POTUS supporters are, and I am surrounded by them, so I decided to live free from social media and suspended my account.

Honestly, it has freed me. What a waste of time these sites are! Furthermore, these platforms have been hijacked and used to spread conspiracy theories, misinformation, and downright lies. I mainly used Facebook to post my hiking photos, wish people a happy birthday, and respond to any messages. I usually refrained from engaging in political discussions unless something earth-shattering happened, like the insurrection at the Capitol, where both Democrats and Republicans were endangered by a madman's misguided maniacs.

Republicans in the Senate will be given the opportunity to do the right thing after Bright's inauguration. They can and should uphold the impeachment, convicting the traitor for inciting the insurrection, therefore preventing him from ever holding office again. One would think they would relish the chance to effectively remove him from the Republican Party and send a clear message to his base that the party no longer chooses to align itself with white supremacists and ignorant conspiracy theorists. The likelihood of them doing so is slim, unfortunately. I fail to understand how these elected officials can sleep at night. I just don't *understand* them, and this failure to relate to the other side is part of the problem, I know.

I am a white person of privilege who does not understand how other white people can continue to hate Americans who are black and brown. Furthermore, I also don't understand hatred of immigrants, gays, females, poor, Jewish, Democrats, the government, the educated, atheists, fat people, and old people. Of course, I am guilty of having harbored hatred in my heart, too. The thing is, I realize that hatred in my heart is a *cancer*, so I choose to love instead. It is a daily choice that each of us can consciously make every day. We must make this choice in order to be *well*.

Doctor King knew this, and he always advocated for peaceful protest. He tried to be Christ-like. Eventually, his efforts paid off, and many acts were passed throughout the country. He paid for it with his own life. I pray that his sacrifice will finally be recognized and valued by all of us in 2021. Let the words in the Declaration of Independence finally ring true for all Americans: "We hold these truths to be self-evident, that all men are created equal, that they are endowed by their Creator with certain unalienable Rights, that among these are Life, Liberty, and the pursuit of Happiness."

Dr. King had a dream that "little black boys and black girls will be able to join hands with little white boys and white girls and walk together as sisters and brothers." Will that come to fruition in my lifetime?

Growing up in the South, I've seen that many whites disrespect MLK day. Just the other day, as I delivered Meals on Wheels to several elderly people in town, one of them asked me why they were getting an extra meal. I explained to her that Monday was Martin Luther King Day and that food was not delivered on holidays.

She shook her head and said, "That n***er. I don't know why we celebrate him anyway. Do you?"

I kindly told her that he was a great man and wished her a good holiday.

Growing up in Georgia, I don't recall ever learning about this hero in public schools, nor did I ever attend any MLK parades or events during my life. And I am pretty sure that holds true for many other white Americans, too.

It makes me sad that I've had so many years without a Black friend. I had one once...a long time ago. Her name was Josie, and she was the only African American student in my fifth grade class, and probably only one of a handful who attended that school. Honestly, I never even thought about her race. I guess my experience at Mother's Head Start job had thankfully made me a colorblind child. The first time I experienced racism was when another white student in class chastened me for letting Josie use my hairbrush. She told me that all blacks had lice and were nasty. I ignored her and told her to shut up. Then I invited Josie to my birthday party at the skating rink, and my other friends were appalled that I included her. Josie didn't come, and thinking back on the hell she must have endured at that school, I am not surprised. She moved away later, and I never saw her again. I played basketball and worked with several blacks in high school, and I even carpooled with one girl named Estelle, but we never got close.

Lately, I have been virtually attending a Black church in North Carolina, one that is preaching God's Word, not the Republican agenda. I hope that when the pandemic ends, I can meet these good people in person and form lasting friendships. I know I need Black people in my life. I need to heal the racism in myself. I pray I don't let them, and myself, down.

Amantha

Wednesday, January 20th
Inauguration Day

I decide to watch the big event at Mother's house, so after letting the chickens out and feeding them a mixture of corn and mealy worms, I walk through the fresh snow by the Diamond. El Camino's welcoming crow breaks the silence of the new day.

I just *love* being the first one to observe the winter animals' tracks. It makes me feel like a brave explorer in a new world. I see the tracks of deer, raccoons, birds of some kind—probably crows, as Jewell feeds them old bread in her front yard—and some other big animal that doesn't leave a heavy print. I wonder if it's a bobcat or a fox or some river creature. These fascinate me, and I crouch over to inspect them up close.

I wish my trail camera would capture some of these mysterious animals that are parading around at night. I would love to see what they're up to! Are they sniffing around the chicken coop? Are they hunting rodents? What are their lives like? I'm sure they have difficult lives, constantly having to search for food in order to stay warm, not hibernating in a cozy den all winter like the bears.

I ponder the tracks of my own life. Are they deep and heavy or barely perceptible? Have they obliterated the path of others while trying to make their mark, leaving blood and destruction along the way, or is my trail more obscure and faint? I hope to leave a gentle trace, for I have no desire for fame or fortune. I do, however, want to help others climb the sacred mountain of life in ways that may seem insignificant to others. I know that I've helped a few students find their way, and now I choose to accompany my mother on her final push to the summit. I can also show kindness to others whose paths may cross mine. We may decide to walk together for a while and then part ways. If we're lucky, we may find a special someone with whom we share the same path, our footprints becoming one. We provide for one another while leaving very little trace in the pure beauty of the wilderness, becoming strong in body and in spirit.

When predators come along, we will join forces and fight, hoping to overcome evil with strength. Sometimes it may be necessary to hide in the rock or by the stream until the danger passes. Perhaps this has been the lesson of 2020. I wonder if we will need to continue hiding in 2021, or must we come out of our caves and fight?

I enter the statue garden in the Zebra Room, named in honor of my dearly departed Aunt Dena, who always pleaded with anyone who would listen to make her a "zebra" to go in her yard. Matthew and I finally honored her request after her death and built the gazebo on our property, facing the river. I climb up and sit on the padded bench under its shelter, then look out at the icy river. My favorite meditation rock is underwater, and I search the opposite bank for signs of life. I'd love to see the playful otter or even a mink or weasel, but the only aquatic life I've seen this winter are the elegant wood ducks.

I continue walking upriver, searching for the elusive ducks. I know to be quiet, for they are easily spooked. Finally, I see them ducking under the water playfully, getting their breakfasts. They don't see me yet, so I remain hidden behind the butterfly bush that's still decorated with Christmas bows. The distinctive male circles around the female and lets her have the choice hunting spots while he's on guard for any danger. I watch them for several minutes before the cold turns me toward Mother's house. I hear their wings beating as they fly away, and I turn around to bid them adieu and to reassure them that I mean them no harm. I just wish to observe their tracks and share this moment of life.

Mother must have been observing me from the "man-chair" in the living room, because her door is unlocked. I enter the very warm house. I immediately shed several layers and call out for her. I hear her in the basement, and I go downstairs to find her. She's got all of her rug-hooking materials out—baskets of yarn, burlap, the frame that Matthew made, and handmade hooks that belonged to Pennie.

"Have you decided to start a new rug? Who's going to get this one?" I ask, happy that she's found something to do.

I worry that she's getting bored with the never-ending quarantine, one that won't be going away any time soon, I predict. The vaccination effort, at least in these parts, is going at a turtle's pace. I was thrilled when Momma told me that she was finally able to get on the list for people seventy-five and older to get vaccinated, but two weeks have already gone by, and they still haven't given her an appointment. Who knows when Matthew and I will be able to get it? I also wonder how effective the vaccine is going to be considering the new variants of the virus are now starting to show up around the globe. The virus seems to be several steps ahead of humans, who can barely keep up with the tiny microbe's evolution.

"This one I'm going to keep for myself, to remind me of Mom. I know exactly the design I want—one big flower in the middle, with vines connecting it to four smaller flowers in the corners. What color do you think should be the background?"

She pulls out several possibilities, including gray, beige, brown, and white. I point to the dark brown, and she agrees. I help her take it all upstairs, and we quickly move things around in the living room to make room for the rug. We place burlap on the frame and tightly fasten it to the corners, then place it on top of two sawhorses. We pick out various shades of pink and green yarn for the flowers, vines, and leaves, and all of this leaves Momma exhausted.

"I think I'll draw the design later. I'm worn out," she says as she sinks down onto the couch.

I sit next to her and pull her big feet onto my lap to gently start massaging them. She relaxes and lets me comfort her. We sit in silence for a few moments, and then I suggest that we go lie down in the bed and watch the inauguration of Bright. She agrees, so I get settled in bed as she makes us some hot chocolate. The president-elect has just arrived to a beautifully transformed Capitol. I don't know how those workers—most of them black, I'm sure—managed to clean up the horrible mess from January 6th in time for this historical event, but they certainly did make it look like a shining city. So many American flags, not the current POTUS's or Confederate flags, wave in the breeze on the cold, windy winter day.

Those flags seem to represent hope to me, hope that nothing bad could happen on this day. Deep down, I am aware that the division between Americans will not simply vanish along with the almost-previous POTUS and the old year, but *we need this day*. My God, how I long for normalcy again! How I long for a leader to show us the way, and Bright just may be the wise, gentle old sage that America cries out for. He certainly looks the part, and as he places his wrinkled hand on his faded, leather-bound Bible, the tears start to release from my eyes and, much to my surprise, Mom's too.

"This is the Washington *I* choose to remember," she declares weakly, "*Not* one that's been defiled and trampled upon. After what happened on the sixth, I had decided I *never* wanted to step foot in that city again, but seeing the beauty now, the possibility of better times ahead, maybe, just maybe, I would like to see it one more time."

I take her hand and tell her we will make plans to go, perhaps in the sweet summertime, and mention that Aunt Macie and her family should join us there for an epic reunion.

We listen to an amazing rendition of the National Anthem, and then a beautiful, young African American poet steps on the stage, and her eloquent mannerisms and words make us cry again:

"We have to be the shining light," she says.

It is amazing to me that a person of color in our country, after the year of racial injustice and the long history of violence and hatred toward her people, is the one showing us the way forward. Again, I find myself so encouraged by the youth in our country. They seem wise beyond their years.

After a moving bilingual rendition of "This Land Is Your Land" brings forth more tears, I decide that I've had enough and leave Momma in bed, blowing her nose into her endless supply of paper towels.

I retrace my own tracks in the snow at first, then decide to go a different way. *Sometimes,* I think, *the old way is not the best way, because if we keep doing things the same way, we'll keep making the same tragic mistakes. Let us start something new, something better, something where all of our tracks are appreciated and none are trampled upon.*

Matthew

February 2nd
Groundhog Day

About an hour before my alarm goes off, I get up and look out the window at the falling snow. There's already about four inches, and I know it's going to take more than an hour to drive in to work. I turn off the alarm and begin my day at 3:30 AM. I turn on CNN in the living room and pull on the pile of clothes I left on the couch the night before.

Groundhog Day. I don't expect the poor critter to even peek out of his hole on a day like this, not even to give his prognosis of more winter to come. Up north, it's much worse than here, with several feet predicted, and down in the Smokies they are calling for a foot or more. We may get another three inches here today, but in town there probably won't be more than an inch or so. It does make for an even longer drive, and it is beginning to wear on me this winter. Sometimes I do wish we lived closer to town.

Amantha and I have talked about getting out of Mavie one day, away from the trash, the previous POTUS's banners, the Confederate flags, and the long drive to work, closer to the doctor, and the grocery stores. I do think it would be nice to be able to go out to dinner or to a concert without having to drive an hour to get there. We could even go dancing again!

Amantha and I met, nearly seventeen years ago, at a dance in Junction City. While we lived there, we would go Contra dancing just about every month, or we'd go to a concert or a bluegrass festival. Those days seem so long ago. Before Covid, we did still try to go to concerts and festivals from time to time, but the dancing days disappeared. There's always so much to do around home, too, and I'm always *so tired.*

On the news, I hear them say that the new strains of the virus, from Africa and Europe, have arrived here in the US. I wonder if the vaccine will still be as effective. I wonder when Amantha and I will be able to get the vaccine. Nancy Mae finally got her first shot last Friday and will get the second one in about three weeks. She said that the whole operation was very organized and didn't take long at all. The health department set up a tent near my factory in Betsyville, and she and Amantha stayed in the car the entire time. They only had to wait fifteen minutes! Of course, only Nancy Mae had an appointment, as she is in phase 1B—people over seventy-five—but Amantha did ask if she could also get one since she is her mother's caretaker. They told her no but took both of our names and our phone number in case they had any leftover doses.

They haven't called yet, but Nancy Mae's friends who have a house in North Carolina told her that we should go to the hospital in Linview, just over the state line, around 6:00 PM to try to get one there. Their daughter got one that way. We are going to try to go this Thursday, weather permitting. (They are surely getting more snow than we are due to the high elevation in that mountain town.) Apparently, they don't care if you're not a resident of NC, as these people are from Florida and got theirs.

I know it will be such a relief to get the vaccine. I am the only person on the factory floor who wears a mask. Even Tim, one of the supers, still refuses to cover his face. After a whistleblower—a woman who used to work in the office—alerted the health department about the company's lack of Covid precautions, management took action with a mask mandate. It lasted *one day*! I don't understand these people. You'd think that they would at least care about their own families.

My thoughts turn to my own brother, Waylon, who now has the virus. He got it from his wife and daughter, who got it while working at a supermarket. They were told by management not to tell anyone about it or they would have to shut down. Is this what we have become? A nation that cares more about the almighty dollar than its own citizens? I know what the Bible says about that: "the love of money is the root of all evil."

ClothTreat sure does love money. I now have to work Sundays, and I *hate* not being able to attend church, even though it's just been parking-lot service at our old church up at Birch Springs, and I go alone. Amantha's been listening to a virtual service of a Black church in the town of Danielton, about forty minutes away. I understand what she's doing and will always support her need to be "part of the change, not part of the problem," as she says, but I have to admit that it makes me so sad that we don't go to church together anymore.

There, I said it. I miss sitting in our pew at Gentry Gap. I miss our friends there. I miss singing in the choir. I miss hearing *her* sing. Amantha doesn't sing anymore, and that *really* makes me sad because I know she loved it. Her eyes would just light up, the Spirit would get ahold of her, and she would belt out a hymn that always moved people to tears. I asked her a few weeks ago why she quit singing and playing her flute, guitar, dulcimer, and psaltery, and she said she just lost the heart to play right now. I hope God gives her this joy again, though there is nowhere for her to play during a pandemic. Maybe she will become part of the wonderful gospel choir at this new church of hers once it opens back up to live services. She has asked me if I plan to go with her when it does, and I tell her I just don't want to travel that far, which is true.

I rest on Sundays, or I did before ClothTreat took that away. I guess each of us has to make his or her own decisions, just like Nancy Mae always says. I know I have to trust God, wait on Him, and know that He has a plan for each one of us. That has to be enough right now.

I've been so lost in thought that at first I don't recognize the furry animal sticking its head up through the snow as I drive slowly next to Bent River, which winds its way behind our factory and many others that also surely contaminate its banks. I laugh out loud. *It's a groundhog!* Good Lord, I think, *what on Earth is she doing showing up on such a frigid day?* I slow down even more and watch the mammal pivot its head slowly, as if it's in a daze, and then it spots me, pauses to take me in, and, in a split second, convey to me its message of hope and assurance: *Breathe, Matthew. Better days are ahead.* Then, as quick as a frozen rodent can go, she ducks back into her winter hole and waits for springtime.

Amantha

Superbowl Sunday

It snowed again last night, and it's a really pretty one, covering every limb, bush, and twig with its white velvet. I know it won't last long, so I take my phone with me as I head down to let the chickens out and then visit with Mom. I take pictures of the hens and El Camino as they stare down at the white stuff, refusing to leave their warm, dry house. The flock looks at me expectantly, and I comply by shoveling a path from the henhouse to the frozen bank, where I scatter several piles of mealworms mixed with corn for a morning meal. The rooster has adjusted to his new surroundings now and no longer seems to fear me. He, along with the hungry hens, is already at my feet, eagerly gobbling up the protein-rich feed. I'm sure they are sick of the snow and ready to consume fresh grass and live bugs, but we still have to get through February.

I leave the birds and continue walking up Mother's driveway, noticing the quietness of this day. Snow does seem to muffle all sounds, and I wonder why this is. I suppose every season has its own peculiar sound. Springtime chirps with new life, summertime buzzes with mosquitoes and lawnmowers, autumn sighs with the death throes of cicadas, and winter quietly mourns her dead.

Before I climb the stairs leading up to the warmth and comfort of Mother, I decide to investigate the banks of the river. I walk quietly so I won't startle any of the Diamond's permanent or guest residents. I watch, transfixed, as a graceful blue heron rises from the swirling mist, touching me deep down in my soul. *Wow! They are here early*, I think, and I feel grateful for the magnificent sight of this harbinger of spring. I know we are so fortunate to live surrounded by nature and witness all its beauty, and I hope I never take it for granted.

Just yesterday, on Bent Lake, as a group of "Keep Elk County Beautiful" members picked up trash on its shores, I heard a familiar sound coming from the treetops and quietly alerted the group by signaling above. There were two bald eagles perched on their nest! Wilderness continuing to thrive amongst the mounds of Styrofoam, plastic and glass bottles, lighters, tires, inner tubes, and hypodermic needles, but for how long?

Humans continue to view all animals as disposable, like the plastic containers we use, giving no thought or care to the inevitable pollution in our rivers, lakes, and oceans. We selfishly view other lifeforms in terms of how they benefit us instead of considering that they are inherently valuable just as they are. Why do we think we are so special that we have the right to eradicate other species this way? I have heard the term "human supremacy" tossed around lately to try to explain what is happening on Earth—this fifth extinction event that is being caused by us.

This is similar to white supremacists, who think that Caucasian genes are biologically superior to other humans. Human supremacists think that this planet belongs to Homo sapiens and that we can use it up as we wish. They think that we are to *conquer and subdue* all other lifeforms that we deem inferior.

It makes me sad to recognize that this language comes from Christianity. "Yours is the earth and everything in it." I suspect that this selfish view may be present in other religions, as well. Being a Christian myself, I personally think that God is appalled by our actions. I cannot possibly believe that our Creator would want us to destroy the Eden that He bestowed to *all* creatures. No, I know He would expect us to be good stewards of the land. I also wonder if the belief that heaven, not Earth, is our ultimate home contributes to our apparent lack of concern over ruining this planet.

"This world is not my home, I'm just a-passing through." How many times have I sung that old gospel song, one that my grandpa loved dearly, without really thinking about the repercussions of living this way? Planet Earth *is* our home, and it is home to every living being we share it with. There has got to be a *reckoning* within our human souls *now*. Our present lifestyle is not sustainable to *any* lifeform. We have to begin to see that we are all connected. We are all made up of the same star stuff. We are all created by the same God. We all deserve to live, and die, with dignity. *Don't we?*

So, it is after such soul-searching that I make my plans to evolve even more as an earthling, to do my part. What can *I* do? Writing this book is one thing, but will I walk the talk? I know Mother is trying to become a vegetarian. That is definitely one way to evolve. Would Matthew and I be willing to omit meat from our diets...say, three times a week? That would be better than the once or twice we now go meatless. Am I willing to completely omit plastic from our lives? Yes, I think it's about time. I already use a reusable water bottle and never buy sodas. Now Matthew, he'll have to make that decision for himself. I know he likes his sodas, and I try not to fuss at him, but he'd feel better drinking more water.

I already have enough cloth bags in the back of Cielito Lindo. So what if I have to bag my groceries myself? That's *not* a big deal. The world would be so much healthier without all those plastic bags choking the life out of everything! I will be more diligent while shopping, too, avoiding prepackaged foods. We already grow most of our organic vegetables and can everything we can. We never have any food waste, as we've been composting for years now, and the chickens eat practically everything we give them. We recycle aluminum and burn our paper trash. I use glass bottles in my bottle gardens, so really, we only generate about one bag of trash a month that goes to the landfill, and that's mainly metal cans that aren't recycled.

I know that each person has to start with herself. If everyone does that, if everyone recognizes the *need* to do her part, then that's how minds will be changed, I think. If minds are changed, maybe then we *will* evolve into a higher lifeform, something that God would be proud of.

Nancy Mae

Valentine's Day

I like to look out my bedroom window while I'm lying in bed, but only if I'm a-waitin' on somebody, and right now it's a little before 3:00 PM on a Sunday, time to begin watching for Matthew to get home. I carefully ease out of bed to open the curtain so I can see down the drive. I keep it closed the rest of the time because the light now hurts my eyes. I declare, I do believe my old body has aged more this past year than in the last ten combined! Every little task takes me forever to do now, including just getting up to walk the five feet to the window.

I look out at the gray, depressing day and notice the chickens next to the Stairway to Heaven, as Amantha likes to call the stairs that lead from my place up to the Treehouse. That rooster, El Something, is with them. They seem content, so I decide to get back in bed to continue my lookout in comfort.

Just before I turn my head, I see something odd: something brown is shooting down out of the sky like a bullet, heading toward the flock. All the chickens scatter away, including the timid cock. I continue watching, and very soon I see red and white feathers begin to carpet the ground, and with a sickening feeling my brain registers what is happening. *A hawk!* As fast as my old body can move, I exit the bedroom and carefully descend the basement stairs. I find my shoes and coat waiting for me by the door. I open the door and grab my walking stick, then start walking toward the massacre. Sure enough, a big red-tailed hawk stares at me for just a split second before I scream at him, and he leaves the poor, mangled red chicken lying there in the red mud. I see him fly to a big hemlock in the Zebra room, where he perches on a branch, glaring down at me.

Oh, the poor chickens, I think as I look over the fence at the pile of feathers. I hear the others squawking nearby, probably near their house, scared to death. I continue down the drive, open the gate to their lot, and look inside the house. They are all there, huddled together and as still as statues. *I cannot take this*, I think, and I shut them up in there for the rest of the day in order to prevent the predator from taking more lives.

My heart feels heavy as I go back home, and I wonder about the cruelty of nature. I know that hawks have to eat, too, but why did God create some animals to eat others? Why can't we all eat plants? My son Jay, an avid meat and plant eater, speculates that plants may have feelings, too. Do they scream when we devour their leaves? If so, what on Earth *are* we to eat?

My thoughts are dark as I climb the basement stairs, stopping to catch my breath more than usual. I hold on to the railing and breathe in slowly until I'm able to continue. *I'm just so tired*, I think. *Maybe a few chocolates will give me some energy.* I get the box of chocolates that Sally gave me and a fresh supply of paper towels, and then I sit in the "man-chair," where I can turn my attention to the river. I stare out at the foaming whitewater until it becomes too blurry to see, and then I realize that I'm crying. The salty tears are mixing with the sweet taste of chocolate, and I'm quickly becoming a mess. I put the box down, blow my nose into the paper towel, and then let the tears have free reign.

I cry for the chickens first. How sad that the sweet creatures—whose only desires in life are to eat, scratch, dig, dust, and sun themselves—can so quickly be devoured from all directions, this time from above. They lay eggs and become broody, but we gather their eggs to consume, denying them motherhood. We also eat *them* as nuggets, strips, dumplings, pies, casseroles, and soups, and I know we forget that they were once living creatures. We refuse to think of them as such and pretend that they don't have brains, hearts, or souls, but I'm not so sure about that. I'm not so sure about anything anymore.

I glance over at the rug that Amantha and I are hooking and immediately think of Momma. She simply *adored* her chickens. I remember one time when Cousin Homer ran over one as he was speeding down Mavie Road, which ran right by our house. He didn't even stop, as if that was a life that didn't matter. Momma was waiting for him, though. She knew he would be returning soon, because old Homer was a creature of habit. Just like that hen had the bad habit of standing in the road, he had the bad habit of drinking at the beer joint down on The Nowhere. He never had much money, though—no one did in Mavie—so he never stayed there long and would soon be returning home. Momma waited for the sound of the muffler-less Ford as it neared the sharp curve out front, and when it arrived, Homer had to slam on the brakes to keep from hitting her. She had that old hen in one hand, and when he leaned out the window to ask her what was going on, Momma began to beat him with that dead chicken. He managed to escape, finally, but was covered with blood and feathers, and he later returned to our house with a new chicken, which he presented to Pennie with shaking hands.

Yep, Momma loved her chickens, yet she also could wring one's neck with one practiced hand and fry it up with the other for the preacher's dinner. How she could do that to her beloved pets, I'll never know. I guess hunger makes all creatures behave badly in order to survive.

Does the hawk feel remorse when he decapitates the chicken before eating it? Or is he like us, thinking that the chicken is a stupid, unfeeling animal who is put here on this Earth to feed him? I just don't know, and right now I don't care. I just need to cry some more.

Now I cry for the sins of our country. The second impeachment trial of the past POTUS is over, and he was not convicted for causing the insurrection. I wonder how those Republicans can sleep at night! Just a few of them, though not enough, voted with the Democrats to convict, and now their party is turning on these brave patriots. The media continues to give him attention, which he craves, and I worry he's still in control of the Republican party and will run again in four years. They had the chance to rid the party of him once and for all, and instead they refused to do the right thing for the country. Why would they want their party to be affiliated with the likes of him, white supremacists, conspiracy theorists, and crazy, hate-filled people? People who refuse to accept truth. People who cannot stand the thought of a changing America, one with more black and brown skin.

The past POTUS is just like that hawk, swooping down on America to gut her of her ideal of equality for all. I'm afraid we will never be given the chance for this lofty ideal to materialize now.

I am afraid for our country. If we lose this democracy, what will become of other democracies around the world who look to us as the beacon of hope? Will they, too, crumble? If democracies fall, what will take their place? The alternative will not be good, I believe. When truth can no longer be found, when truth can no longer be trusted, when people greedily consume warped headlines without even wanting to read the fine print, and when people see those being consumed as "them instead of us," then fellow citizens become the enemy of the state. Hawks consuming chickens. Then the rule by people is replaced by a set of falsehoods controlled by those in power—rich, greedy corporations who use these falsehoods to get the brainwashed masses to commit atrocities on one another. *History repeating itself over and over again, I think. We take one step forward and three steps back.*

Today is Valentine's Day, a day that is supposed to represent *love*. What is love, really? I think it has to be love for *all* of us, starting with the stinkbug who invades our homes in the winter, trying to stay warm. We must love the homeless man we pretend not to see lying in his own mess on the curb. *We are all connected to this Earth.* We all have a destiny to fulfill—God's will, if you choose to call it that. We all have a perfect design and purpose, and even though we may not understand that design and purpose in other beings, we must begin to *see* our connectedness. Yes, I think that's it. In order to *love* one another, we must first learn to *see* each other. In order to see one another, we must remove the blinders from our eyes. False preconceptions about who we are, about who *they* are, prevent us from true vision. We need vision right now, *all* of us on planet Earth, if we are to coexist and survive.

Love one another.

I am finished crying. As I get up from the "man-chair," I spot a wasp struggling under it. I bend over to get a better look at the insect. *I see you,* I tell it. *I see your pretty, delicate wings that have such intricate, lacy details, and I leave you to your destiny. You are free to live and love another day.*

Amantha

February 23rd

Today is my dear friend Becky's birthday, and I celebrate our long friendship by dancing to welcome the soft morning light that is beginning to reveal the woods behind the Treehouse. She is only one month older than me, and as I dance I pray that her day is truly beautiful and filled with joy, not pain and sorrow.

Becky's mother died suddenly just last month after suffering a stroke. It happened so quickly, which is a blessing, I suppose. She was able to die in her home, too, not a hospital. I know that gives Becky and her father some comfort, but I also know that they are grieving her death tremendously. It's so hard to find the right words to say to her, but I just try to be there for her. I hope that is enough.

I decide to call her right now even though it's early. She answers right away, and I can tell from her voice that she is strong today and feels well. We talk for a while, and I am so grateful for these talks because, honestly, Becky and I have *always* been able to say whatever is in our hearts. That is a rare thing, I realize, not to be taken for granted. There is nobody else with whom I feel so at ease. I am so grateful to have this friendship in my life and to have her in this world.

After we hang up, I fall on my knees and give God thanks for this gift, and I pray that He will comfort her and heal her. I know that God will never give us more than we can bear, and I can see Him holding up my childhood friend. I see her tremendous strength and wisdom in this dark hour of her life, and I know that she will be okay.

2021 can be a year of growth for all of us, I think, if we choose to seek wisdom and understanding. It has to start within each of us. It is a *choice*. We can choose to move toward the light, or we can wallow in the darkness.

For me, the darkness of 2020 has revealed past hurts, and I am now truly ready to release them, to release myself from further suffering. Hurt and suffering has kept me trapped, and I can clearly see this now. Yes, people have hurt me, whether intentionally or not, though that really doesn't even matter anymore. The end result hasn't affected anyone but *me*, causing me to withdraw from people, causing me to turn to food for comfort, and causing me to blame and hate myself for engaging in these self-destructive behaviors.

I have made a lot of progress over the years, and I give God credit. I quit drinking and smoking over ten years ago and allowed God to change my desires. I am in a healthy, loving relationship with my husband of more than fifteen years. I engage in healthy activities now, such as hiking, playing music, volunteering, and painting, and I removed myself from an unhealthy work environment and retired at fifty-six.

Once retired, I was able to help Mother more and spend more time with her, yet anger and resentment were still residing below the surface. They had been a part of my life for so long, but the time for me to confront them had come. 2020 was that teacher. Last year did not timidly knock; it *demanded* to be heard. Instead of burying these ugly truths, I decided to reckon with them. I have decided to hear them and to honor the little girl inside me who is finally ready to be free from the bondage of past resentments. These feelings are an accumulation of a lifetime of hurt, I now realize, and I am sure that many people have similar unresolved feelings in themselves. Some people choose to never deal with the hurts, instead covering them up with possessions, pride, or power.

Perhaps this is the past POTUS's story. Only he has the power to know that...if he chooses to do the work.

Others give up their own happiness and self-worth to serve others, mistakenly believing that if they make others happy, then surely they will finally be recognized for being a good person. I have been guilty of this in the past, but now I see that we should be good to others because it is the right thing to do. We should choose to love one another and then release that gift into the universe, not expecting anything in return. I like to think that by releasing enough love into the universe, we can heal not only ourselves but the entire world.

Will we succeed? We *must try*. *I must try*. I know I will have setbacks. I know I will have doubts. I also know where to turn for help, as God resides inside me and is my guide and compass. I may not have a physical church building right now, but I do have a church. It is on a mountain trail, where the sunlight is sparkling on the ice crystals hanging from the branches, causing them to break and scatter on the snow like shards of quartz.

The ice that formed on my heart is melting, and I am grateful to feel. I am grateful for myself, so wondrously made by God's hand, and will strive to practice self-love from now on. I know now that I cannot truly love another being if I do not love myself. God made me and knows the goodness in me, for which I rejoice today.

I get dressed and exit into a beautiful world—one filled with hope, birdsong, and the promise of spring. I can't wait to share the day with Momma. I'm so blessed to be alive on this patch of dirt called Nowhere.

Epilogue

Amantha

Spring Forward

M atthew and I are climbing up the steep hill leading out of our No Place on The Nowhere, and as the U-Haul chugs slowly beside the cliffs, I spot the pearly white petals of the bloodroot waving goodbye in the brisk wind. I can't believe we are leaving our beautiful home on the Diamond River, yet I am filled with the promise that only springtime can bring. It is time to leave. That is clear to both of us. This haven sheltered us for twenty years, but even though its roots run through my blood, they were never strong enough to keep us here indefinitely. I will always love these mountains and the people they nourished: Pennie, Dena, and Momma.

We make it to the top, and we both breathe a sigh of relief. Before we turn right and head up The Nowhere, I get out and check the mailbox one last time. Shuffling through the endless junk mail and catalogues, I find a long-awaited treasure: a letter from Hawaii. A letter from Sarah! I smile and tuck it into my pocket. I'll read it in the comfort of the heated truck later.

Hope Knocking

Sunlight bathes the cliffs as we continue our ascent of Mavie Road, and I look to my right, in the direction of the river and our Treehouse, which is perched above the sparkling waters. I see a hawk circling above, searching for his breakfast, and I say a small, silent prayer for him, knowing that he has to eat, too, and has a place in this beautiful world.

When we get to the stop sign at the top of the road, I look over at Matthew and squeeze his hand. He smiles and turns left twice, then parks at the cemetery. I smile at the sign there: "No Digging up Graves Without Permission." *Apparently, someone must have done this, or there wouldn't be a sign here,* I think. *I wish I had asked Momma about this. That has to be a good story.*

We both get out, Matthew carrying a homemade cake—Pennie's Plum Good Plain Cake, to be exact—and make our way over to Momma's cremation bench. We sit there, surrounded by all the other granite sentinels of my mountain family.

"We've come to say happy birthday, Momma. You were stubborn enough to make it to ninety, just as you wanted, but I guess you figured that after that you were too tired to go any further. You rest easy now. I won't be far away, just over these mountains to the west. Matthew and I will come visit as much as we can. I promise. You are with family, back on Nowhere Road, just like my song says."

"Back on Nowhere Road"

A mountain girl born in '34
On a road that led to Nowhere
In a two-room shack that was filled with cracks
And love to last forever

Her dad called her Mule
'Cause she wouldn't quit school
Even though he tried to make her

She got up at four and was out the door
Caught the bus way down The Nowhere
The Nowhere

CHORUS
Back on Nowhere Road
Way back on Nowhere Road
With a hoe in her hand and her toes in the sand
On the banks of that river
The Diamond River

Her folks beamed with pride graduation night
The first to finish high school
Got a job up North up in Washington
Packed her bags and left The Nowhere,
The Nowhere

Now her kids are grown, but she's not alone
She's back up on that Nowhere
With her dog, Pedro, she can be seen
At No Place on The Nowhere
The Nowhere

I continue, saying, "You are not alone. I will always carry part of you with me. I thank you for teaching me about my mountain heritage—the songs, the crafts, the food, and the stories. They are now woven into me, like one of the rugs we made on those snowy winter days. We go now into a new place and a new year, replenished with light from the old, an unbroken circle. I make a promise to you that I will share the gifts you gave me with anyone who wants them. Now, let's eat some of this plum good cake, and you can share the rest with any critters you are now communing with."

We sit there, eating our fill of cake while looking out over the ancient mountains, and then we see a lovely, pearly gray mourning dove perched on the split-rail fence, looking in our direction. She seems to be waiting for her piece of cake, so we brush the crumbs off our traveling clothes and empty the pan onto the bench. We return to the full U-Haul, toss the Tupperware into the back, and depart.

I slowly breathe into my heart space, and I feel light and unburdened as we bump along the narrow road, trying to avoid the ever-present potholes. We finally arrive to the highway and turn west toward the promise of a new home. The rising sun is at our backs, lighting up the horizon.

Acknowledgments

First and foremost, I acknowledge that *Hope Knocking* would never have materialized without God to direct and guide my writing. With God, nothing is impossible.

I must also acknowledge my parents, who have always believed and encouraged my dreams and led me to believe that I was capable of doing anything. Authors themselves, my parents have definitely inspired me to pick up the torch and carry on. My mother's love of Appalachia will forever live on in her six regional books on the subject and in the character of Nancy Mae in *Hope Knocking*.

Furthermore, I received tremendous support and encouragement from my dear husband, who commented after reading the first two chapters, "I believe this writing's got a hold on you."

I thank my best friend, Cece, who was always interested in what I had to say and kept asking for more to review.

I owe a debt of gratitude to my friend MW, who recorded all of my songs for the book in his studio, at no charge.

Finally, I thank my publisher, Janie Jessee, for taking a chance on me.

It is important to have a tribe that loves and accepts you as you are, so I know I am blessed with mine.

About the Author

This is Nova Mann's first novel, but she is already working on a sequel to *Hope Knocking*, which will hopefully be released sometime in 2023.

Ms. Mann is a former high school teacher who began her career in North Carolina and retired in Tennessee. She received her undergraduate degree from the University of Georgia and her graduate degree from Appalachian State University. As a lifelong learner, she continues to explore the world through hiking, sustainable gardening, writing, and playing old-time mountain music.

One of her life's biggest accomplishments was spent as a Fulbright scholar in South America, teaching English at a public high school. She later led many American students on trips throughout Latin America and Europe, believing that travel is the best way to uproot intolerance and replace it with respect for all cultures.

She lives with her husband in the mountains of Tennessee, embraced by the Cherokee Forest.

Hope Knocking Album

1. Mountain Heart
2. The Birthday Song
3. Coronavirus Blues
4. Old Bent Town
5. Peace Be Unto You
6. Dear Jesus
7. Bury Me in Zinnias
8. Apple Butter Pickin' Party
9. Inmigrante
10. Up There in Heaven
11. Trail of Tears
12. Pennie's Packages
13. Back on Nowhere Road

This album of original songs written by Nova Mann is available for download, as is each individual song, on her website: novamann.com.

NovaMann20
novamann500@gmail.com
novamann.com

FLIGHT
of the
Mourning Dove

The next book by
Nova Mann

PROLOGUE

I scan my river world perched high up on a dead hemlock spire, turning my head left and right, trying to pick up scents on the early spring breeze. There...I have it....downriver. My stomach leads the way and I launch myself off the branch and glide effortlessly over the twisting waterfall. I gaze down and see my reflection in the deep pool below: a magnificent red hawk! I try to take this information in as I continue downstream.

I AM A BIRD! I have always wondered what it would feel like to fly above the Diamond River, and now I am experiencing the wonderment of this secret world. There standing in the sparkling water below me is a recent arrival—a great blue heron—hoping to snag a rainbow trout from the depth. My shadow spooks it and it freezes and crouches low, hoping to avoid detection...but I mean it no harm. I have chicken on my bird brain.